THE MONCALVOS

Works by Enrico Castelnuovo:

Racconti e bozzetti, 1872
Nuovi racconti, 1876
Il professore Romualdo, 1878
Dal primo piano alla soffitta, 1880
Nella lotta, 1880
Alla finestra, 1885
Troppo amata, 1891
L'onorevole Paolo Leonforte, 1894
Il fallo di una donna onesta, 1897
I Coniugi Varedo, 1899
Natalia ed altri racconti, 1899
Sulla laguna, 1899
Ultime novelle, 1906
I Moncalvo, 1908

THE MONCALVOS

Enrico Castelnuovo

Translated from the Italian by

Brenda Webster
and ## Gabriella Romani

Introduction by Gabriella Romani

WingsPress

San Antonio, Texas
2017

Cover image: "Villa Doria Pamphili" by Fratelli Alinari, 1870.
Used by permission of Museo di Roma.

First Edition

ISBN: 978-1-60940-532-8
paperback original

epub ISBN: 978-1-60940-533-5
Mobipocket/Kindle ISBN: 978-1-60940-534-2
Library PDF ISBN: 978-1-60940-535-9

Wings Press
627 E. Guenther
San Antonio, Texas 78210
Phone/fax: (210) 271-7805
On-line catalogue and ordering: www.wingspress.com
All Wings Press titles are distributed to the trade by
Independent Publishers Group
www.ipgbook.com

Library of Congress Cataloging-in-Publication Data:

Names: Castelnuovo, Enrico, 1839-1915, author. | Romani, Gabriella,
    translator. | Webster, Brenda S., translator.
Title: The Moncalvos / Enrico Castelnuova ; translated by Gabriella Romani;
    translated by Brenda Webster.
Other titles: Moncalvo. English
Description: San Antonio, Texas : Wings Press, 2017.
Identifiers: LCCN 2016036913| ISBN 9781609405328 (paperback original) |
    ISBN 9781609405335 (ePub ebook) | ISBN 9781609405342 (kindle/mobipocket)
    | ISBN 9781609405359 (library pdf)
Subjects: LCSH: Jewish families--Italy--History--19th century--Fiction. |
    Brothers--Fiction. | Social mobility--Fiction. | Judaism--Fiction. |
    Conversion--Catholic Church--Fiction. | Italy--Fiction. | Jewish fiction. |
    Historical fiction. | BISAC: FICTION / Jewish. | FICTION / Classics.

LCC PQ4687.C3 M613 2017
DDC 853/.8--dc23
LC record available at https://lccn.loc.gov/2016036913

Contents

Introduction

Enrico Castelnuovo and Italian Jews at the Turn of the Twentieth Century

As the anecdote goes, Enrico Castelnuovo was such a creature of habit that, when he would return home in the early evening from his daily stop after work at the iconic Venetian Florian Cafè in Saint Mark's square, housewives who lived on his street, on hearing his footsteps would know that it was time to prepare dinner.[1] Such was his reputation among contemporaries, a methodic and habitual man in his daily life as well as in his writing.

A prolific and renowned writer of his day, albeit almost forgotten today, Castelnuovo wrote many novels and short stories which, for the most part, depict the life of the Italian bourgeoisie at the turn of the twentieth century. Published and reviewed in the main literary periodicals of the time, from the Florentine *Nuova Antologia* to the Milanese *Perseveranza* and *Illustrazione italiana*, as well as the Roman *Fanfulla della Domenica*, Castelnuovo was praised by critics for the naturalness and vivacity of his prose which, some critics contended, was a welcome change from the sometimes too-academic and pedantic style adopted by Italian writers. Widely read by an Italian readership that not too uncommonly favored foreign novels, especially French and English, for cultural entertainment, Castelnuovo produced a fictional representation of contemporary life which, filled with psychological insights and realistic descriptions, provided readers with situations and characters with which they could identify and recognize as part of their own reality. Castelnuovo himself, with a good dose of self-irony, had commented on the modesty of his literary ambitions when, in the preface to a collection of four short stories titled *Sulla laguna* ("On the Lagoon," 1899), he wrote "I don't assume that they [short stories] are four masterpieces; I have never expected so much from my writings, and I have never believed either, as certain rabid critics pretend to believe, that art is vile and contemptible when it does not manifest itself as a masterpiece. To spark an honest smile on the lips, to squeeze a merciful tear from the eye, to invigorate a gentle sentiment in the soul, to wake up the dormant virtues of fantasy in a reader afflicted by the daily chores, all this has for the last twenty-five years seemed to me a task neither useless nor unworthy of literature."[2]

The novel for which Castelnuovo is most remembered today, *The Moncalvos*, here translated into English for the first time, is centered on the life of the Italian Jewish bourgeoisie at the turn of the twentieth century, thematically a rarity even for Castelnuovo who usually did not include Jewish characters in his fiction. A secular Jew, who professed that he would neither convert to Catholicism nor embrace Zionism, Castelnuovo represents that generation of Italian Jews who were born when the majority of the Jewish people in Italy were still living in ghettos and who enthusiastically welcomed the creation of a unified Italy under the Savoy Royal House, finding in the new monarchic nation, at least on legal grounds, the end of centuries-long persecutions and discrimination. Castelnuovo embraced wholeheartedly the Italian culture and identity as the core, especially, of his artistic persona.

The revolutions of 1848 were an important turning point for the history of the Jewish people in Europe. On the Italian peninsula, Jews' participation in the 1848 first war of Italy's Independence from foreign domination inaugurated a season of civic and political activism which eventually brought Italian Jews full citizenship. On March 29 of 1848, Carlo Alberto of Savoy signed an edict of emancipation,[3] which extended civil rights to Jews and Protestants in the kingdom of Piedmont and Sardinia, and, in 1861, when the country was politically unified, to the entire Italian nation. The annexation of Rome in 1870, finally, marked the completion of Italy's political process of political unification, and, for Italian Jews, the beginning of a new era as equal citizens under the law. Not surprisingly, many Italian Jews participated in the movement for Italy's political unification: they joined the secret revolutionary group of *Carbonari*, became close collaborators with the founders of Italy's movement for independence (Angelo Usiglio, for instance, was the so-called "guardian angel" of Giuseppe Mazzini, and Isacco Artom, the private secretary of the Count Camillo Benso di Cavour, the mastermind of Italy's unification). And starting in the 1860s, Italian Jews enthusiastically joined the rank and files of the new state. By the time World War I broke out, Italy had already had Europe's first Jewish general, Giuseppe Ottolenghi, who in 1902 became Minister of War; a Jewish Prime Minister, Luigi Luzzatti, who served from 1910 to 1911; a Jewish mayor in Rome from 1907 to 1913, Ernesto Nathan, still remembered today as one of the most effective mayors in the history of capital Rome; as well as a myriad of professors and civil servants who worked in schools, universities, and public offices. The lower illiteracy rates (5.8 percent among the Italian Jewish community as compared to 72.9 percent of the general population, according to the 1872 census) certainly facilitated the entrance of Jews in the nation's public institutions, but the wide participation of Italian Jews in the formation of the Italian national state was also the result of a deep sense of belonging to the Italian identity and culture.[4]

Nevertheless, such integration was anything but natural. Not only was there disagreement within the various Jewish communities, primarily established throughout central and northern Italy, on how to go about adopting habits of majority society without losing the traditional Jewish identity (among the contentious points: fear of mixed marriages, conversions, and secularization especially among the new generation), but the very Italian identity of Jews was contested by those who, for mere prejudice or political calculation, did not welcome the full integration of the Jewish people in Italian society. Suffice it to mention the so-called Pasqualigo case, when a member of Parliament, Francesco Pasqualigo, wrote to the king of Italy in 1873 to discourage him from approving the nomination of Isacco Pesaro Maurogonato for the position of Minister of Finance; or the case of Alessandro D'Ancona whose nomination for a professorship in the Italian department at the university of Pisa was challenged in 1861 by those who considered him unfit to teach Dante. In both cases, the contention was that they could not be considered fully Italian (insofar as they held a double nationality, Italian and Jewish) and therefore were untrustworthy in crucial positions of national interest—an argument that found fertile terrain both in secular and clerical circles of Italian society. While nineteenth-century Italy did not witness the persecutions and violence perpetrated against Jews in other parts of Europe, the question of integration was far from being a simple and natural process. A subtle and yet effective process of cultural and social stereotyping of Jews existed in Italy already at the turn of the twentieth century—something that must have played a significant role in creating popular consent when, in 1938, the fascist government passed the Racial Laws, which banned Jews from civil society and excluded them from public offices, military service, as well as schools and universities.

Though legally emancipated and well integrated in civil society, many Jewish public figures of the post-unification period preferred to keep their Jewish identity private, according to the old patriotic formula "Jewish at home and citizens outside," which many Jews adopted to maintain ties with their community while promoting a national Italian identity, but also, consciously or unconsciously, as a reaction to the understanding that a display of diversity came with a price. In 1892, for instance, Tullo Massarani, renowned literary critic, journalist, and politician of Jewish origin, rejected a request by the lawyer Leone Ravenna to formally protest the publication in a Milanese newspaper of anti-Semitic remarks, as he believed that "the only way for persecuted races to combat intolerance was to emulate good citizenship and, without ostentation, to demonstrate in word and deed that they could surpass others in honesty, charity and patriotism."[5] The lack of a Jewish visibility in the public arena corresponded in cultural terms with the absence of a meaningful Jewish representation in the literary imagination of Italians, at least until post-World War II, when, with the writings of authors such as Primo Levi and Giorgio Bassani, Jewish identity gained a visibility in Italian culture never encountered before.

The cultural representations of Jews in nineteenth-century Italian literature is rare, and the few Jewish characters who managed to find a place on the pages of novels and short stories, especially in popular literature, were in most cases marginal and stereotyped (sinister and devious characters, who had to be redeemed through conversion to Catholicism). Emblematic of this cultural anti-Semitism were two very popular novels of the time, *L'ebreo di Verona* (1850) by Antonio Bresciani, a Jesuit priest who wrote for the widely circulated journal *Civiltà Cattolica*, and *L'orfana del ghetto* (1887) by Carolina Invernizio, a prolific and best-selling author of the time. We have to wait until the twentieth century to find fictional representations that not only portray Jews in a more sympathetic fashion but that turn them into the protagonists of the narrated events. Enrico Castelnuovo's *The Moncalvos* is the first novel in Italian literature to be centered on the life of a Jewish family and to be meant for the general Italian readership, among which he had gained some fame as a writer during the previous thirty years. Published in 1908 by the most important publisher of the time, Emilio Treves, and also serialized in *Nuova Antologia* (from November 16, 1907 to January 1 1908), a prestigious national periodical, Castelnuovo's novel is a true rarity as it offers a story focused on a Jewish family, presented through the lens of a double and ambitious narrative project: the portrayal of a moment in Italian history, the late nineteenth century, marked by great social and economic changes, as seen from the point of view of the Jewish community as well as of Italian society as a whole. Anticipating some of the thematic threads developed later in two masterpieces of Italian literature, Giuseppe Tomasi di Lampedusa's *The Leopard* (1958) and Giorgio Bassani's *The Garden of the Finzi-Contini* (1962), *The Moncalvos* narrates the story of the rise of the bourgeoisie in Italian society and its entrance through marriage into a prestigious but financially insolvent family of the local nobility—as well as the clash between a wealthy Jewish family and a bourgeois one over how best to reconcile their Jewish identity with the role they chose for themselves in society.

Gabriele and Giacomo Moncalvo are the main protagonists of the novel. Two brothers, originally from Ferrara, but living in Rome at the end of the nineteenth century, in the midst of Italy's economic and urban development after its political unification, both aspire to climb the social ladder of the newly formed Italian nation. Gabriele, a wealthy businessman, seeks assimilation and encourages his daughter, Mariannina, to marry the sickly offspring of the Orobonis, an old aristocratic Roman Catholic family—a marriage which will grant the Jewish family access to the most exclusive echelon of Roman society but which will also entail the conversion of the daughter, and eventually of both her parents. Giacomo, on the contrary, fully embraces the national Italian identity without abjuring his Jewish roots, as well as the values, inherited from the rhetorical tradition of the Risorgimento, of sacrifice and integrity deemed as the moral foundation of social progress.[6] A positivist and a secular Jew, Giacomo is a university professor, a character with whom the author is most sympathetic and, probably, inspired by Castelnuovo's own son, Guido, a renowned mathematician at the time when novel was written.

A sentiment of deep disappointment in the present and nostalgia for the past pervades Castelnuovo's novel, although the author seems all too aware that the process of Italy's modernization is not only inevitable but necessary. "Ah, why wasn't I born two generations before when one fought for Italy and Garibaldi gathered around himself the flower of youth and there was a magnificent fervor of generous ideals—a robust faith in the future of the country?" (p. 216) laments Giorgio, Giacomo's son, expressing his frustrations with his present life and voicing Castelnuovo's concern for the future of the country. Giorgio and his father, Giacomo, are the characters who most vividly express the author's critical view of contemporary Italy, seen as politically ineffective and morally corrupted. Not surprisingly, the novel takes place in Rome, the new capital city of modern Italy, which disillusioned intellectuals of the time referred to as Byzantium, an ancient but still effective symbol of decadence and corruption.[7]

The 1880s, known as the infamous era of *trasformismo*—a centrist government coalition forged by Prime Minister Agostino Depretis—saw the fast growth of unregulated banking ventures and property speculations, which favored the empowerment of the status quo, and, according to those who were highly critical of government economic policies, betrayed the very ideals of democratic progress on which the Italian nation had been created. Gabriele, a banker and a political candidate who unsuccessfully attempts to run for election to Parliament with the Left and then shifts his political ideology towards the Right, crystallizes the author's criticism of the financial world as he personifies unbridled ambition for power at any cost. Yet, Castelnuovo is not totally unsympathetic to him. Gabrio, as he is called familiarly by relatives and friends, is a devoted father, husband and brother, who cares deeply about his family, and while Castelnuovo condemns his thirst for power, he also shows us his positive traits, such as generosity and affability of personality, as well as how his desire for upward mobility cannot be separated from his legitimate aspiration to compete on equal footing in society—a right only recently gained by Jews. Such ambiguity may well represent the essence of Castelnuovo's idea and representation of modernity: a reflection on the contradictory and complex transformation of Italy from a past of inequalities, which was, as the author seems to suggest, even when compared to the failures of the present, far worse not only for Jews but society as a whole.

Crucial to Castelnuovo's depiction of the complexity of integration is his portrayal of the new generation of Jewish Italians, represented by Giorgio and Mariannina. If, on one side, Mariannina, beautiful and ambitious, seeks full integration, along with power and social status, on the other, Giorgio, an aspiring university professor like his father, idealistically rejects the opportunity he is given by his uncle to make a fortune in business in order to pursue fame and knowledge in a poorly paid academic career. Neither finds true happiness in life, nor, in this scenario of heartache, can they redeem their parents' failure to create a morally acceptable society. Paradoxically, however, Mariannina is the truly self-realized character here. Not only does she affirm her right to marry whomever she wishes (a choice rarely available to young women of the time), but she shows an awareness of her desires and potential as an individual, rarely encountered in the portrayal of a female character in Italian literature of the time. Neither a victim nor a heroine, Mariannina is a young woman who pursues her own life objectives and who, most importantly, understands without hypocrisy the realities of power dynamics in which she is operating. An actor and a designer of her own fate, Mariannina is above all a female character of great modernity.

About half a century before Castelnuovo wrote *The Moncalvos*, Massimo D'Azeglio, a writer, painter and patriot of aristocratic extraction and one of the intellectual fathers of unified Italy, had published a pamphlet titled *Dell'emancipazione civile degl'Israeliti* ("On the civil emancipation of Israelites," 1848) in which he expressed his solidarity with the Jewish people and advocated their civil emancipation and legal equality. In his pamphlet, endorsing a belief commonly held in those years by democratic patriots, Massimo D'Azeglio wrote: "the cause of the Jewish regeneration is closely connected to that of Italy's regeneration; because justice is one and the same for all."[8] Perhaps it was this maxim of patriotic idealism, which united the fate of Italy to that of the Jewish people at the dawn of Italy's political unification, that Castelnuovo, like many of his generation, was most nostalgic for in his novel. As Alessandro D'Ancona wrote, reminiscing happily about the past and the years, the 1840s and 1850s, when he was growing up in the midst of Italy's quest for independence and political unification: "Isn't it better to have lived in those years of sacred enthusiasm, when century-old misfortunes were thought to be the earned expiation of ancient guilt, but when we were also preparing together for well-deserved fortunes, and for the final victory— the prize for good sense, valor, and abnegation? Isn't it better to have been part of a generation which was industrious and inspired exclusively by the love for common good, rather than by one's personal interest?"[9]

Whether Castelnuovo was truly nostalgic for the past, or was, like many other writers of the time (Giovanni Verga and Luigi Pirandello, for instance), artistically giving voice to a social malaise he recognized around himself, he created with *The Moncalvos* a remarkable novel, which portrays the ideas, fears and aspirations of a whole generation of Italians, Jewish and non-Jewish.

Gabriella Romani
Philadelphia, 2016

Notes

1. From Alessandro Levi, "Enrico Castelnuovo, l'autore dei Moncalvo," in *La Rassegna mensile di Israel* XV.8-9 (August-September 1949): 388.

2. Enrico Castelnuovo, *Sulla laguna* (Catania: Giannotta, 1899), xv.

3. Often referred to as the "second emancipation," after Napoleon's 1806 emancipation of Italian Jews, which brought, among other things, freedom from ghettos.

4. For a history of Jews in the nineteenth- and early twentieth-century Italy see: Tullia Catalan, "Italian Jews and the 1848-49 Revolutions: Patriotism and Multiple Identities" in *The Risorgimento Revisited: Nationalism and Culture in Nineteenth-Century Italy*, edited by Silvana Patriarca and Lucy Riall (New York: Palgrave Macmillan, 2012), 214-231; Elizabeth Schächter, *The Jews of Italy 1848-1915: Between Tradition and Transformation* (London-Portland: Vallentine Mitchell, 2011); Cristina Bettin, *Italian Jews from Emancipation to the Racial Laws* (New York: Palgrave Macmillan, 2010); *The Most Ancient of Minorities: the Jews of Italy*, edited by Stanislao G. Pugliese (Westport, CT : Greenwood Press, 2002).

5. See Elisabeth Schächter's *The Jews of Italy 1848-1915*, 26. In his letter to Ravenna, Massarani specified that he did not want to join the sensational journalism developed around this issue, and would rather intervene by talking to people privately.

6. The Risorgimento ("resurgence" in Italian) was the nineteenth-century political and literary movement that culminated with the 1861 establishment of the Kingdom of Italy under the reign of the Savoy House.

7. See Richard Drake, *Byzantium for Rome: The Politics of Nostalgia in Umbertian Italy, 1878-1900* (Chapel Hill: The University of North Carolina Press, 1980).

8. Massimo D'Azeglio. *Dell'emancipazione civile degl'Israeliti* (Florence: Felice Le Monnier, 1848), 56.

9. Alessandro D'Ancona, "Rimembranze gradevoli," in *Pagine sparse di letteratura e di storia* (Florence: Sansoni Editore, 1914), 306.

To Vittoria Aganoor Pompilj

In this book of modest art but rich sincerity, I tried to portray some strange events of our contemporary life. And given that you didn't dislike the book, I dare ask you to accept my dedication to you. I am most delighted to be given the opportunity to have, if only for a moment, my name appear next to your illustrious name and affirm publicly the high regard with which I hold your mind, soul, and precious friendship.

Enrico Castelnuovo
Venice, January 1908

(Vittoria Aganoor Pompilj [1855-1910] was an Italian poet and writer of Armenian origin.)

THE MONCALVOS

Chapter 1

At Villa Borghese

Drawn by memories of his youth, Giorgio Moncalvo was looking forward to visiting Villa Borghese upon his return from a long stay abroad. He was coming home from a great metropolis rich with all the comforts of life: refinements of taste, the latest advances in knowledge—a city proud of its recent triumphs, of its over-bearing and dominant civilization. He had returned, in short, from Berlin, which had offered his scientific mind means of study not available in Italy.

Still, he had returned to Italy, which was neither rich nor victorious, with the humility of a son almost ashamed of his mother. Yet it had reconquered him from the moment he came out of the Gotthard tunnel and looked over the plains and lakes of Lombardy.

Little by little as he continued his journey along the coasts of the Ligurian and Tyrrhenian Seas, his love of country stirred with increasing warmth. How beautiful his Italy was at the end of October. In the North where he'd been, there were already the warning signs of winter. Wind-spun leaves abandoned their branches to clutter the well-groomed parks. Everything was already fading beneath the cold, wet sky. Here in the South, nature only hinted at a voluptuous fatigue and summer seemed to linger, smiling through the warm, bright air.

This was Giorgio Moncalvo's impression as he walked the wide paths of Villa Borghese, pausing from time to time to admire the meadows, enameled with flowers, where horses grazed freely. Great tree trunks wove together, blending infinite gradations of green, from the deep green of the pines to the dusty green of the oaks to the tender green of the locust tree.

The villa, seemingly deserted when he entered, grew suddenly animated: there were the carriages of a few foreigners guided by their coach men, some romantic couples and solitary cyclists, governesses with children, a group of priests, some policemen on horseback. A company of soldiers passed by, followed by a dusty automobile roaring like an enormous insect, leaving behind it a strong smell of gasoline. A cheerful group of students passed directly in front of Moncalvo.

He thought: "Once I was like that...."

Where had that time gone? Though he was still young, what had happened to the flexibility of his muscles, his urge to jump, to laugh, to make noise? Where were the friends, his companions who, at the first sound of the bell announcing the yearned-for end of lessons, flew with him to the Villa Borghese to tumble on the grass and practice on their bikes? Where was his mother who, used to living in a quiet city in the Veneto, unwillingly crossed the threshold of the noisy and magnificent villa and, shaking her head, remarked "Yes, it's a fine place but too many people, too many carriages, too much noise. No, I'll never get used to it."

Giorgio remembered how the happy meetings of Villa Borghese had stopped after the illness and death of that unhappy woman. Poor mamma! Good and intelligent but born with a talent for unhappiness. For as long as her husband had been a lecturer at a technical college at 2,500 lire a year, she had continued to deafen her husband with her hysterical complaints, while praising his brother Gabriele. Gabriele didn't waste his nights on books but threw himself into business, accumulating a vast fortune, drowning his family in abundance.

"If at least you would give us some satisfaction," she sighed. "Instead, even with all your brains, you'll rot in some little provincial school."

And then, unexpectedly, Giacomo Moncalvo became a famous man. He received the *Royal Lincei* prize[1] for mathematics with his work in geometry and won a position at the University of Rome.

"Are you happy?" he had asked his wife.

"Yes," she answered—and maybe in the beginning she had been content, but it was a contentment that didn't last long. Complications arose: the difficulties of the journey and accommodations and the even greater aggravation of organizing a household in a city where everything cost infinitely more. This led to new and endless fights.

"Here you spend double, triple. Is it really worth the trouble of changing our position and household only to be reduced to having to watch every cent? And then, what confusion, what a Babylon. It's a miracle if you aren't run over by a carriage or a tram. Ah, where's my peace?"

She found her peace soon enough in the cemetery, after a brief illness and an easy death that allowed her to bid an affectionate farewell to her husband and son. She begged their pardon if, out of love, she had tormented them with the ups and downs of her anxious, preoccupied personality. Addressing herself to Giorgio in particular, she had added: "Ah, if only your Aunt Clara were able to come and stay a few weeks with you!"

In fact, as soon as she had heard of the disaster, she had come spontaneously—from Cairo no less—where she had lived for several years with her brother Gabriele, the one with the talent for business. She came and stayed some nine months, re-organizing the house and making Giacomo and Giorgio appreciate the value of a good housewife.

"Why don't you stay with us forever?" the professor asked her.

"I can't. Everyone needs me down there."

"What can they need from you?"

"Maybe more than you others do." And those down there, as aunt Clara referred to her brother Gabriele, her sister-in-law, Rachele and her niece Mariannina, took her away in November after they, too, had spent a few weeks in Rome at the end of their yearly visit to northern Europe.

Those millionaire relatives who stayed at the Hotel del Quirinale—displaying their princely wealth, keeping horses and carriages and having their meals apart with a great profusion of Bordeaux and champagne—had caught the imagination of the young student. They treated him with noisy cordiality as an honored guest at their table, a sought-after guide in their visits to the Roman monuments.

For the most part, Giorgio was with the women because his uncle, Gabriele, arriving suddenly in Italy during a period of general elections, had the unfortunate idea of running for political office in the district of Lazio. He visited his presumed constituency often to dazzle them with his promises and his money.

The women disapproved of these expensive whims.

"It would have been better to buy that yacht we were offered," said the daughter, a lively twelve year-old. And the wife, a mature beauty with markedly oriental features, looking at her bejeweled white hands, complained of her husband's unusual stinginess in refusing to buy her a diamond ring exhibited at Marchesini's on the Corso with the miserable excuse that she had too many already.

"If uncle succeeds," Giorgio asked one evening, "will you want to settle in Italy?"

"Sooner or later," answered his Aunt Rachele, "We'll certainly leave Egypt. But there is no hurry. Meanwhile, Gabrio"—she often used this diminutive with her husband—"Gabrio can go back and forth. It's such a short trip."

This didn't merit further thought since Gabriele Moncalvo was roundly beaten by his competitor, who was supported by the clergy and had an easy victory against a foreign candidate who was both a Jew and a socialist sympathizer.

Even though he felt his defeat bitterly, Moncalvo pretended to take no notice and limited himself with deploring Italy's continued domination by the priests, enemies of any progress. As for him, he had to be grateful to the voters who hadn't chosen him and thus allowed him not to be distracted from his profitable labors. Since he was now free of his political preoccupations and it was almost time for his departure to Egypt, he wanted to dedicate the last two weeks of his stay in Italy to the beauties of Rome.

In these excursions, Giorgio, fresh from his classical studies, provided an excellent guide for his uncle who, to his nephew's amazement, showed more taste in art and knowledge of archeology than could be expected in a businessman. His uncle, in turn, admiring the quick intelligence of the young man, had immediately toyed with the idea of bringing him into his business.

"Would you like to make your fortune?"

Giorgio recalled the question that his uncle had asked him point blank just here at the Villa Borghese as he was getting into the carriage waiting for him at the exit of the museum.

"If you want to make your fortune," these had been the precise words said to him by Gabriele Moncalvo seating Giorgio beside him, "leave the University, that factory of useless doctors, and come with us to Africa. Spend a couple of months in Cairo as my personal secretary. Take some lessons in Arabic and, in February or March, go to our family house in Khartoum. New people, new countries: there you'll learn more than in all the libraries of the world. And along the way you'll see more antiquities that rival Rome's. In five or six years, I guarantee you will have enough money to return to Europe and live on your income. In five or six years we'll all go back. I don't insist that you decide right away. Think about it. Consult your father. Let me hear something tomorrow or the next day."

Nothing was decided. Professor Giacomo, although he told his son that he didn't want to restrict his freedom, had counseled him to refuse the offer, and Giorgio himself didn't have the strength to abandon his father, his country and his studies.

"I expected this," Gabriele Moncalvo said, "You are crazy like all contemporary Italians. Your ideal is a job and a pension. What's more, your father is a stoic philosopher who despises money…. Never mind. If you change your mind before the end of the year, all you have to do is set sail for Alexandria and telegraph me. In the meantime, we'll sail with my sister Clara whom you will so kindly return to us.

Seven years had passed and yet, for a variety of reasons Giorgio hadn't seen his relatives though they were in Europe every summer. One could almost think that he had forgotten them, except of course Aunt Clara, whose placid and kind features were engraved in his memory and with whom he exchanged affectionate letters from time to time. "It will be a joy to embrace you again," she had written him when she announced her imminent return to Rome. "Now thank God we, too, will be Italians again and, God willing, we will stop traveling the world. The uncles and Mariannina send greetings and hope that you won't be aloof now like your papa, who honestly is a little too reclusive."

Giorgio Moncalvo looked forward to embracing his aunt again, certainly, but not the rest of his relatives who figured as suspect in his father's letters. "They are immensely wealthy," admonished the professor, "much richer than they were seven years ago. They are not our kind of people. I appreciate my brother's excellent qualities. I have nothing against my sister-in-law; I admire Mariannina who is extremely beautiful; but, when possible, I keep my distance and I recommend you keep yours too."

"I'll follow this advice easily," thought Giorgio. In truth, if his relatives had become much richer in those seven years, he had become much more serious, avoiding luxury and fun-loving companions at all costs. And how many new images, new impressions overcame the former memories in his mind and heart.

Passionate about his physiological studies, he had made a name for himself with some original monographs while he was at the university. As soon as he had taken his degree, his father had sent him to Berlin to the celebrated Professor Raucher, who had been enthusiastic about Giorgio and had invited him to help in his lab. He was only supposed to stay for a few months but had spent three years enclosed, as it were, by the four walls of the laboratory, full of reverent admiration for the eminent master who, in a science devoted to the service of humanity, sought comfort for the two great sorrows of his life—his wife's death and his daughter's fatal illness.

Welcomed to the intimacy of the household, Giorgio Moncalvo made the acquaintance of the pallid, blond Frida who spoke with marvelous serenity of the fate awaiting her. Knowing that she had to renounce love and maternity and yet thirsty for affection, she invented the story of a spiritual and fraternal love.

And there was a moment in which Giorgio Moncalvo became aware that he himself was the hero of this story. Frida wrapped him in a warm and discreet sympathy. When he sat at Raucher's table as an honored guest, he was sure to find his favorite dishes prepared by the young woman's hand. In the evening, when he came for tea in the cozy little room where the professor rested from the day's labor, she sat at the piano and played exquisitely the music he loved most: Bach, Beethoven, Schumann. Other times instead she recited, in her faint, sweet voice, the verses of Goethe, Schiller or Heine and begged him to read them or to explain a poem of Leopardi, a chorus of

Manzoni, an ode of Carducci. She would listen to him captivated, moved by the melodious Italian she had learned as a child spending two winters in Pisa with her mother. She still pronounced it correctly enough and not without her delicate grace.

From time to time, suffering an attack of her chronic illness, Frida would stay in her room for three or four days, invisible to everyone except her father. In those days, the unhappy wrinkles that always furrowed the scientist's brow became deeper and his small, sharp eyes, used to scrutinizing the secrets of the atom, couldn't stand the effort of the microscope. "You look, Moncalvo. Today I can't."

"Ah, Moncalvo, Moncalvo," the professor exclaimed one morning, giving in to a sudden need to express the feelings he usually mastered. "If you knew what I feel when they call me illustrious, when they praise my discoveries! I would trade places with the first yokel who passed me on the street if I could have a healthy daughter. I would give away my scientific baggage for the nostrums of a charlatan who could cure my Frida. And there's no hope. A year, maybe two, and I'll see them carry her out the way they carried her mother. Why did I bring her into the world? Why did I marry a woman afflicted by an illness that is transmitted to the children? She, poor woman, had the right to ignore it but I, the great physiologist? Believe me, Moncalvo, it's a mistake for which I'll never pardon myself. And if Frida wasn't an angel, what reason she'd have to curse me! At any rate, her firm resolution not to marry...I myself wouldn't permit it... isn't that a tacit condemnation of me? Ah, if things had gone differently, if Frida were a girl like others, free to follow her inclinations. Enough. It's useless to talk about what can never happen. Thank you, Moncalvo, for the attention you give my Frida. Don't disillusion her. Let her believe that you love her the way a brother loves his sister. Frida won't ask for more."

Now, Giorgio Moncalvo asked himself what his feelings for Frida Raucher might really be. Certainly he didn't love her like a lover; still, he thought of her with tenderness made of compassion and gratitude and, at the thought that she was far away and he probably wouldn't see her again, he felt tears making a lump in his throat. How pale and lifeless she was the day she saw him off! How her voice trembled when, with a forced smile she said: "Your return to Italy to be close to your father was inevitable. It would have been a bad mistake to turn down the assistantship that was offered you in Rome. We'll remain friends just the same, won't we? Our affection isn't the sort that requires living near each other. You'll write to me in Italian and I'll answer also in Italian. It will be a useful exercise. Don't be shocked by my proposition. Goodbye Signor Giorgio, and good luck."

The moist, slender little hand that Moncalvo had taken in his own was gently withdrawn. The shy, sad eyes turned in another direction and, with a final wave, Frida disappeared.

Giorgio Moncalvo had been wandering through the park for about two hours. He had entered Porta del Popolo and was slowly heading towards Porta Pinciana with the intention of looking into the Ludovisi[2] quarter that had been in the planning phase when he left Rome. But precisely when he slowed down, he saw on a small rise to his left the monument to Goethe, outlined in the sharp clarity of white marble among the greenery. His attention was distracted by the sound of hoof beats. The riders, three women and a man, were coming the way he had come and were probably also going to Porta Pinciana. The three women, very elegant in their long Amazons' outfits, were young and beautiful; their companion, who looked nearer to fifty than forty, had a lordly aristocratic air.

Moncalvo had drawn to the side of the road to let the group pass, moving as they were at a brisk trot; but what was his astonishment when one of the cavalcade, precisely the one who seemed the youngest and most beautiful, greeted him warmly and broke away from her friends calling loudly:

"*Go on! I'll be with you in a moment.*"[3]

The same voice, addressed to him continued in perfect Italian: "Oh Giorgio! Don't you remember me? Isn't it polite to greet your friends?"

The unknown beauty leaned from the saddle and, reaching out her small gloved hand, added with slight impatience: "It's Mariannina, come on! See, it's easy!"

"Mariannina! I apologize.... You have changed so much."

"Why do you *apologize*? And what does it mean *changed so much*? Or that you address me formally?"

He blushed, stammering, wracking his brain to put together two words, humiliated by the wretched figure he made with this cousin whom he hadn't seen in seven years; she, however, continued to smile at him encouragingly, benevolent, pleased by the admiration that she sensed she'd inspired.

"It's agreed. You'll come to see us," she said, patting the neck of her magnificent sorrel with the starred face who trembled with agitation and pawed the ground. "Wait! Not tonight, because we're out...tomorrow night at quarter-to-eight for dinner. You'll get an invitation for you and uncle Giacomo. Palazzo Gandi, Via Nazionale, almost opposite the Banca d'Italia. Your father might have forgotten the address, but tomorrow he won't escape. See you tomorrow—without fail." And she raced away in a cloud of dust.

Giorgio Moncalvo remained frozen for a spell as this vision dwindled. Was this the Mariannina he remembered in short skirts, pretty perhaps, but in that critical period when the most beautiful girl in the world has something harsh and shrill about her that is disturbing and offensive and stops even her complacent family from predicting the future? Was it this the same Mariannina who today was so fascinating in the remarkable harmony of her limbs, the mysterious depth of her glance, the raven mass of shining, wavy hair, the bewitching smile and velvety sweet voice that searched out the secret corners of his soul?

How Frida's bloodless, melancholy shadow seemed to flee and melt into a cloud before this superb creature so full of force and life! For the past three years, he had lived in a little dream world in the peace of his studies, deaf to the din and unreceptive to the flatteries of a great city. That little dream world was fast fading away.

"I am a fool to think something could come of this," the young scientist said to himself hunching his shoulders. "I'm a fool...notwithstanding my family relations with Mariannina. What can there be in common between she and I? She is a girl with many millions and I, I am an assistant physiologist with a salary of 1,200 lire. I have met her today by chance, and tomorrow I'm going to dinner at her house...and then I'll manage with a visit once every blue moon.... And what if I don't go to dinner? But what would my excuse be? I would have to confess that I'm afraid.... Afraid of what? Fool! Fool!"

And he set out slowly. From the height of his Corinthian pillar the statue of Goethe looked out at Rome. At the base of the monument, Mignon leaning against the harpist seemed to murmur the pathetic song repeated so often by Frida:

Kennst du das Land wo die Zitronen blühn,
Im dunkeln Laub die Gold-Orangen glühn...[4]

Chapter 2

After Dinner

I t had been a family dinner. In order not to disappoint his brother and nephew, Commendatore[5] Gabrio Moncalvo didn't invite anyone else except the painter Brulati, who was practically one of the family and couldn't possibly be intimidating. This didn't mean that Commendatore Moncalvo was not wearing tails and that Signora Rachele, still a beautiful woman in spite of her forty-three or forty-four years, was not showing off her full shoulders, overflowing from the top of a dress in black tulle with sequins. Mariannina was dressed in white folded silk, with a light blue belt on her waist and pearls around her neck.

Now the guests were gathered in the living room and Aunt Clara, the unmarried and elderly sister of the two Moncalvos, was in charge of distributing coffee and liquors. She always had a kindly expression, but had aged considerably in the last few years. She looked tired, her grey hair matching the color of her silk dress. *Ma soeur grise*—my grey sister—Gabrio Moncalvo used to call her sometimes, jokingly.

The large living room, full of chairs and divans of all shapes and sizes, was lit by electric lights and furnished richly, but inelegantly. On the walls hung ceramic plates, old pieces of fabric, Japanese mats, among which it was hard to discern those three or four valuable Roman watercolors. A group of plants added a green note in a corner; in the opposite corner, above a turning pedestal, one could see a little bronze statue by Cifariello.[6] Between a sideboard in a corner, with its shelves full of knick-knacks, and other shelves holding several elegantly bound books there was a small upright piano. Some artistic volumes were thrown casually on a bigger table. A lacquered table held the cup service for the coffee and liquors.

"You have no religion," Signora Rachele said to her brother-in-law, as if she wanted to continue an interrupted conversation.

Commendatore Gabrio began to laugh.

"Tonight my wife doesn't want to leave you in peace."

"Oh well," added Signora Clara, offering cigarettes around. "Leave him in peace. He never comes, and when he does you tease him."

"Oh!" Signora Rachele intervened "Giacomo is not a man who gets offended for so little. And as for you, she added looking at Clara, you are just like him, we all were...."

Professor Giacomo raised his eyes from a book he was leafing through.

'It would be helpful to know what you mean by religion."

"What a question!" replied Signora Rachele, more embarrassed than she cared to appear. "As if anyone wouldn't know what religion is. I mean a set of unassailable beliefs, as sure as your mathematical theories, on which one may rely as a norm for life."

"And you consider that these dogmas are real and that they force us to act for the good of friends and enemies, and to refrain from any evil and base act, and so regulate the conformity of our behavior?"

"No, no, it's not enough to consider them. There must be the certainty that these precepts come from God, that by obeying them we receive a prize, and that transgressing them will bring a punishment."

The usual investment of capital, thought the professor. But he didn't say it. He only said, "You believe what you want."

"There you are," uttered Signora Rachele, getting angry. "I know too well that I can believe what I want, but I need to reinforce my faith with the faith of others. I need a religion, a set of common practices. Gabrio is silent, but he shares my view."

"Ah, she is not that wrong," agreed her husband, puffing out the smoke of his cigarette. "The materialistic doctrines are obsolete."

Giorgio Moncalvo, who was chatting with his cousin near the window, couldn't suppress a sense of surprise. He could remember the strong anticlerical invectives he'd heard from his uncle seven years ago.

Mariannina could guess his thoughts. "Oh, papa no longer has the ideas he once had…there is nothing wrong in changing when you change for the better. *Au présent, nous sommes de gens rangés.*[7]

In the meantime, the discussion between Giacomo Moncalvo and his sister-in-law, was becoming ever more lively.

"Well," the professor said, "you are becoming a conservative…and when you were young, if I remember well, you came across as a rebel, a heretic, and your grandfather…"

Signora Rachele raised her shoulders.

"Just as in your household, my grandparents were strictly orthodox, attached to antiquated and ridiculous ways."

"They had a certain poetry," noted the professor.

"Are you defending them?"

"No, but I consider them dispassionately, as I do all rituals and symbols in which humanity has invested its soul."

"But how can we be interested in those stories, three or four thousand years old, expressed in a language nobody any longer understands?…those patriarchs, the Exodus across the red sea, that Moses who comes down the mountain with horns on his forehead!"

"Come on, they even built the new religion on it."

"It's something else, something else," the Signora protested. "In any case, to return to what we were saying: our grandparents were stubbornly orthodox; the next generation pretended to believe, but didn't; and we of the third generation couldn't have been raised in any other way."

The professor nodded. "Certainly the old faith was dying, making it all the more necessary for every one of us to assimilate what is permanent in it, what has proven to be indestructible in religion, to strengthen the moral law which must govern our lives."

"Here is where you are wrong," Commendatore Moncalvo jumped in and threw away the *Tribuna* which he was holding at the moment. "First a different morality corresponds to each religion. The Turkish one, for instance, which has its own attractions...well, it would be good to start with choosing a religion whose juice you want to squeeze...then, make sure you can preserve this juice once you throw the fruit away.

"You misunderstood me. I didn't mean to say that religion is the only basis for morality—many factors contribute to creating it, race, customs, civility—actually today, in some civilized countries, the morals of truly virtuous individuals are superior in many ways to those taught by religion. But it is a fact that religion represents people's best effort towards an ideal perfection, and this effort in itself is an element of moral greatness."

"Ah, so you admit it?" Signora Rachele exclaimed triumphantly.

"I don't have the least difficulty admitting it. This doesn't mean that I don't wish for the time when morality stands on its own the way a monument stands without a frame. You see, religion is like a dictionary, which is always outdated when compared with the spoken language."

Signora Rachele prepared to answer but her husband signaled her not to insist.

"And what is the opinion of our Brulati?" he asked, turning to the painter, who was sketching caricatures in a pocket notebook.

"Brulati has no opinion," the artist responded, "I don't want to wear out my brain."

"Well then let's see your album."

"It's not worth the effort."

Brulati was about to replace the little book in the pocket of his overcoat but changed his mind in the middle and added: "If you promise not to take offense."

Everyone stood around Brulati laughing heartily at his ability to catch the comic aspect of a face.

The most enthusiastic was Gabrio Moncalvo, even though he was given the hardest time by the caricaturist.

"That can't be beaten! With two strokes this man kills you. And there's no mistaking; you could recognize yourself among a thousand. I've always said so. Brulati's paintings are good but there are many others like his. Where he has no rival is in caricature. In France, in Germany, in England, working for the *Journal pour rire,* for the *Fliegende Blätter* or *Punch,* he would be rich. We are a penniless people."

And the Commendatore went on comparing the various caricatures.

"Mine is the masterpiece without a doubt, but he got you too, Rachele."

Signora Rachele smiled with tight lips.

"I won't deny it. But I don't like the genre."

"You're wrong, But isn't it true, Brulati? You can't expect beautiful women to be happy to see themselves reduced to this state."

"It's the fate of all beautiful things to be parodied," Brulati said immediately.

"Don't tease me," replied the Signora softened by the compliment "now I'm a ruin."

"I wish there were more ruins like you! And here is my sister"—continued the banker—"the sketch is her to perfection and yet there's nothing but a little nose and two dots for eyes."

Signora Clara, who was in a good mood and who never had any pretenses said in a joking tone, "That's right; there is really nothing else."

"Giacomo too is just right," the Commendatore took up his newspaper again, "a pair of glasses, a tuft of hair on his forehead and nothing left over."

"It must be a fine hobby for you," the professor remarked, turning to Brulati. "If we could only do the same when we are attending the sessions of the Academy of the Lincei."

"Besides the eminent professor—has Brulati also done the aspiring one?" asked Signora Rachele, referring to her brother-in-law and nephew.

"Well, and haven't you done my caricature or Giorgio's?" Marianinna added petulantly, standing on tiptoe behind her father's back as she watched the pages of the album turn.

"You try it!" challenged Brulati, "you were in total shadow."

"You ought to have told us to move to the light."

"No chance of that. You were too comfortable where you were."

That was also Giorgio's opinion. He moved to the window seat where Marianinna joined him.

Despite his own proud resolutions, the young scientist suffered from a fascination with his beautiful cousin, now so different from the way she'd been seven years before: the budding girl he had seen then had flowered, proud and shining.

Everything about her was enchanting: her face, her person, her voice, even the perfume that she spread around her. And he, the austere young man immersed in his studies who had conceded little or nothing to the pleasures of his age, today hung inebriated by that bewitching mouth, those eyes lit at times by a sudden flame, at times veiled by a sweet melancholy. This heavenly girl addressed him with the familiar "*tu*" and he used it with her, and she encouraged him to evoke the past and listened benevolently when he talked about his designs for the future.

"Do you remember our walks at the Roman Forum?"

"Of course! And those on the Palatine hills?"

"Do you remember? Do you remember?"

"Certainly. And how you confounded me with your erudition! The little I know of Roman history comes from you."

"Oh, I was a pedant. We scholarly men are all pedants. You were right on the Palatine. While I lectured you about Augustus, Caligula, Tiberius...you were enchanted to hear the happy twittering of sparrows in the leaves."

"Really. What a good memory you have!"

"And remember also at the Forum you were more interested in the lilies that were growing at the base of the temple of Saturn than you were in my learned speeches."

"I was a child. But now I know a lot more, since I've had no less than the archaeologist Giacomo Boni as a guide." [8]

"Bravo!"

The familiarity so easily established between the cousins did not worry the Moncalvo parents, who by now were hoping for a great marriage for their daughter. They were certain that Mariannina wouldn't get excited over a person with no money. A different worry disturbed Signora Clara, who in order to interrupt the talk of the young people asked her nephew a question.

"Well, Giorgio, when do you start your classes?"

"When the University opens next month. Meanwhile Salvieni asked me to work in his clinic."

"You're Salvieni's assistant?" asked the Commendatore. "Who has the Chair of...of...?"

Giorgio pronounced a difficult word.

"Yes. Well, well, one doesn't understand but it doesn't matter. How much do they pay you?"

"A thousand two hundred lira."

"For cigars."

"But I don't smoke!" Giorgio objected.

"I mean for small pleasures…very small."

"And then I'll prepare the publications to compete for a position."

"In a secondary school?"

"At the University I hope."

"And if you succeed you'll enter as an untenured professor?"

"Naturally."

"With three thousand lira a year."

"Understood."

"To become a full professor at your leisure with a salary of five thousand lira."

"It will take time."

"As if I didn't know that. That's how long it took your father who today, after ten years, earns the beauty of six thousand lira, less the deductions. Isn't it so?"

Father and son started laughing.

"You're better informed than the tax collector."

"I've always kept my eyes on my nearest relatives," said the Commendatore—"and anyway, as long as poor Lisa was alive she kept us informed about everything. Isn't that so Rachele?"

This allusion to Giorgio's mother and the professor's dead wife displeased both Professor Giacomo and Giorgio. They were not unaware that poor Lisa never accepted with calm her modest financial position. She complained about it in her letters to her sister-in-law, from whom she accepted and sometimes even solicited gifts of some value. And if it depended on her, she wouldn't have hesitated a moment to accept Gabrio's offer. Liberal-hearted and used to managing millions, the Commendatore would gladly have come to help his brother. But woe to anyone who mentioned this to Giacomo. To listen to him, his family had no need of anything.

"You are philosophers…" the Commendatore started again to mitigate the effect of his previous words. "It's a beautiful quality that I admire in other people. *Multa petentibus desunt multa,* those who want much are much in need—I haven't entirely forgotten my Latin."

The professor finished the citation with a laugh. "*Bene est cui deus obtulit, parca quod satis est manu,* happy is he whom God has given, with sparing hand, as much as enough," and added, "Lisa was an angel. Her one fault was not turning to look at those who are worse off. Good God! Between my pay and the fruit of her dowry and that little that I had, we always had the means to make ends meet. Even when I was only a miserable little school teacher. We were never more than three, and Giorgio was a child."

"Still, you did well not touching your capital in those early years."

"To be honest. I broke into my capital two years running to take Lisa and this boy to the mountains. Thank heaven I was able to fill the gap, and at my death Giorgio will have twenty-five thousand lira to add to a similar amount inherited from his mother. He will almost be rich."

"You're not very demanding," said the Commendatore shaking his cigar into the ashtray. "He would have been rich without the 'almost' if he'd accepted my proposal seven years ago."

Mariannina interrupted with a phrase that had no importance for her but that produced a lively impression on her cousin. "If he becomes famous he will console himself for not being a millionaire. Glory is worth as much as riches."

"Glory, glory," muttered the Commendatore, "at twenty everyone dreams of it. How many get it? At any rate, glory also has its injustices. Why should it be reserved for scientists, poets, politicians, warriors? Do you think it requires less brains to conduct a great financial enterprise to a successful conclusion than to make a discovery, write verses, govern a country or win a battle? Men like Morgan or Carnegie."

"I prefer Marconi," the girl jumped in.

Just then the servant opened the door and introduced a mature, fine-looking gentleman whom Giorgio Moncalvo recognized as the elegant cavalier he'd seen at the Villa Borghese with Mariannina.

"How are you, Signora Rachele?" asked the new arrival, bending to kiss the hand that the lady of the house extended to him.

"My brother Giacomo, my nephew Giorgio, Count Ugolini-Ruschi," said Commendatore Gabrio to introduce them. "But perhaps you have met Giacomo already?"

"With the professor? Yes, certainly. I met him some months ago."

"My nephew is a budding professor as well," added Gabrio Moncalvo. "It's a hereditary sickness. He's arrived fresh from Berlin where he completed his studies in physiology. Now he is assistant to Salvieni".

"Berlin!" exclaimed the count. "What a city! We were there ten years ago for the wedding of my cousin Wartenburg, a third cousin on the female side. Have you had an occasion to meet them? A great family, a family that entertains."

"Oh, but I lived such a secluded life," noted Giorgio.

"Many professors frequent my relatives," Ugolini took up again, "and my cousin is a specialist in heraldry. He also knows Italian extremely well."

He turned to Signora Moncalvo and added, "If you permit me, Signora Rachele, I'll introduce them when he comes to Rome for a session of the Order."

"It would be an honor," babbled Signora Rachele, confused until she realized that Ugolini was referring to the Order of Malta, which had knighted him as well. "Ah that villa of theirs on the Aventine! And to think that they never go there! If only that were my villa!"

"We'll go back there, Signora Rachele. We'll go back there when my cousin comes."

Some years ago, Count Ugolini-Ruschi had accompanied the Moncalvo ladies, mother and daughter, and the visit had left, especially in the mind of the mother, a profound impression. A sort of mystical exaltation had overcome her while the Knight of Malta guided her through thick boxwood hedges that defined the rectilinear paths of the modest garden. He showed them the tombs of the ancient Grand Masters. He sat next to them on the splendid terrace, the Tiber and all of Rome spread out at their feet.

"Saint Peter's dominates everything," the Count said with emphasis, pointing out Michelangelo's cupola. Everything else is diminished by comparison. Saint Peter will stay. And it will continue to dominate."

Having no more Turks to fight, the knight of the faith lost no opportunity to magnify the glories of Catholicism to these infidels. And given the women's different characters, Count Ugolini-Ruschi's religious effusions found in Signora Rachele a benevolent hearing.

"You are blessed to be a believer," she repeatedly sighed.

And in her talks with Mariannina she exalted to the sky the perfect gentleman who united so many worldly graces and so much religious piety.

Mariannina agreed that it had been fortunate to know Ugolini. It had enabled her to be present at the canonization of two saints and to be admitted to a reception of the Pope who had deigned to sketch a vague sign of blessing on the head of the heretic. In any case, her maternal mawkishness seemed excessive and brought forth an ironic smile and a disrespectful grimace.

That evening the prospect of returning to the villa on the Aventine at the side of two knights of the Order thrilled even Signora Rachele.

"Ah Ugolini, how kind you are, how courteous. Did you hear, Mariannina?"

"I heard, I heard," answered the girl. "By the way, Count, have you seen Miss May after our ride the day before yesterday?"

"No, I haven't seen her, but she wrote to me sending me a check for a hundred sterling for the destitute women."

"Yes, I knew she planned to do that."

"She sent it yesterday and, as you can imagine, I answered right away. What a generosity that Signorina has!"

"Her father has a billion," muttered the painter Brulati.

"And he makes the most of it," added Gabrio Moncalvo.

"May I?" asked an insinuating voice from the threshold.

It was a little priest, at least fifty years old who but appeared much younger. He came forward into the room.

"Oh, Monsignor Don Paolo de Luchi," said the Commendatore and the two ladies, almost in chorus. "What good fortune brings you here?"

"Indeed, Signora Rachele. I was passing by, saw light in the windows and thought to myself: The Moncalvos are at home. Let's go and greet them."

"Bravo."

The introductions were hardly finished when yet more people entered. Everyone was in evening dress; a secretary of the Minister of the Interior, a deputy of the majority, an important person in foreign affairs. The latter looked around instinctively for a couch where he was in the habit of taking a nap and, seeing it occupied, was perplexed for a moment. The observant Signora Clara pushed him towards a similar one.

"Oh Signora Clara, you will think me a sybarite," said the diplomat hurrying to stretch out in the comfortable seat. "And you will also think that I sleep," he added. "I bet you will."

"Not by any means," returned the Signora. "You pretend to sleep so as not to reveal secrets of the Senate."

"That's it exactly, dear Signora, you understand right away. Don't reveal your own secrets and try to catch out the secrets of others—that's the alpha and omega of our profession."

While the counselor of the insurance company discussed business with Gabrio Moncalvo, the majority deputy and the secretary of the Minister of the Interior made an effort to attract Mariannina's attention. She paid attention to them both without neglecting her cousin Giorgio. Meanwhile, Signora Rachele, seated between Count Ugolini-Ruschi and Monsignor Paolo de Luchi, listened with obvious pleasure to certain communications made by the Monsignor. At one point she couldn't refrain from calling her daughter.

"Mariannina! Mariannina!"

"I'm here. What do you want?"

The Signora signaled her to come over. "Do you know?" she said quietly "I will sign the manifesto for the charity fair right after Princess Oroboni."

"What an honor! Still, you're the one who gave the most."

"But I'm the only one who doesn't have an aristocratic name...and I'm also the only one...you understand me?"

"Yes, the great blemish of your origin..."

"And then next week our good Monsignor says we can go with him to see the palace and the gardens."

"Oh, oh, they deign to spend time with us!"

"The owners won't be there they are at Loreto."

"Well then," Mariannina said with a scornful gesture.

"They never let anyone come when they're not at home," explained the Monsignor. "But I secured permission from them."

"Yes," continued Signora Rachele "and we must be grateful for the privilege."

Giorgio and Giacomo got up.

"Already?" asked the Commendatore.

"We are but savages," Giacomo said smiling.

"We'll expect you soon. We're always home in the early evening."

"I want a visit just for myself," declared Aunt Clara to her nephew. "From noon to four you'll be sure of finding me at home."

"And if you phone in time, you'll find me too," added Mariannina accompanying her relatives to the door." I want to show you my watercolors."

"You paint?"

"Absolutely, I study with Brulati. Some mornings we go to the country in the car. One morning I'll invite you."

"Thank you."

Professor Giacomo cut short the goodbyes, "Good night. Come along Giorgio."

Chapter 3

Two Sleepless People

When the front door of Palazzo Gandi closed behind them, the professor said to his son, "You must be totally convinced this is not the ambiance for us."

Giorgio avoided a definitive answer.

"There's something I don't understand. They are always so open with us, especially uncle and Mariannina, but they aren't the way they were seven years ago. They've changed direction."

"Completely. My brother was radical; now he is conservative; he had strong opinions; now he flirts with the priests."

"But how? But why?"

"Ah, my dear, everyone has his defects…Gabriele…"

"Incidentally now everyone calls him Gabrio."

"It's more chic…. Gabrio, then, is ambitious. Since he didn't succeed in one direction, he's turning the other way."

"And deludes himself that he has the clergy's support to enter Parliament?"

"I believe he's renounced politics."

"What ambitions does he have then?"

"He has some of the ambitions of his wife. She is ambitious too, but like other women she pays more attention to appearances than to substance—entering into the most closed and exclusive salons, being present at the places reserved for the activities of the Vatican, belonging to charity committees where aristocratic ladies of the Catholic aristocracy reign—those are your aunt's great ideals. Gabrio, who is a forward-looking man, toys with the idea of using his International Bank to participate in financial operations with the Vatican."

"It remains to be seen if we'll have the moving spectacle of a conversion!"

"I wouldn't be surprised...though I think that my brother will think twice before burning his bridges. It is useful to him to have a foothold in the liberal camp as well."

"In fact" noted Giorgio, "he receives a very mixed society: a Monsignor, a Knight of Malta, a deputy, an important functionary of the Ministry of Foreign Affairs, what a mosaic!"

"There's someone for every taste."

"And the knight, what kind of man is he?" continued Giorgio. "He seems very intimate with the family. The other morning I saw him at the Villa Borghese with Mariannina and her American friends."

The professor shook his head.

"I hardly know him. He seems like a sly priestling, meddling under the mask of discretion, not at all sincere in the ideals of tolerance he uses to get easy access to the less orthodox salons."

After a pause Giorgio asked, hesitantly: "And what do you think of Mariannina? Listening to her, you'd say that she was clear-headed."

Professor Giacomo looked uneasily at his son. "For heaven's sake, Giorgio, don't trust her. My brother and sister-in-law have the great merit of showing who they are; and that's why, although I don't approve of the ideas or the conduct of Gabrio, I still love him. Along with his weaknesses, he has precious qualities of intellect and heart. After Clara, who is an angel, he's the best head of our family...and maybe not even Rachele is wicked."

"So only Mariannina is wicked," the young man replied with a certain bitterness.

"Let's not exaggerate. Mariannina is an extremely beautiful, much-courted girl whose every whim is granted, with a dowry of a million, not counting the money she'll have when her parents die."

"But she doesn't seem to subscribe to the cult of money," objected Giorgio, "she understands the worth of intelligence, of learning."

"Maybe she understands glory—or rather fame—sounding its thousand trumpets and calling the attention of the crowd to a name. She might be perhaps...capable of falling in love with a famous man...for the fifteen minutes his fame lasts. The day on which another more brilliant sun obscures the star, she will consider herself loosed from her commitment. She is not a woman who will sacrifice herself for the obscure genius or the genius without fortune."

"You are harsh."

"I'm fair. But why are we quarreling now? Thank heaven you don't have to marry her."

"Me?" said Giorgio with feigned indifference. "That's all I need. On the contrary. I'm amazed she isn't married yet. She's nineteen."

"That's not much. Anyway suitors aren't lacking."

"And she hasn't found anyone yet of her station?"

"It appears so."

"What does she want? A prince?"

"Who knows?"

"There are so many here.... But she'll have competition from her American girl friends. And they have more money than she does."

"True...but her money is at hand and theirs is on the other side of the ocean."

Chatting this way, father and son arrived at the opening of the tunnel of the Quirinale. A tram heading to the Prati neighborhood stopped next to them to let someone off.

"We could get on," the professor suggested.

"Gladly."

Without further talk, they arrived at Piazza Della Libertà

and continued on foot the four or five hundred meters to their house near Piazza Cavour.

"We are housed with less luxury than our relatives," the professor joked.

Giacomo had already opened the door and lit a candle with a match.

"In Berlin I always lived in ugly student rooms half the size of my room here," said Giorgio. He tried to take the light from his father's hand but Giacomo wouldn't let him.

"No, for today I'll go first. I have more practice." When, after climbing the 150 steps, they entered the apartment, the professor said, "You know how our little quarter is arranged... your bedroom is there. Do you need anything? Our housekeeper is accustomed to go to bed early. I'd rather not have her wait for me, but if you want..."

"No, papa, why should I have more needs than you?" Giorgio answered exchanging good nights....

In his room, at the desk near a partially unpacked box of books, Giorgio Moncalvo thought about his father with an admiration made up of tenderness and envy. By now Giacomo was known both in Italy and abroad as one of the country's major mathematicians, but the simplicity of his tastes and manners remained unchanged. The brief and fleeting contacts with his incredibly rich brother only increased his love of his sober life, his almost monastic habits, the classrooms of his school, the silent walls of his office.

Similarly, in Berlin, Giorgio—taking his mentor Raucher as a model, a man like his father in so many ways—had lived and dreamed of continuing his own existence undisturbed by passions, undistracted by extreme pleasures or disheartened by a thirst for gold. The sweet adoration of Frida had touched his spirit with the gentleness of a caress, tempering with a breath of poetry the rigid austerity of science.

But today he didn't recognize himself. It had been enough to see Mariannina, brush against her dress, touch her hand, hear her voice, breath her perfume for him to feel like another man, a man similar to those he used to look at from on high as beings of an inferior race. He too felt those fevers of the blood that had seemed up until now a mark of mere bestiality. He too was distracted in his meditations by profane thoughts and lascivious images. At moments he even abandoned himself to the dual illusion he had derided so often: reaching glory more quickly through love and of conquering love though glory. Hadn't Mariannina said she preferred Guglielmo Marconi to Andrew Carnegie?

Nevertheless, Giorgio Moncalvo was one of those madmen who recognized their madness. That night, curved over a German academic article which he'd begun translating in Berlin and wanted to present to the Academy of the Lincei, he was overcome by bitter spasmodic laughter when he read this sentence: "It doesn't matter if a cell is born by splitting, germination, endogenesis or genesis."

"I'm such an idiot!" He exclaimed springing from his chair and giving the table a blow with his fist that made the lamp flame quiver.

"A real idiot! I'll overcome the abyss that separates me from my cousin with my dissertation on genesis and endogenesis!"

And after walking to and fro in his room, he sat down again with the belief that, at least for that night, he had uprooted Mariannina from his mind. He went on writing: "In the end, the content of a living anatomic element doesn't differ in any essential way from the blastema that surrounds it; here and there are organized substances in whose depth there is the incessant movement of molecules."

And yet, "Bravo!" hisses a mocking voice next to Moncalvo. It is the banished image of Mariannina, returned petulant and provocative to disturb him. The mocking voice continued with cold cynicism: "Don't hope to free yourself from me…when you think I'm dead in your memory, I'll revive. I am a toxin that has penetrated your veins and I won't leave until I've drained you. I'm an image fixed in your pupils. It may fade but will never be erased. I am not the colorless and lymphatic Frida Raucher, diaphanous and white like a ray of moonlight. My lips burn, my eyes flame like the sun; I am the eternal feminine that you think to strike with your scorn. I am the eternal feminine and I'll revenge…. I'm not here to love you but to torment you."

Giorgio Moncalvo tried to write again but, that night, he didn't manage to put together two lines. When he decided to go to bed it was already almost five.

In Palazzo Gandi there was also one who didn't sleep. It was Mariannina. But it wasn't the thought of Giorgio Moncalvo that kept her awake. Certainly she had to admit that the young scientist was much more interesting than the dandies who courted her. There was no comparison, for instance, between him and the majority deputy or the Secretary of the Ministry of the Interior who, but a little while ago, had besieged her with their gallantries. But if this was an excellent reason to desire her cousin's company, it wasn't as good a reason to chase shadows and weave the plot of a schoolgirl romance. Mariannina's poorly concealed uneasiness had a different cause altogether. She had received her mother's communication about the possibility of a visit to the palace and the Oroboni gardens with simulated coldness; but the news was in fact unexpectedly pleasant. Entering the jealously guarded enclosure seemed like a first victory, and perhaps a prelude to bigger victories.

How many times since she came to Rome had she looked curiously, insistently, at those massive walls that rose opposite her villa? All along the other side of the noisy street they continued uninterrupted, then along two smaller lateral streets which were badly paved and deserted. In the face of the wall—beyond which the tops of some pine and poplars emerged swaying in the wind—there was no opening at all. Or it would be more exact to say that an earlier great doorway had been closed and bared with solid iron bars. The only visible opening were some small windows, in a little tower on one of the corners—windows defended only by wooden blinds. A fortress or a convent... that was the impression made on anyone walking alongside the inhospitable enclosure whose only entrance, a small door, was to be found at the end of one of the side streets.

However, Mariannina Moncalvo, looking from her second story window, had successfully penetrated the mysterious place. And she had noted that what seemed a simple wall was—at least on the front—in fact a long, narrow terrace, lined with tubs of lemon trees. Certainly an interior stair must lead to the terrace that communicated with the tower. Mariannina could only see a small part of the garden beneath, but it was enough to lead her to believe that it must be ample, rich with water, shade and flowers. By comparison, a ruined seventeenth-century edifice that emerged among the plants—a gray façade and protruding cornice—didn't seem large at all. Mariannina had informed herself about the ancient and most noble Oroboni family that lived there long before Count Ugolini-Ruschi and Monsignor de Luchi began to hang around the house. As they were both members of the nobility that sided with the Pope, and were tied to the Oroboni, they tried to put those pure champions of Roman intransigence in a better light. The original information that Mariannina Moncalvo had collected was true nonetheless. The family was now reduced to two people, the Princess Olimpia and her son, Don Cesarino. Prince Ottavio, Olimpia's father-in-law, had died in 1885. After September 20, 1870,[9] he had protested against the new order of things by never leaving his house except in a closed carriage to go to the Vatican and, to isolate himself even further from the impious and corrupt world, had spent an infinite amount of money on the surrounding wall. The son and successor, Prince Gregorio, had followed the example of his father, but with the addition of an arthritis that made movement painful and difficult—until his last trip undertaken in 1890. Don Cesarino was thus orphaned at fifteen with a wasted patrimony and his own poor health—his only companion his sickly and bigoted mother. He had never felt any need to change his mode of life and vegetated in his palace and his garden, dealing with very few people even of his political party.

Mariannina saw him wandering the garden paths, losing himself in the little ways, bending over the flowerbeds, alone or on the arm of his mother. Once she saw him and the Princess Olimpia closer up, both on the upper terrace in the company of a priest, that same Monsignor de Luchi whom she would soon meet. And she recalled that the priest seemed younger than Don Cesarino, which certainly could not be. The two moved slowly along with the air of a tired old couple, annoyed by all the noises from outside. The priest, who walked a few feet ahead of them, turned at every moment, talked, gesticulated as if he were inciting them to make an effort and overcome their reluctance. Somehow he accomplished the miracle of inducing them to enter the tower, and to look out one of the windows where he had hastened to raise the blinds. Marianinna had the impression of having two ancient portraits presented in front of her: the princess, thin and pale, with grey unmoving eyes and greying hair adhering to her temples, wearing a starched white collar that fell back over her shoulders to emphasize the black silk of her dress; Don Cesarino, tall and thin, pale without the shadow of a beard, of uncertain glance and bloodless lips, his head leaning a little towards his shoulders. Still, he had a certain distinction in his appearance, with that stamp of race that in certain families is preserved until extreme degeneration. Now behind the princess, now behind the son, the jovial physiognomy of Monsignor de Luchi appeared, white, rosy, plump with the malicious glance of someone who knew what's what not just through his ministry but through direct experience. And Mariannina well remembered that on that day, Monsignor had drawn Don Cesarino's attention to *her*. In fact, after the priest whispered in his ear, the young man had turned his eyes to the window where she appeared, leaning next to the blind. He had stared at her obstinately while a light redness suffused his pallid cheeks. She too had blushed, torn between the desire to withdraw from an indiscreet curiosity and the satisfaction of being noticed by a Roman prince. On just this point, Mariannina had a memory as fresh as yesterday's, when Queen Elena with the beautiful Princess Yolanda had passed in an elegant carriage going to the Quirinale.[10] People took off their hats respectfully; the queen inclined her head with a benevolent smile. But not so the Princess Oroboni, who drew back abruptly. Prince Cesarino and Monsignor de Luchi also withdrew, though not so quickly. This last hesitated a moment before closing the shutters. A short while later, all three reappeared on the terrace; the princess walked more swiftly on the arm of her son; the Monsignor talked and gesticulated as before.

After that, Mariannina hadn't seen the young prince and his mother except at a distance among the flower beds and the paths of the garden. Instead, she had met Monsignor de Luchi, who was brought to her own house by Count Ugolini-Ruschi. And the Monsignor, amiable, spontaneous, had quickly won the favor of the family: he accepted a couple of invitations to meals and at dinner he had wormed several hundred lire from the women for a children's hospital, a night shelter, a safe haven for destitute women—he compensated them by sending tickets to functions of Saint Peter's and with the promise to introduce them to the aristocratic patronesses of some charitable work.

"How frivolous we are," said Signora Rachele. "To listen to my brother-in-law Giacomo, Catholic priests are intolerant, fanatical, imbued with prejudice. Instead, I challenge you to find a person more conciliatory than Monsignor de Luchi. Never an unsuitable allusion, never an ironic word.

And Mariannina often repeated half joking, half serious, "that priest is my passion."

Now, with the help of the priest, she was about to cross the forbidden threshold of Casa Oroboni and one day, who knows, that same priest might present her to Donna Olimpia and Don Cesarino.

It was warm and Mariannina, who had begun to undress, opened her window. The trams had stopped, the shops were closed, and half of the electric lamps were extinguished. On the street there were only some hotel buses and a few carriages; a woman seated at the street corner offered pedestrians the *Tribuna* and the *Giornale d'Italia* in a monotonous voice. Opposite, the wall of the Oroboni seemed darker, higher, and more inhospitable than ever. Inside the wall, the garden stretched like a shadowy sea. Breaths of air stirred the masses of plants drawing sighs and fragrance. All of a sudden, Mariannina's eye fixed on a point of light that shone behind the blinds of one of the tower windows. Was it possible that someone was there? It occurred to her that the window was about the same height as her own, and that just as she—if the blind had not been lowered—could have seen clearly who was in there, she herself could be seen. A sudden modesty seized her, a sudden shame at being surprised by an indiscreet glance, half undressed, with her hair loose on her shoulders. She quickly closed the shades, finished undressing and hid herself under the covers. But she couldn't sleep and twice got out of bed and, without turning on the light, drew near the window, opened the edge of the curtain and focused her eye on the tower where the point of light had been before. All was dark. Certainly there wasn't a living soul in the tower. But who could have been there before? A servant come to get an object that had been forgotten? The princess, or Don Cesarino? It would be truly strange for them to come at night to a place they so rarely frequented during the day. But everything was strange about the Orobonis—and it was just this strangeness that exercised such a special attraction on Mariannina Moncalvo. It seemed to her that there must be an extraordinary satisfaction in being admitted to that holiest of places, to belong to that circle of the elect. Everyone went to the Quirinale; she too had been presented to the queen, invited to the court balls where she found herself among the petit bourgeois, with the wives and sons of lawyers and doctors. At the Vatican, it was more or less the same thing—and the Pope received millions of people of every race and every social rank, blessing right and left the human flock that prostrated itself at his feet. Instead, houses like the Oroboni were closed with two chains, and just for this reason it would be a great triumph to penetrate....

During that sleepless night, Mariannina, stretched out on the bed with her hands clasped behind her neck, continued to fantasize. Certain proposals of marriage that she had rejected with the agreement of her family came to her mind. In Cairo a couple of years ago, two barons of finance of Semitic origin; in Rome, newly arrived, the lieutenant of a naval vessel and an official of the cavalry, both of them boasting the crest of Count but without any money.

"It would be easier with money," said Signora Rachele, "but if one is going to make sacrifices, you need a prince."

A bizarre thought made Mariannina smile.

"Here's the prince! Don Cesarino!" she mused. And for a moment she saw herself by the side of this young man who had never known youth; she saw herself the daughter-in-law of that woman who spent her days mumbling orations and protesting against the breach of Porta Pia.[11] Admittedly, it would have been one of the most singular spectacles of these times so rich in surprises.

"Bah!" Mariannina concluded. "I have a million lire dowry; I'm the only daughter and later on I'll have an immense patrimony. I can't fail to get a prince. If it's not him, it will be someone else."

And she turned on her side to try and sleep. It was dawn.

Chapter 4

A Morning Well Spent

Commendatore Gabrio Moncalvo had the habit of rising early, but this morning (a gray morning in November) he got up earlier than usual and went down the stairs to his office, which was composed of an antechamber and three modestly furnished rooms. Usually there was an errand boy in the antechamber, ready for every call; the secretary Fanoli occupied the first of the three rooms—a little dark and thus often lit with electric lights even during the day. The Commendatore was usually in the second, a more cheerful and spacious room which looked out on an ample courtyard. The third was a small, austere room used only for more important visitors or those who had something very important and delicate to discuss.

Secretary Fanoli arrived around nine, so when the Commendatore entered the office there was only the errand boy, intent on dusting the furniture. "The door is still closed," said Moncalvo to him. "Go to the porter's lodge and open it. I'm expecting someone."

He sat at his desk beside a window, and set about correcting the proof of an article that was supposed to appear in the next issue of a financial journal. The light was low but his eyes were good and there was no need to light the lamp.

A little while later the errand boy introduced the expected person, who bowed deeply.

The Commendatore stood up and greeted him.

"Ah, you've arrived. If you don't mind, let's go in here."

In the private room, Moncalvo stretched out on an easy chair and offered another to his visitor.

"Well, do you have the letter?" he asked him.

The man to whom he posed the question—a smallish middle-aged man with neglected and soiled clothes, responded hurriedly: "Of course."

And he took a yellowed letter from a greasy and worn portfolio.

"Give it here."

The man hesitated, not seeing the promised 500 lire appear.

"Don't you trust me?" Gabrio Moncalvo asked sarcastically. "Go then, go with your precious document. If you imagine that I care so much about having it!"

"Oh, Signor Commendatore," the other protested making himself smaller and smaller. "How could you imagine such a thing?"

Moncalvo cautiously took, between two fingers, the letter that this suspicious fellow offered him and moved to the window to examine it.

It was really the one. It was a letter written seven years before to a journalist friend of Zanardelli to obtain the support of the government in an election. Besides professing the most liberal sentiments, Moncalvo solemnly had promised to vote for the law on divorce which, at that time, the Minister seemed determined to pass at any cost.

"You worked at the *Tribuna*?"

"Yes sir."

"And you no longer work there?"

"For some years."

"And for some years you have had this letter?"

"Exactly."

"How did you get it?"

"In an editorial office you know…so many papers get dispersed."

"Oh, I see—you stole it."

"Oh, Commendatore!"

"It doesn't matter. Getting it back I am only exercising my right."

The ex-reporter at the *Tribuna* opened his eyes wide.

"I mean a moral right," added the Commendatore ironically. "Though I believe that, even if this letter were published, I wouldn't lose anything. Who doesn't change his opinion in seven years? In any case I'll keep my word. Here are the 500 lire. Go ahead open, open and verify." And Gabrio Moncalvo gave the journalist an envelope with brand new notes from the Bank of Italy.

With a deeper bow than the one with which he had entered, the anonymous man took his leave.

The banker rubbed his hands.

"That man doesn't know his business," he mused to himself. "He could have made more money. Not that a letter of seven years ago means so much, but it's always better to destroy such evidence. God! A formal pledge to uphold the law on divorce. What would my current friends say?"

As Moncalvo was about to leave the room and return to the correction of his article, the errand boy came back with a visiting card and a letter, given him right then by a foreign gentleman who insisted on being received.

After glancing at the card, inscribed with a name he did not know, the Commendatore opened the letter and looked at the signature. It must have had a hidden power because he immediately welcomed the stranger with an enthusiastic, "Come in, come in!"

The person who was furnished with such a notable recommendation was middle-aged, a man of imposing height, an olive complexion, thick jet-black beard and hair, hook-nosed, with penetrating eyes behind his glasses. He wore a black great coat closed from top to bottom. In his left hand he held a black bowler hat and gloves. He stopped a few feet from the Commendatore and said in French in a doubtful voice, "Signor Commendatore Giorgio Moncalvo?"

"That's me, exactly."

"Doctor Löwe," resumed the other, presenting himself.

"Please sit down," said the Commendatore bringing the stranger into the reserved room and seating him on a sofa. He sat facing him and asked "Have you seen the baron lately?"

"Three days ago in Frankfurt."

"Is he well?"

"So-so...he took the cure at Carlsbad again this summer."

"I haven't seen him in over a year...but we're always in touch about business."

"I know. The baron has spoken of you with much respect as the person who could help me with making my ideas known in Italy. I suppose that you imagine the reason for my visit."

"No...to be honest," answered Moncalvo pretending to be surprised, though he did in fact have an idea of what the doctor wanted. He tried a middle way between open solidarity which he thought contrary to his interests and a decided refusal that might have displeased the magnificent baron of Frankfurt.

The doctor unbuttoned his suit and spread out on a little table several newspaper clippings and pamphlets. "At any rate, the question can't be new to you. That will allow me not to waste too much of your time."

The banker inclined his head ceremoniously. "I would never consider it time lost spent listening to someone who enjoys the confidence of the baron."

After making a gesture of thanks, Doctor Löwe approached the heart of the subject.

His testimony was brief and clear. He was one of the leaders of the Zionist movement and was touring Europe to proselytize for his idea and assure its triumph by finding material and moral help. German by birth, he had lived in Galicia a long time. In Russia and Romania he had seen with his own eyes the persecution of the Jews. He was persuaded because of the profound roots of anti-Semitism in those countries that—even if the laws changed and the legal disabilities that weighed heavily on the Jewish race were abolished and the governments became as favorable to them as they were now against them—the situation of the Jews would remain more or less the same. The only remedy, he argued, was abandoning these inhospitable lands en masse and forming a Hebrew state in the lands of the temple ruins, the biblical traditions, and the history of the glories and sorrows of the Jewish people.

Doctor Löwe spoke with warmth and conviction, without losing self-control and without taking his eyes from his interlocutor, whom he sensed was more hostile than indifferent. And several times he anticipated the Commendatore's objections.

"I know, I know: Western Jews aren't aware of the real state of things...they've won so many rights, they can become magistrates, generals, ministers...but they shouldn't deceive themselves. Anti-Semitism, rather than attenuating in the most affected countries, is reappearing in those that were immune. Where it isn't manifest, it is latent.... In France anti-Semitism is growing and...even in Italy you can see signs of it."

The doctor seemed highly gratified by his own statements and continued unperturbed.

"That could be fortunate, because the blindfold will fall from the eyes of the most reluctant and all our admirable faculties will be turned to the final triumph of the race. Israel hasn't fulfilled its mission in the world... I know, I know," he repeated himself with apostolic emphasis, thinking that he noticed a smile on the lips of Giorgio Moncalvo. "They are skeptical about the destiny of our people. They look to the nationality they hope to assimilate to...never, never..."

"And still," Moncalvo insinuated, "through intermarriage…"

"Mixed marriages!" exclaimed the doctor. "If a Christian enters our house and, without abjuring her faith, allows the family to continue Jewish as before, there is nothing to be said. But if it's a question of creating a family without religion, or if they agree to baptize their children, only misfortune can come from it…. Believe me, Signor Commendatore, even from the point of view of material interests these calculations are wrong. Neither the baptism of their children, nor their own baptism is enough to realize the fusion they dream of. Through three or four generations the stamp of the race will reveal itself and triumphant prejudice will punish the apostates and the descendants of apostates."

"Wait a minute," objected the Commendatore. "There is more than one Rothschild who has taken the holy water. There are some in Paris in the Saint Germaine district, there are some in London, the wife of Rosebery for example…."

The face of the doctor contracted woefully. "Unfortunately… it is one of the Baron's great afflictions…but the few who desert don't break the complex structure of an army. We are still a great family."

At this point the apostle, following the nature of his people and uniting the imagination of the visionary to the positive spirit of a practical man, thought it time to reach a conclusion. "Let's leave general considerations aside," he said, "and, for the moment, content ourselves with what is possible. The resurrection of the kingdom of Israel is a beautiful dream that will be realized with time. But now it is a question of helping our persecuted brethren, finding them a strip of land where they can live in peace and worship their God. If it isn't a state it will be a colony, if not in Palestine then somewhere else. I'm not one of the intransigents. We will study the proposals that will be made… including that of Uganda which it seems England wants. The important thing is to procure a stable seat for those who have no country...that which we Germans call *eine Heimstätte für die Heimatlosen*.... And note that using the word *Heimstätte*, homeland, we put aside the political concept. If we put it in these terms, no one ought to be skeptical and our enterprise will be deemed philanthropic and civilized."

"Oh, without a doubt," began Moncalvo but he stopped, having heard the ringing voice of Marianinna talking to the secretary, who must have just come in.

"He isn't available? Patience. You'll let him know that I..."

"Excuse me," said the Commendatore to Doctor Löwe."I have to go and see what my daughter wants; I'll be back...."

"Please, don't stand on ceremony."

When Mariannina saw her father she kissed him effusively. "Fanoli," she said playfully, "was resolved to let himself be killed rather than let me go to you."

"It's a precise instruction," explained the banker. "No one is allowed to enter the little room unless I call them."

"What mysteries are in the little room then? Is it reserved only to grown-ups...like in certain guard houses?" Mariannina went on, shaking her head. "However, if Fanoli had precise orders, he did his duty and I propose him for a promotion...."

Moncalvo looked at the lovely girl with paternal pride. She was in her bonnet, ready to go out. "Silly! Tell me what you want. Hurry. I have someone inside."

"I wanted to tell you that I'm going with Brulati and Aunt Clara in the car and I won't be eating at home."

"And where are you going?"

"To Mentana to sketch an old Borghese Palace that according to Brulati is very picturesque."

"You're not going to drive the car?"

"You know I drive very well."

"Umm!"

"But there's the chauffeur, Giovanni."

"That's good. He's a prudent man."

"Apropos of automobiles, our eight horsepower Panhard that goes 35 kilometers an hour isn't worthy of us. Miss May's Mercedes has more that forty horsepower and can get up to 90 kilometers an hour."

"It's exactly what I don't want," the Commendatore clarified. "This is mad. I don't have Miss May's millions."

"At least a Fiat with 24 horsepower—that's not going to ruin you."

"Enough. For now I'm not going to buy anything.... Instead, tell me how you persuaded Aunt Clara...with her rheumatism? With her fears?"

"As far as fears go, she hasn't any except when I drive. And I have sworn not even to put my hand on the steering wheel. And as for the rheumatism, we'll wrap her in shawls...we take so many with us."

"Well, do take care. The day will be chilly."

"We'll be well covered. I told you that we have lots of shawls. See you later!" Mariannina blew a kiss at her father, gave a friendly wave to Fanoli, and went out the door.

"I'll see the mail later," said Moncalvo to his secretary. "Now I'll finish with the gentleman" And he added a gesture which kept him from exclaiming: "What a nuisance."

Naturally, reentering the little room he renewed his apologies to Dr Löwe.

"Don't give it another thought!" the doctor mumbled and took up where he left off. "If I'm not mistaken, you agree that given the limits to which we restrict our campaign, no one has a motive to take umbrage." Encouraged by a sign of assent, the doctor continued. "I have no doubt that you will want to be part of the Zionist committee of Rome.... I'd even hoped you would preside over it."

Moncalvo immediately gauged the consequences of the step he was being urged to take and he became guarded. "Dear doctor. You caught me unprepared and must permit me not to answer on the spot. On one point though I can answer immediately, and I'm sorry to have to respond in the negative. As far as the presidency don't even think of it. Among your co-religionists who live in the capital…"

"Ours," emphasized Doctor Löwe.

"As you wish…ours. Among the Israelites in Rome there are many more notable than I. Many who have a reputation in politics, in science, in art, there are many of the most orthodox whom you ought to consider."

"Orthodoxy isn't indispensable. We manifest the solidarity of the race independent of religious questions."

"That's a more subtle point," responded the Commendatore. "You insist on this godforsaken race, on this assumed nationality. But we westerners don't believe in a Jewish nationality and as for race, after centuries it is now bastardized. My God! How many races there are in Italy—Longobards, Etruscans, Romans and whatever else…. Who distinguishes them? And also our women…"

"Don't doubt it: the Hebrew will always be distinguishable," the doctor interrupted in a lively fashion, fixing his eyes on Moncalvo's face—which was of a pronouncedly Semitic type. "At any rate, the baron assures me that you're not one of those who disdain their origins."

"There is nothing to be ashamed of," replied the Commendatore, a little annoyed. "But it's quite another thing to take an active part in the movement, to enter the Committee…."

"Won't you even join the committee? We spoke first of the presidency."

"There is nothing more to say about that."

"And the Committee?'

"Slow, slow.... I'll think about it. I'll give you a positive answer, in any case..." added Moncalvo, who was afraid of compromising the good relationship he had with the Rothschilds. "Don't think that I won't help the enterprise...to the limits of my powers, which cannot be compared to the Baron's! Is there a social fund?"

Doctor Löwe pointed to the pamphlets he had brought with him. "I'll leave you these publications. You'll see that the members of the Association pledge an annual contribution that has nothing to do with extraordinary obligations."

"That's fine." responded Moncalvo. "I'll make my gift as well, don't doubt it."

"We accept everything with gratitude. However, your collaboration would be more precious to us than any gift of money. And before the final agreement on the committee I'll come back to you."

"It will always be an honor. Are you staying awhile?"

"I need to hurry and finish this week."

"And where are you staying?"

The commercial traveler for Zionism named a modest inn in old Rome run by an Israelite.

"I would like to have you at my table" said Moncalvo, sure that the other wouldn't accept. "Tomorrow? The day after?"

"Thank you, but I'll be taking all my meals at the inn," the doctor responded, bowing. His rigid orthodoxy did not permit him to sit at a table where the food wasn't set out according to orthodox Jewish practice. And so he took his leave, accompanied by the Commendatore to the stair landing.

The banker went back to Fanoli's room to glance at the mail.

"Look at this telegram first," said the secretary, showing his employer the dispatch which had arrived minutes before.

"Ah, they offer us three hundred thousand lire to put off the sale of the thousand shares of Terni to be delivered at the end of the month. Send them the agreement by telegraph."

"I think that, if we insisted, they'd give us ten thousand more lire," suggested Fanoli.

Commendatore Moncalvo shook his head. "Don't insist. Who tightens the cord too much breaks it. I've always followed this maxim in my dealings and I was always able to congratulate myself for it."

Correct, respectful, the secretary didn't add a word and set about writing the telegram of consent, after he had passed his employer a private letter.

"Umm!" mused Moncalvo, twisting his nose. "I smell the odor of the Count. This is Ugolini...."

"His promissory note will be due in a few days," added Fanoli.

"I'm sure he's not going to pay," returned the banker opening the envelope. "Here it is.... He is asking for the payment to be extended six months."

"For the second time."

"Ah, dear Fanoli, a third is to be expected, a fourth and so on. I've never counted on the repayment of those fifteen thousand lire. But Ugolini is a reasonable man.... If instead of those fifteen thousand he had asked twenty or twenty-five, I would have been embarrassed to say no. That Ugolini is a precious man.... He takes my women here and there. He saves me from a great deal of annoyance...above all with my wife who never finishes singing his praises to me. And he is a Knight of Malta, which imposes silence on malicious tongues."

Fanoli kept himself from smiling at the naiveté of his employer and asked, curling his mustaches, "Therefore the extension is approved?"

"Absolutely, most approved. Fifteen thousand lire from me, an equal amount from the International Bank isn't excessive for one with so many connections—and it even does good to the Bank indirectly."

(Here we note, in parentheses, that the Commendatore Gabrio Moncalvo was the soul of the Bank and passed most afternoons there deciding on everything.)

After a quick glance at the other letters and telegrams, our banker set himself again to the revision of his proofs. But even now he wasn't left in peace for, announced by a mellifluous, "Am I bothering you?" the ruddy, smooth face of Monsignor de Luchi appeared before him.

"Oh, you?" exclaimed Gabrio Moncalvo. "Come in."

"Good morning, Commmendatore. You look surprised to see me. Perhaps because of the unusual time."

"Not the time, I'll explain, I'll tell you.... Come into the reserved room...go ahead, sit down." And, making him sit where the apostle of Zionism had been sitting before, he explained in a few words who his predecessor was and what he wanted.

"That's the reason for my exclamation of surprise. These are contrasts of ideas that we only see in our time and only in Rome.... What a confusion of tongues, isn't that true, Monsignor? A priest of the Catholic Church, a Hebrew of the old type, and one who is neither fish now fowl...."

"We're in the City of Rome," noted the ecclesiast.

"But before the 1870s certain differences weren't possible."

"Why not, why not?" responded the Monsignor who said that all the time. He went on, "The Church is inflexible in its principles and intransigent in appearances but, in the end, it has always been exceedingly tolerant."

"You jest?"

"I'm serious. The Popes have never excluded anyone from their presence."

"If you say so. What's certain is that you, Monsignor, are a true man of the world, a truly modern man."

"The Church is always ancient and always modern. It's contemporary in every century and is well acquainted with all the issues."

"Even Zionism?"

"Why not? The Church knows that the temple of Solomon won't be rebuilt. The Church will not permit the rise of an Israelite kingdom in the same place as the tomb of Christ, but it doesn't disapprove of the emigration of the Hebrews towards whatever region where they can live in peace. It will be all the more probable that those who are assimilated into our civilization will embrace our faith."

"Therefore—excuse me if for a moment I pretend to be a good Catholic and take you for my spiritual advisor—you don't think that my support of the enterprise could harm me among your friends?"

"Of the Zionist enterprise?"

"Exactly."

"Not at all. It would just be necessary to see their plan.... Have you also signed?"

"No, no," the Commendatore replied, who had already decided not to subscribe. "Not the signature. Everything will be limited to a monetary contribution."

"That's quite natural. A person with your financial position and who belongs, at least officially, to the Israelite persuasion can't close his purse."

Moncalvo who, after all, was satisfied by the response of Monsignor de Luchi, shook his head. "They think my purse is inexhaustible...but it would only take a crisis...."

"Never mind, never mind...someone with your capital, your ability, your connections, isn't afraid of crises. But let's get to us...."

"I'm here, all ears."

"Well, it has to do with the Oroboni business. Has the

council of the International Bank met?"

"Yes, it met, has discussed…but it is a bone that sticks in the throat. I won't hide it from you. The business deal doesn't present the necessary guarantees to justify the loan. And also, the law itself demands them. You see, the Bank is in a great hurry to get out of it."

"It's a leftover from the Roman bank, and it's understandable that the Bank of Italy wishes to sell as soon as possible. The law itself demands unfreezing the capital—what a horrid expression! If only all investments were as secure as this one. Curious, though…for two years now this large property hasn't yielded enough to pay the interest…especially curious since there are only two Orobonis and they don't live in luxury."

"Far from it…but the administration has been neglected. Leaving aside the city palace, the properties could return four times what they do now."

"If they don't know how to administer it, they should sell."

"Up until now the princess hasn't wanted to, and Don Cesarino is so obsequious to his mother! That doesn't mean he couldn't change his mind…if there were an advantageous proposal…. Dear Commendatore," added the ecclesiastic as if an unexpected thought had come to him, "have you ever thought that acquiring it could be an advantage to you?"

"Me?" exclaimed Moncalvo, pretending to be surprised. "How can you think I could take a million from my company? We bankers need live money."

"Oh, really! Even with a million less your business would prosper. There will always be enough…and in the worst case credit works miracles. Two lines of a telegram to your friend Rothschild and those coffers will be available to you."

"You want to joke, Monsignor. No, no this isn't an operation for me."

"It would be a golden business deal. The palace in Rome

and the small villa of Porto d'Anzio together are worth a million. And all the properties in Albano will go to you in the bargain and in your hands they will yield six percent and more.

"Ha! For all I know about agriculture!"

"You'll get a good agent."

"The Oroboni's agent, for example?"

"No, their agent wouldn't suit you. But the new owner won't be tied by any obligation."

"Stop now, this is a useless discussion, and as for the loan with the International Bank, what do you want me to say? I'm sorry, but I'm afraid nothing will come of it. I can try again."

"It's important to hurry before the Bank of Italy sends it to public auction. Not that the auction is necessarily ruinous. I bet that there will be applicants for even more than a million…. But it's the effect on the morale of the princess and Don Cesarino… and the prospect of having to leave their palace."

"That would happen even with a private sale."

Monsignor de Luchi adjusted his collar.

"That depends on the buyer. It could be someone who agrees to rent it to the present proprietors."

"Bravo! Never collecting the rent! No, no, dear Monsignor… whoever buys the palace and the garden would have to make a fresh start and profit from the area by building…five or six floors, small rooms, all the modern comforts…with time it could be a pretty good investment."

Ah Commendatore," exclaimed the priest clasping his hands, "what sacrilege! To destroy one of the few oases that remain! As if they hadn't defaced our Rome enough! And what would be said to the ladies who have such an exquisite sense of art. You remember several days ago when I had the honor to accompany them to the palace and the Oroboni gardens, you remember how enthusiastic your Mariannina was."

"It's very true. Demolishing it would be a sin, but the buyer couldn't do anything else."

"I bet that you wouldn't demolish it."

"I'm afraid you'd lose that bet."

"You wouldn't want to displease your wife and daughter...."

Moncalvo shook his head.

"But on the other hand my wife and daughter wouldn't suggest a ruinous speculation. They also have an instinct for business. It's in the blood." Saying this the Commendatore smiled. Then changing the argument he made this proposal. "Let's leave business aside for the moment. Do something pleasant...come to lunch with us. My wife and I are alone...Mariannina and my sister-in-law are in the car and won't be back till afternoon.... Come, what obligations do you have?"

"But...really," mumbled Monsignor.

"Don't look for excuses," insisted Moncalvo.

Actually, the Monsignor was extremely disposed to accept. He was sure that staying for lunch wouldn't have the consequence of leaving aside the business, but rather of putting it back on the table in more favorable conditions—with an efficacious ally beside him. Donna Rachele had great sympathy for the Orobonis, and hearing about their economic problems she would be delighted if her husband might save them from the shipwreck.

"A disinterested sympathy?" the Monsignor wondered.

He believed that he read the soul of that woman to be full of vanity and ambition. And perhaps he wasn't mistaken. But he wasn't a closed book to her either, and maybe she understood something as well. Who knows if they wouldn't come to an understanding?

"Well, what are you thinking?" asked the banker.

"What would you have me say? One can't resist your courtesy. What time would it be?"

"We go to table at twelve fifteen."

"And I will be with you by twelve fifteen. It's half past ten. I have time to go to the Cancelleria and return."

"That's quite a walk. Would you like me to hitch the horse to the fiacre?'

"Goodness, no. I walk willingly and at any rate there is a tram right at the door."

"As you like. In a few minutes the fiacre could be ready."

"No, but thanks."

"Thank you for accepting the invitation." And the Commendatore accompanied the priest to the landing as he had previously accompanied the Zionist.

Two stockbrokers waited in the antechamber. On Fanoli's desk were some open telegrams whose content seemed to give much satisfaction to Gabrio Moncalvo.

"Some money leaves but fortunately much more enters," he said to himself. Then he called the errand boy. "Go to the house and let my wife know that Monsignor de Luchi will be coming to lunch with us." Finished with the brokers, Moncalvo dictated a letter in French to his secretary:

Signor Doctor,

I am putting 25,000 francs at the disposition of the noble work to which you have consecrated your efforts. I will charge my friends the barons Rothschild of Frankfurt to release the money in my stead to the central fund. I naturally agree that my name will figure among the Donors. However, I regret that I cannot enter the Roman committee. Wishing you the greatest success in your endeavor, I beg you to accept the assurance of my profound esteem.

Yours Sincerely,
Gabrio Moncalvo

After having added his signature, the Commendatore dictated the address and ordered his secretary to send off the letter as quickly as possible.

"This business has been taken care of too," he said rubbing his hands together.

Chapter 5

In the Car

The car crossed Piazza delle Terme and Via XX Settembre at a sedate pace. Inside were four people: Mariannina Moncalvo with her Aunt Clara, the painter Brulati and the chauffeur, Giovanni.

At a certain point Mariannina cried out: "Stop!"

Giovanni put on the brakes and the car stopped at the corner of the Grand Hotel. The porter of the hotel took a couple of steps thinking that someone wanted to get out; then, seeing that the matter had nothing to do with him, he turned back yawning.

"What is it?" asked Aunt Clara, frightened.

"Nothing, nothing," answered Giovanni turning around.

But Mariannina made a sign with her hand to a young man who came running up, saying, "It's Giorgio."

The young professor who had obeyed his cousin's call (and how could he not obey her?), came up red faced and breathless to the car, around which some loafers were already buzzing.

"Good morning," he said, greeting everyone but having eyes only for Mariannina. "Are you on an excursion?"

"An artistic tour," replied the girl. "We're gong to Mentana to paint with Brulati."

"To Mentana!" exclaimed Giorgio struck by the name. "Where they fought the battle of November 1867?"[12]

"If you say so. There's a very picturesque castle of the Borghese's...at least according to my illustrious maestro. I'm going there for the first time." She looked maliciously at the young man. "You too have a wild desire to see Mentana, I'm sure…for love of the battle, naturally, the battle with Garibaldi, now I remember. Come with us…."

"What if we don't all fit in the car?" insinuated Aunt Clara.

"We'll fit fine," returned her niece. "He can ride between us …squeezing a little…take heart, get in. It's a favor that you don't deserve because you haven't visited for ages."

Signora Clara, who had a high opinion and affection for Giorgio and wanted to save him from the flirtatiousness of her niece, renewed her objections.

"We'll make him uncomfortable and we'll be uncomfortable as well. And probably he has work to do, and his father will be expecting him for lunch."

"No," said the young man. "Today my father won't be eating at home. He is in Frascati at a colleague's. He wanted me to come too, but it bored me. I know I am more retiring than he is."

"So there are no more excuses…. Come on, Signorino."

Giorgio hesitated.

"I don't want to displease Aunt Clara."

"What displeasure could you give me?" returned Aunt Clara. "Your company is always dear to me, but this naughty one will make you lose half a day."

"And all of your wits," muttered Brulati almost incomprehensibly. He had a boundless admiration for the beautiful girl and, despite his fifty-five years, he sighed platonically for her.

Meanwhile Giorgio had taken his place between his cousin and his aunt as best he could.

"I was sure that we'd fit comfortably," exclaimed Mariannina triumphantly, and she ordered the chauffeur, "Go ahead!"

"Are you sure of the weather?" asked Giorgio looking at the sky which was covered by large clouds.

Signora Clara drew the plush cover over her knees, "I'm also afraid it's going to rain."

"It won't rain," pronounced Mariannina "and the sky and the countryside are more picturesque this way than when it's clear."

In a flash, the car exited Porta Pia and they found themselves on Via Nomentana, flanked by villas left and right.

"Ah, these Roman villas!" said Mariannina, pressing Giorgio's elbow. He jumped at the touch of her white hand. And she added, immediately, "Incidentally, we haven't seen each other since I visited the Oroboni's garden and palace. You know of my great curiosity about it."

"I know," the young man responded, disturbed by this announcement without being able to say why. "And how did you manage to penetrate the palace?"

"It was the work of Monsignor de Luchi…my Monsignor."

Giorgio shrugged his shoulders. "It's a strange taste to have a priest underfoot at every moment."

"Eh, my dear, we're not intolerant. That little priest would throw himself into the fire for me."

"You think so? He'll have his ulterior motives."

"You're quick to accuse him. You'll have to prove your accusation."

Giorgio didn't take back his challenge and continued: "Well, and what wonders are at these Oroboni's villa?"

"Everything is singular and has its particular character. Ask Brulati."

"He was there too?"

The artist who was sitting next to the chauffeur turned to respond. "Yes, I didn't let the opportunity pass. But perhaps the place wouldn't be such a draw if it were not almost inaccessible to the profane…. In Rome, there are gardens infinitely larger and better maintained, with a greater richness of plants, of water, of flowers."

"Now Brulati is willfully misleading," said Mariannina. "He also agreed that one of the attractions of the garden was its being so neglected."

"I don't deny it. It reminds me a little of the painting by Calderini, *Abandoned Gardens*."

"Exactly. Ah, those paths where grass is growing, those trees that no one dreams of trimming..."

"Let's hear Aunt Clara's opinion," said Giorgio.

"Clara has no opinion," responded the interrogated aunt, "because Aunt Clara wasn't there."

"If Aunt Clara were or weren't there," Mariannina resumed heatedly, "that doesn't alter the fact, my handsome Signorino, that that villa of the Oroboni in the center of Rome is a marvel."

"You have strange tastes!" countered Giorgio. "Putrification, death...but I love life in the appearance of things and people."

And he enveloped his beautiful cousin—who was in fact the symbol of life and youth—in a passionate look.

Mariannina, who had just come from a lecture on the *Virgin of the Rocks*, told Giorgio that he wasn't an artist, that he didn't understand the poetry of the ruins, of still water, of decayed leaves, of the dying aristocracy."

"And the champions of this aristocracy were there? Did you meet them?"

"I wish! But they weren't there. They were at Loreto."

"To fulfill a vow?"

"Who knows? Loreto must be beautiful."

"The fair of indulgences and the meeting place of the misguided."

"Have you been there?"

"No, but I was nearby, in Recanati."

"The home of Leopardi?"

"Yes, that was a man...quite different from your Orobonis."

"Who makes such a comparison? And yet I haven't given up hope of meeting them."

"Are you going back?"

"Why not? As Monsignor de Luchi always says."

"The Monsignor will take you there?"

"The Monsignor, of course…what's the harm? What has my good little priest done to you?"

"What do you want me to say?" replied Giorgio. "I don't know what possible common interests can there be between Monsignor de Luchi and the daughter of Commendatore Gabrio Moncalvo. Once…"

"Once," added Mariannina vivaciously, "the Monsignor would have found a way to burn me alive. Now he comes to dinner with us…. Doesn't that seem better?"

"Surely it's better…but it doesn't negate the fact that your Monsignor and those mummified Oroboni you rave about represent a world, an order of ideas very different from our ideas and our world. I call on Aunt Clara…."

The good woman, somewhat discomforted by the speed of the car had enveloped herself deeper in her shawls. She secretly agreed with Giorgio, but wanted to avoid discussion and contented herself by responding: "Dear children, above all don't argue. Let everyone think in their own way."

"But it's this young professor who wants to impose his views," responded the girl with a petulant voice.

"You stop, too," urged the Aunt.

"I amuse myself by making him angry," Mariannina answered in a softened voice, "and then I want to have the credit of refining his tastes. He is a scientist, but he's a bourgeois…"

"What does that mean?"

"It means…it means…," said Mariannina feeling her way, "one who accepts current opinions."

Giorgio shook his head, disagreeing.

"Yes sir. Today it's the fashion to protest against obscurantism, clericalism…," Mariannina said.

"What? What?" interrupted her cousin, "On the contrary, clerics are back in favor."

"Slow down, Giovanni" cried Signora Clara, "there's a cart up ahead."

"Eh. I see it."

The two-wheeled cart drawn by two horses with red ribbons came noisily down from the Nomentano Bridge. Under the characteristic blue umbrella, the cart driver hardly gave a glance at the car that brushed by him. A snarling dog barked.

From the Nomentano Bridge, the road, that had been wide and straight, shrunk, becoming irregular and torturous, sinking and rising until it dominated the melancholy and suggestive landscape. Several *butteri* on horses crossed the large meadows where their cattle grazed.[13] A few eucalyptus, a solitary oak, some pines, interrupted the monotony of the gently undulating green plain.

"Please. Slowly!" Signora Clara frequently implored.

Under the heavy felt cover that was big enough for three—and of which Mariannina had reclaimed her part—Giorgio Moncalvo sought for the hand of his beautiful cousin and squeezed it firmly. She, always calm, responded with a light pressure of her fingers; then she freed her imprisoned hand and readjusted her veil. An enigmatic little smile played across her lips.

"Soon it will rain," sighed the Aunt, looking at the sky that was darker than before.

Mariannina gestured impatiently. "That's impossible. I bet on the way back it's going to be sunny."

And Giorgio, now ready to agree to anything, added: "In fact, down there there's a strip of blue."

Brulati who, instead was in a terrible mood, turned to contradict him. "But what blue? Those mountains were clear earlier and now they are covered. Without a doubt it will rain and if it were up to me I'd turn the car around and go back to Rome. It is not a day for drawing."

"I think Brulati's right," said Aunt Clara, but the two young people cried out, almost with one voice: Turn back? Now that they'd almost arrived? For fear of a little rain? As if in any case it weren't better to arrive in a little village where it should be easy to find shelter.

Mariannina was particularly harsh with the painter. Wasn't he ashamed at being so cowardly?

Giorgio declared that for himself rather than renounce seeing Mentana, which by now was only a few kilometers away, he'd go the rest of the way on foot. "Bravo!" exclaimed Mariannina, "I'll come too."

"You want to?" asked Giorgio gazing in her eyes.

"Are you two mad?" interrupted Aunt Clara. Mariannina shrugged. "Dear Aunt, you need to be catechized by Miss May."

"Miss May doesn't have to catechize me at all," responded Signora Clara. "She can regulate herself according to the American way of doing things. We follow the European ways." Signora Clara said these things without losing her composure, without raising her voice but with an intonation that contrasted with her slender, sickly, submissive appearance.

Mariannina didn't rebel even though at heart she was fuming and found the subjection that her aunt inspired in certain moments inexplicable.

"Is this blessed Mentana near by?" Aunt Clara asked Giovanni.

"If you'll permit me to go a little faster we'd be there in five or six minutes."

"Go ahead then, but prudently."

"Of course."

The car accelerated its speed; the squeals of the horn echoed almost uninterrupted along the solitary road.

Aunt Clara closed her eyes and rested her head against the back of the seat. The two young people, on the other hand, with their lungs expanding, breathed in voluptuously the tingling air that beat against their faces.

"Auff!" said Mariannina, raising the veil sticking to her temples and cheeks.

"This is what I like...to cut the wind, devour space, be masters of the road...."

"I would like to go around the world like this," declared Giorgio in a low voice.

"It's long."

"In the right company it would seem short to me," added the young professor speaking close to his cousin's ear.

She took up her ironic tone.

"The good company would be me, that's understood...?"

"Of course!"

"An abduction by automobile... there are so many examples. We have to see if the chauffeur would agree."

"Without a chauffeur...for heaven's sake!"

"Then I'll drive...because you don't even know how to hold the wheel, that's obvious at once.

"Unfortunately," confessed Giorgio, mortified.

"In this case...because I also drive any which way, it would be a disaster."

"It would be a beautiful death."

"Thank you...for you...but I would be there too."

"Here's Mentana," announced Brulati and pointed at a group of houses. "The highest one is the Borghese castle.... They call it a castle, but really it's just a big old broken down palace...picturesque enough when there is sun...today unfortunately..."

"And the battle," Giorgio asked anxiously, "where was it fought?"

Brulati, though he was from Rome, knew little about it. "Around here," he said. "I think that Garibaldi with his men was in Mentana, marching towards Tivoli. The Pope's men had occupied the houses, the hills.... I was only a boy then... further on there is an altar to the fallen—and they are building a museum to bring together the relics of the battle."

Giorgio kept up his questions.

"Oh," said Mariannina, "it's the history of forty years ago. Who cares about it!"

Aunt Clara shook herself and protested energetically: "It's history, it's our history and it's necessary to remember it. I was, like Brulati, little more than a girl at that time and still I remember how much it was spoken of. At our house, they criticized the young men who had responded to Garibaldi's call and I scandalized my grandparents by saying that if I'd been a man I would have immediately enlisted."

Giorgio said with a sigh, "I always envy people born half a century before me.... They at least had the possibility of dying as heroes."

"Bah," responded Mariannina with a grimace. "As if, to be a hero it is enough to die in battle. A bullet could also find a man who was running away."

They had reached the edge of the village and Brulati suggested they stop and get out. If it was necessary to return by the same route it was better to turn the car right away. Those who wanted to see the monument to the fallen could get there on foot. It was only a few steps to the little piazza that was in the middle of Via III November. He knew the monument very well and preferred to go towards the castle to familiarize himself with the place, to choose the spot best suited for a sketch...if not today, another day.

"I'll go with Brulati," announced Mariannina jumping from the car. "Then he'll take me to the monument to meet up with Aunt Clara and Giorgio. Dear Brulati, although you know the monument by heart, nothing stops you from seeing it one more time."

Flattered at the idea of paying cavalier to the fascinating girl, the painter bowed deeply. "You command and I obey."

"Alright," said Signora Clara taking her nephew's arm, "you'll meet us later. Is it this way?"

"Yes Ma'am, this is the street, Via III November," said an old village guide who, without being asked, had come to the strangers' side.

"Are you leaving them alone?" asked Giorgio as he watched the two move away.

The aunt couldn't keep from laughing. "What scruples! Even though earlier you wanted to take a trip around the world alone with Mariannina. You spoke softly but I have good ears!"

Giorgio turned red and babbled some disconnected phrases.

"Oh don't be embarrassed. I'm not afraid that you will turn your cousin's head. There's no one who can excite her. You'll see if I have to worry about leaving her alone with Brulati, who is fifty-five and won't compromise her.... In any case, he's in more danger than she is. But if he doesn't know how to defend himself, so much the worse. He interests me to a point. But you, I really care about you and I don't want you to lose your peace of mind. If it has to be like that, it would have been better for you to have stayed in Germany."

It was more or less the same conversation that Giorgio had had with his father, and he had recognized the strength of their argument.

In order to respond to his aunt, Giorgio denied being in love with Mariannina. She pleased him, of course, and when he was with her he came under the spell she cast on everyone but he still wasn't addled enough not to recognize that she wasn't the girl for him.

Not persuaded, Aunt Clara shook her head, "Don't seek her out, then...she's dangerous, I assure you."

"Like papa, you are hostile to Mariannina," noted Giorgio bitterly.

Signora Clara grew impatient. "I? I wish her well from the bottom of my heart. I've watched her grow up, and the house will feel deserted when she's no longer there. But I know her— her virtues and her defects—she'll make many people suffer a lot. And she's not responsible. She knows how to triumph with her beauty, with her grace, with the vagaries of her character; she knows that men get ecstatic when she smiles or glances at them and she dispenses smiles and glances believing that she will make them happy. Is it her fault that the happiness of today becomes tomorrow's grief? Is the flame guilty if it burns? Flee her, flee her."

"Then I should never, never come to uncle's house anymore? I come there so seldom as it is."

"If you can't arm yourself with indifference, you shouldn't go there. But look—the guide is giving us a sign."

Down a gentle slope, they came to the space where the altar to the fallen of Mentana rose up, girdled by an iron railing. There they read incised the beautiful epitaph of Guerrazzi:[14] "The mouth of this tomb utters a voice to the living, a voice that says: Come on! Be less cowardly and make sure that we did not die in vain, for liberty and our country."

The custodian came up with the keys, opened the gate and a little door that led to the inside of the altar, and lit a candle above a corbel. In the center of that dark and massive square cell, a sarcophagus of marble held, visible through the crystal cover, bones and skulls of the fallen of the November 3 battle.

On the corbel, near the light, was a cup full of visiting cards. Silently Giorgio deposited his.

"Poor young men," sighed Aunt Clara.

"No aunt, don't cry for them," protested Giorgio. "They died for a great cause."

"There are great causes to fight for and, if necessary, to die for in every time." The custodian thought she ought to add her opinion. "I was there."

Aunt and nephew turned. In fact the woman who looked as if she wouldn't live to mid-century could have been there.

"I was a child," she added.

"And what did you see? Did you see Garibaldi?"

"Oh no, I spent the whole day hiding in the cellar."

Just at the moment in which this ocular witness gave such precious information on the battle, Mariannina and Brulati looked through the door.

"We're here," said Mariannina, "today we have to renounce painting. It's begun to rain."

"I predicted it," said Signora Clara. "It would have been better to have listened to Brulati."

"Brulati always gives good advice," the painter asserted with mock solemnity.

Giorgio invited his cousin to enter the monument but she signaled with her finger that she wasn't going to enter.

"Why?"

"I've heard from Brulati that there are horrible things inside. No, no. It's no use, I have no sympathy for ossuaries. Come, Brulati. Let's go and enjoy the beautiful view. You said that the view from up there is a wonder."

"But with a clear sky."

"In any case, I'm going," continued the girl. "Anyone who wants can follow me."

Brulati followed behind her like a little dog.

The custodian gave other explanations, and showed them a skull penetrated by a bullet.

"What a shame!" whispered Signora Clara wringing her hands. And she recalled the sorrowfully celebrated phrase: *The Chassepots rifles did miracles!*

"Who knows if it was a Garibaldino or a Frenchman?" objected Giorgio.

"It's the same," responded Clara. "Maybe he was twenty years old; he had a mother waiting for him.... You are on tenterhooks...let's go. Where are those two?"

"Just a few steps away," said the guide.

From the top of the hill, you could see the whole Sabina region. Brulati enumerated the villages: "There, on the left, Fara Sabina, Montelibretti, Morigoni, Palombara; to the right, Sant'Angelo, Mount Celio. Tivoli is behind those olive trees."

"If you can't do any better than that..." began Mariannina. And she stopped to turn and look at Clara and Giorgio who were just joining them.

"All Brulati's knowledge consists of pouring out a quantity of names. It's like taking a *Baedeker*... when you ask him where were the Pope's men, where were the French, what was the route they took to fall on Garibaldi, Brulati stays with his mouth open."

"I confessed earlier that I didn't know the particulars of the battle."

"I was there," repeated the custodian, putting the tip Giorgio Moncalvo had given her into her pocket.

"Good. Tell us."

Giorgio burst out laughing. "Oh yes, she spent the day hiding in a cellar. She didn't see anything."

"I heard the guns firing."

"The ossuaries horrify me," said Mariannina, "but I'd gladly see a battle. And I bet I wouldn't be afraid, that I'd be drunk on the smoke, the dust, the uproar!"

"It's really raining hard," said Clara. "What shall we do, children?"

After examining the various opinions it was clear that there wasn't an acceptable restaurant for Mariannina. They concluded that the least bad choice was to get back to the car immediately and go to eat at Sant'Agnese. Without hurrying too much, they could reach it in a little more than half an hour. When they started walking, the rain got heavier and the open umbrella of Signora Clara didn't shelter her or anyone else, so she closed it and pulled her shawl up to her face. The bad weather affected everyone's mood; Brulati scolded the driver; the chauffeur blamed the tortuously uneven road; Giorgio pondered the serious words of his aunt; Mariannina sulked, not used to serenely tolerating contraries. She was also annoyed at the reserve of her cousin who had, without a doubt, been lectured by Aunt Clara—he was nothing like the way he'd been at first.

"Bah!" She thought, "still I want..." And under the cover that they had stretched over their legs and that more or less kept the rain off, she made a move similar to the one Giorgio had made earlier; she advanced her hand very slowly until it touched his. But, as soon as she had touched it, she withdrew hers briskly as if she were fleeing the contact. Giorgio turned purple; a flame sparkled in his eyes.

Mariannina didn't move but her expression softened.

"Mariannina!" said Giorgio almost involuntarily. He couldn't continue because the car stopped all of a sudden and almost threw out its occupants. There was a flat tire. "I have one to replace it" said Giovanni who had jumped out before the others.,"but it will take time."

"How much?"

"An hour…three-quarters of an hour."

"Great! You've really done a good job of it." Mariannina said sulkily.

"Misfortunes happen…the road is full of stones."

"My dears," declared Clara, who Giorgio had helped down. "The worst thing would be to stay here in the rain. Let's walk. Sooner or later we'll get someplace."

"We must be near Nomentano Bridge," said Brulati. "There's an inn and we can get out of the rain."

"In the meantime," resumed Signora Clara, "it is absolutely necessary for me to stretch my legs…. Giorgio will hold the umbrella. Come on, take the umbrella. There must be two in the car. One will serve for Brulati and Mariannina. Courage. Forward."

His aunt's orders were so precise and peremptory Giorgio didn't dare disobey.

"And you, Giovanni," Clara resumed, "if you hurry, you'll join us. Give a look at the inn of Nomentano Bridge in case we stopped there. If not, we'll be at Sant'Agnese."

They set out with small steps in the mud. The rain continued to fall slowly and fine. It was all gray, difficult to make out the distant mountains. Mariannina, pulling up her hood, declared that she needed neither the arm nor the umbrella of Brulati. She turned here and there, quick and light, scarcely marking in the mud the form of her elegantly shod little foot. Under the hood, her eyes rested now on Brulati, now on Giorgio, shining with an expression both provocative and ironic.

At Nomentano Bridge they stopped briefly to talk with the host. But, despite the placards announcing "Wines from Frascati—Good food—Upstairs room," the host confessed that besides wine there was nothing ready, not even the upstair room which had been under repairs for a week. On the first floor instead, three or four carters were drinking happily and singing their coarse songs.

Though she was tired, Aunt Clara expressed the desire to press on to Saint Agnese.

"We're in the midst of it now," she said, "We'll rest at Sant'Agnese...and then, God willing, we'll take a carriage or tram and go back home. It will be a trip to remember for quite a time."

"If you'd listened to me," muttered Brulati, "by this time we'd be in Rome."

"Instead of making useless comments," rejoined Mariannina,"you ought to go faster so that you'd precede us at Sant'Agnese to order lunch."

"I don't want to get involved, but if you come to help me with your advice..."

The girl shook her head, no. "I'm not coming. He's too grumpy."

Signora Clara observed that Sant'Agnese wasn't far and that it would be better if they all arrived together. "You others can have lunch. As for me, I'm not hungry and it will be enough to drink a cup of hot tea."

"They walked on, in silence, for a good fifteen minutes. In the proximity of Sant'Agnese, they were joined by a closed carriage with two horses, driven by a coachman dressed in black with a top hat. An elegant young man stuck his head out the little window, recognized the women and Brulati, and ordered the coachman to stop.

"Oh, Signora Moncalvo, why ever are you here on foot in such weather?"

"Hello, Cherasco!" the two women exclaimed, surprised. It was that secretary of the Ministry of the Interior who had come to their house several times in the evening, and whom Giorgio had also seen.

After Mariannina had explained the accident with the tire that forced her, her aunt and friends to the unpleasant walk, the gentlemanly Cherasco got down with great solicitude from the carriage and declared that, if the two ladies were going to Rome, he would be very happy to accompany them wherever they wished. He regretted not being able to offer a seat to the two gentlemen but there was really no way of accommodating them. In order not to weigh too heavily on the government, a Minister of His Majesty the King of Italy had only the right to a miserable carriage—because this was the carriage of the Minister, on whose account Cherasco had to make an inspection. But the Minister would have been very glad to know that his carriage had served to remove the difficulties of two gentlewomen.

"Truthfully," said Signora Clara, "I would almost want to accept…if my niece wasn't in too much of a hurry to have lunch."

"Hurry?" interrupted Mariannina, who was always hungry for novelty and who was diverted to see the disgusted expressions of the artist Brulati and her cousin Giorgio. "I'm not in any hurry. Half hour ago I was hungry. Now I'm not anymore. And in any case I'm sure that at home I'll find something better to eat than at Sant'Agnese. At any rate, Cherasco, we'll take you at your word."

"Naturally. That's what I want."

The secretary, beaming, bowed deeply in thanks for the great honor they were giving him.

Signora Clara's conscience bothered her.

"But you then, how will you be?"

"I, perfectly. All I have to do is to lower this one seat." And Cherasco underlined the phrase to make understood for the second time that there wasn't place for the others.

"Get in, ladies, get in."

"You'll excuse us," said Clara holding out her hand to the

two dispirited men. "It's been a miserable trip but we'll make another when it's good weather."

"Goodbye Giorgio, goodbye Brulati!" added Marianinna brightly. I'm really sorry but I can't leave my aunt…I guess that after lunch you'll go back to Rome with the tram. If you come to Gandi palace you can take tea with us."

The small door of the carriage shut, the driver whipped the horse, and they trotted off.

Brulati threw a cigar stump away scornfully and put the hand that he had freed from the umbrella on Giorgio's shoulder.

"You don't yet know your cousin the way I do. She plays these tricks continually and you have to take her as she is. I'm more amazed at Signora Clara."

Giorgio thought that his aunt had been enthusiastic about an opportunity to separate him from Mariannina and the thought irritated him. Why so much zeal? Did that blessed woman think that he was a baby who didn't know how to defend himself?

"We can't stay here getting soaked," the painter began again, seeing that his companion in the misadventure wasn't moving. "In ten minutes we'll be in Sant'Agnese and we can dry off and restore ourselves. Do you want to share my umbrella?"

"Thank you" Giorgio responded, "the rain doesn't bother me. And now it doesn't seem worth the trouble to stop at Sant' Agnese. I'm not going to stop…I'll go by tram."

"Very well!" replied Brulati moving faster. "I don't intend to follow Count Ugolino's fate.[15] I'll go into the first tavern I pass."

Chapter 6

Between Husband and Wife

The Moncalvo couple, who had finished eating but not yet risen from the table, were having an animated discussion. They were alone. Monsignor de Luchi, their guest that morning, had just left; the servants had been ordered to stay outside until they were called.

"And you didn't know anything? Mariannina didn't tell you anything?" asked the Commendatore.

"Mariannina wouldn't even be aware of it," answered Signora Rachele. "She'd be so far from imagining…"

"As far as I'm concerned, these are mere fantasies of the Monsignor."

"What? Monsignor de Luchi is an intimate of the Orobonis, and he's not a man to speak lightly. Besides, is it such a marvel that our daughter has made an impression on a young man of the Roman high aristocracy?"

"I'm not amazed by the impression," replied Gabrio Moncalvo. "I'm amazed that the Monsignor judges it sufficient for him to want to engineer a marriage…in that family! With those attitudes! With those prejudices!"

Signora Rachele seemed absorbed in a sublime vision. Wasn't it a dream? Her daughter, her own Mariannina, had the possibility of becoming Princess Oroboni?

"It would sound well, wouldn't it, Gabrio, the name, Mariannina Oroboni? What a triumph that would be!"

The Commendatore attempted to calm the enthusiasm of his consort. "A triumph that would cost us dear. We'd have to come up with a million to buy the Orobonis' things; then it would be necessary to give the Roman palace as part of Mariannina's dowry and finally we'd have to supplement this dowry with thousands of lire so that the couple could get by decently."

"Weren't you already planning to give our daughter—our only daughter—a million lire dowry?"

"I did say once that to set her up well I wouldn't mind sacrifices and that I'd willingly give a million; but it isn't clear that a better match couldn't be found for half the price."

Signora Rachele protested with all her strength. "What sort of stinginess is this? Do you think Mariannina can't manage to get more? And what better match could you find?"

"Eh, steady now. Young Don Cesarino is from an esteemed noble family, a great name, but for the rest? Apart from that, it is a family in ruins. And Don Cesarino, what sort of person is he? A young man who looks decrepit, who's always lived under a bell jar; a fossil who knows nothing of the modern world."

"You're talking of other people's prejudices," exclaimed Signora Rachele, scandalized. "And yours? Those people see the world in a manner which isn't ours…. And are you sure they don't see it better? Freedom, freedom! The great efforts undertaken in the name of freedom! Strikes, demonstrations, revolts. The only thing missing is that one day they'll come to our house to rob us."

"Yes, one day they'll come," said the Commendatore who had a philosophic spirit; "but when they've carried away everything there is, we won't be left on the straw. When the storm passes, we'll come back to the top just as we were before. And yet, if the Orobonis and their ilk had continued to have the upper hand, both of us would be in the ghetto of Ferrara, me to sell old clothes and you to pluck the geese."

This allusion to the social position of their ancestors displeased Signora Rachele, who was tormented by not being a

Montmorency, and she responded scornfully: "As far as that goes it's been almost a century since mine left the ghetto."

Moncalvo rubbed his hands. "That's thanks to the liberals, my dear, thanks to the French revolution and the first Kingdom of Italy."

"I don't deny the merits of anybody," replied his wife. But it's certain that even if the Orobonis were governing now, they wouldn't have the same ideas. And the best proof of that is that our daughter has caught their eye."

The Commendatore shook his head. "Not forgetting the clause about conversion."

"Of course! What were you thinking? As if sooner or later this wasn't what it would come to."

"Slow, slow!" said her prudent husband, gesturing at her to stop. "I admit that on this point we have to compromise for Mariannina...if baptism is the indispensable condition for a great marriage, then let her get baptized. But our case is different than Mariannina's."

Signora Rachele twisted her mouth into a look of disgust. "This is the first time that I see you so attached to your religion."

Gabrio Moncalvo smiled with a condescending air.

"I'm not attached to my religion or anyone else's, but just for this reason I see no need to convert."

"I, instead, feel the need!" Signora Rachele exclaimed with force. "I feel that I could bring all the passion of a neophyte to the new faith."

"That could be," Moncalvo said placidly, "but it would be a big nuisance in the family. But you'd better convince yourself that whatever your zeal, it would not be enough to make your origins forgotten. You and I, in spite of the great cleanse, will be considered the same."

Signora Rachele made a negative sign with her head.

"You're completely free to deny it. But I tell you that

our social position wouldn't change a jot, not even with the Orobonis—given the hypothesis that Don Cesarino becomes our son-in-law. Yes, yes, but if you believe that having a prince for a son-in-law will give you the right of being an equal in their society, you are deceiving yourself. Hebrew or Catholic, liberal or reactionary, for them we'll continue to be of an inferior race. Maybe they'll stroke us on the days when they need to draw from our funds, invite us to their official receptions, but they'll always look at us from above.... That's what we'd gain from having our daughter become a princess."

"And if it were that way, which I don't believe," Signora Rachele asked uneasily, "do you want to create obstacles to Mariannina's happiness?"

"That's another matter," said the banker. "Our daughter is ambitious, and we have to think of her above all. Many girls would find happiness in a very different marriage, and Mariannina herself some time ago... Who knows? Enough, it's water under the bridge. Today, Mariannina has grand ideas...I'm persuaded that she dreams of a coat of arms and a title and that in order to be a princess she is prepared to renounce—besides the so-called faith of our ancestors—many of the satisfactions longed for by romantic and sentimental natures. I will keep her desires in mind, but until now they are all castles in the air and there is never enough prudence...."

Signora Rachele agreed with that, but not without observing that there was one positive thing: the new visit they were to make to the garden of the Orobonis with the full assent of Don Cesarino and the princess mother and with the probability of meeting them.

"Certainly," replied the Commendatore. "They want to see the merchandise. It's even more necessary to avoid untimely gossip, with Mariannina as well. There is nothing concrete... everything is in a cloudy state and I have to walk with leaden feet. Let's not forget that when this bomb explodes, if it does explode, we'll have half a world against us, beginning with Giacomo and Clara."

"I sincerely hope you won't pay attention to them," interrupted Signora Rachele with irritation. "Clara is an excellent creature, full of good sense—but she is a pragmatic sort of person who was born to be the wife of a working man who makes three thousand lire a year. And as for your brother, he may be a fine man, everyone thinks so, but he is also an antiquated man who doesn't understand our times. And basically he doesn't forgive you for having made money."

"Oh, he's not tempted by money."

"I know…and I don't think that he envies it, but he always throws it in our face."

"Ever since I was a boy," said the banker evoking the earlier times, "he lived on nothing. He isolated himself from the family dedicated to its small businesses, he buried himself in his books, and at school he was always first…while I barely passed."

Signora Rachele, who was proud of her husband's millions, rolled her shoulders scornfully.

"That's what the triumphs at school are worth. Truthfully one wouldn't think you were brothers."

"A common phenomenon," the Commendatore said.

After a moment of silence, Signora Rachele began again: "By the way, I confess that I don't look kindly on the friendship of your nephew Giorgio with Mariannina."

"Giorgio comes to us so little!"

"Yes, but when he comes he takes too many liberties."

"He doesn't take them, it's Mariannina who gives them to him."

"Mariannina is made that way. She's a Lucifer at heart, but she has never been condescending and she won't tolerate our interference…but don't worry—when it's necessary, she knows how to show her claws. Giorgio himself ought to be able to see that things have changed."

"That Giorgio," the Commendatore went on—and in his voice there was sorrow for a beautiful lost dream. "Seven years ago, he let a fortune get away from him. If he'd gone to Khartoum, by now he would have put away a good sum."

"Better this way," interrupted his wife. "At the time you nourished the idea of a union between the cousins."

"It wouldn't have been an enormous disgrace," noted Gabrio Moncalvo. "Not having any sons, it wouldn't be bad to have a son-in-law who would occupy himself with our affairs. If Mariannina marries Don Cesarino, it certainly wouldn't be him to help me run my business."

"Your nephew doesn't have any better aptitude for commerce than Don Cesarino would have," replied Signora Rachele.

"Who knows if he wouldn't have had it," the husband responded. "He's an intelligent young man."

"Oh yes, with his father's nature. Giorgio's one of those who will remain penniless for their lifetime."

"At least they don't get themselves in debt the way the Orobonis do. They don't ruin themselves."

Signora Rachele lost her patience: "It seems impossible to me that an intelligent man like you cannot see the abyss that there is between the old nobility and us. They can indebt themselves up to their eyebrows, they can ruin themselves without losing their reputations and without losing their place in society. They keep their name, their past, their connections.... Us no: we're rich or we're nothing. And it isn't worth the trouble to try and found a dynasty. The day on which the Rothschilds become destitute no one will remember them. And you lament not having sons! Maybe they would devour what you've earned. You, when you are tired you can withdraw and if Mariannina becomes a Roman princess, she is the only heir of your patrimony, she'll put a family that is in decline back on its feet. I hope that will be better than being the wife of a little professor who is barely able to pay the tailor with his stipend and, for the rest, he would have to play the part of a kept man."

The Commendatore who, during the harangue of his consort had the time to roll and light a cigarette, answered with some irritation: "The young professor is not a contestant... Now neither you nor I will accept him as a son-in-law and Mariannina won't accept him as a husband. And you are the first to understand that, were he thinking of a similar thing (which I don't believe), Mariannina would make him lose his desire.... I can't shut the door in his face. It would be a gratuitous offense to him and to my brother."

Gabrio Moncalvo got up and began to walk around the room with his head lowered and hands behind his back.

His wife's mention of the Rothschilds disturbed him. The great banking house, above all the mother house in Frankfurt, had honored him with its benevolence. Now precisely this same Frankfurt house was the most attached to the Hebrew faith. Who knew what effect Gabrio Moncalvo's news of the conversion of his only daughter would have? It was impossible to keep it hidden. All the newspapers of Rome would surely talk about it! On the other side, the idea of being related by marriage with a princely Roman family flattered the banker's vanity more than he wanted to admit to himself, and destroyed inside him the judicious objections that he had presented to Signora Rachele.

She, who felt sure of victory, thought it was not opportune to insist. She got up from the table and looked out the window. "God, how it rains!" she said.

Distracted first by a discussion with Monsignor de Luchi, then by talking things over themselves, the two spouses were hardly aware that the weather had gotten worse.

"It really is raining hard," added the Commendatore also looking through the window. "I told Mariannina it wasn't a good time to go out in the car."

"I understand that they went to paint."

"I'm sorry for Clara—she's always been disposed to bronchitis. Would it be possible to send the covered carriage to meet them?"

"Where? They were going to Mentana but probably they didn't reach it and sought shelter somewhere."

"And who knows what road they're on! I hope nothing terrible will happen!" said Moncalvo coming closer to his wife.

"Oh, well," sighed the Signora. "You can trust Giovanni."

She fixed her eyes greedily on the other part of Via Nazionale, the great wall of the Orobonis garden and the tops of the trees waving in the wind.

"As long as you agree…" she whispered, placing her hand on her husband's shoulder.

Gabrio smiled. "You're ambitious."

"For our daughter."

"Not only for our daughter," the banker started again. "You wish to see Mariannina a princess but you also want a title for yourself, and you're not content with one that would be easy to have…and even the Rothschilds would remain content with it."

"A barony? No. There are too many of these financial barons. It's almost another mark of race. You ought to demand the crown of Count.

"My dear the Heraldic Council doesn't give so freely anymore."

"You have overcome larger difficulties than this," she suggested.

"Flatterer!"

She continued caressingly: "You came from humble beginnings and you've arrived at the top."

"Fortune has helped me," Moncalvo said with some modesty.

"There were moments in which fortune was eluding you and you recaptured it," added his wife, "and there were also moments in which you doubted your star and someone gave you heart again."

In evoking that past time, the mature, slightly-worn beauty of Signora Rachele came to life and seemed to flower again. Meanwhile her hand, gently resting on Gabrio's shoulder, rose slowly to his chin, soothing his graying beard.

"It was you who gave me heart," he said. "You are a good and faithful companion."

She blushed, knowing that she didn't entirely merit the praise. She had been faithful for more than forty years; then, swept away in the whirlwind of the great world, she had succumbed to temptation. Oh, not much...enough to avoid being laughed at.... He, too, for that matter, had had his little adventures, always for the same reason—not to be less than other people...but never losing his head, never falling in love...just as she had never fallen in love, having loved only one man, her Gabrio. Maybe he ignored her little sins, maybe suspecting them, he forgave her in the same way she forgave his.

Rapid steps could be heard in the adjoining room. The door opened wide.

"Oh, Mariannina!" exclaimed the Commendatore and Signora Rachele at the same time. "Strange that we were by the window and we didn't see you coming. Usually the car makes an awful racket."

"What car? I came in the carriage of his Excellency the Minister of Internal Affairs."

"How? Why? What happened...and Aunt Clara?"

"Aunt Clara came with me. She went to her room. Now I'll

tell you...let me catch my breath...and above all give me something to eat. I'm starving!

The girl pressed the button of the electric bell.

"Haven't you had lunch?"

"No!"

"So can you tell us what happened?"

"It was a very minor accident. No one dead or injured. The car's tire ruptured."

"And what does this have to do with the carriage of his Excellency?"

"I'm not going to say anything more till I've eaten," declared Mariannina who was sitting at the table crumbling a little roll. "Oh, finally," she said turning towards the servant who had run up at the sound of the bell. "Let the cook send me what she has, right away...hot or cold, it makes no difference."

Chapter 7

The Princess Olimpia Oroboni

It was almost eleven at night. A closed carriage stopped in front of the small service door of the Oroboni palace and Monsignor de Luchi descended.

A mature woman holding a little oil lamp came to open.

"Good evening, Pulcheria."

"Is it you, Monsignor?"

"Yes, the princess has asked for me."

"Exactly," answered Pulcheria, closing the door again and bolting it. "And I was here in the caretaker's lodge to wait for you...my husband should be inside, in the entry. He is in an intractable mood. What if you lecture him a little? Not now, not now. At an opportune moment."

"My dear," replied the Monsignor, setting out behind her on the gravel path that crunched under every step. In the night without wind the trees were still and the silence of the place was broken only by the monotonous murmuring of the fountain. "Lecturing your husband is a waste of breath. He's a man who wants the world to go his way."

"Unfortunately," sighed the woman. "Now he has the fixed idea that there will be a kind of revolution inside here and he declares, if that happens, he's going. Where would he go? Here we haven't been paid for awhile, but at least we have a place to stay and food. And at Plinio's age, with his aches and his ideas, it's not easy to find..."

"As long as he doesn't do something idiotic," replied the clergyman. "He mustn't mix in others' affairs...it's he who's making a revolution, insisting on the right to judge his masters...."

"So it's true, Monsignor?" Pulcheria asked anxiously. "There's something going on?" And, turning, she lifted the lamp almost under the nose of the Monsignor to read his response on his face. Monsignor de Luchi covered his eyes with his hands and remained impassive.

"I am giving you the same council as I did your husband. Don't mix with things that shouldn't concern you."

And to rid himself of the annoyance, he walked faster and added: "I see clearly with my glasses. No need to bother yourself walking with me. I know the way well enough."

He went quickly up the few steps and entered.

Less talkative than his wife, the servant, Plinio came to meet them in silence.

"Is the princess in her room?"

Plinio nodded, yes.

"Is there a light on the stairs?"

"Yes, in front of the little altar on the landing…on the little stairs."

"That will be enough. I'll go that way."

Illuminated from below, the painting on the little altar allowed one to make out the head of the Madonna, curved in a loving gesture over the fruit of her womb. The baby was barely visible. You could hardly make out the outlines, disappearing beneath the layers of soot from the continuous smoke of the candle, which was always lit.

"By now, the churches have introduced electric lights," thought Monsignor de Luchi, who had a modern spirit.

"Monsignor de Luchi," announced the servant knocking at Donna Olimpia's door.

The rustle of a silk dress could be heard and a female voice responded: "Come in!"

The princess, who was standing, offered a chair to Monsignor; then, seeing that Plinio wasn't leaving, she said,

"What is it? If I need you, I'll ring."

"The fire is out," mumbled Plinio, eyeing the fireplace.

"It doesn't matter. I'm not cold. Leave now."

The servant obeyed.

With his chest puffed out, the Monsignor waited for Donna Olimpia to speak.

"I was praying," she said, pointing to the crimson velvet prayer stool that bore the sign of the knees that had recently compressed it. "I begged the Lord for guidance in this most critical moment of my life. The Lord is silent. I'm not worthy."

She threw herself down on a easy chair and after a brief pause, went on: "I called you...you who has hatched this plot..."

"It was the only way left to us," murmured the priest opening his arms wide.

"Yes, it's easy for you to say," Donna Olimpia went on. "I called you at this hour because we can talk without being disturbed. Today I talked with Salvucci, our trusted general agent, a man who enjoyed our full confidence and who has ruined us. Do you want to excuse him?" the princess asked in a resonant voice interpreting in her own way a movement by Monsignor de Luchi.

"No, no," said de Luchi. "He has been unfit and improvident, but let's be fair. The situation was very difficult. Twenty or twenty-five years ago, before the building crisis, we should have had the courage to sell the garden and the palace."

"So they could build a hotel?"

"Certainly the speculators don't have archeological scruples."

"Never, never," protested Princess Olimpia. "At any rate if it was necessary to sell, Salvucci ought to have said something and looked for a buyer in our caste among the Roman patricians. Instead he hasn't known how to do anything but get into debt... and now he can't even do that."

"And what does he suggest?" asked the Monsignor.

"You're being ingenuous," said the princess sarcastically. "Naturally he suggests what you suggest...what you told him."

"Not me, Princess...it's the ineluctable force of events."

"Ah, Don Paolo de Luchi, if my son's idiocy weren't mixed up in this, I know what I'd do...I'd put everything up for auction, our lands, our villa in Porto Anzio, this palace...everything. I'd let the furniture be taken away, the paintings, and I'd wait until the policemen came to drive me out of my room or perhaps from the attic where I'd taken refuge. Better, a thousand times better than accepting the propositions of your Moncalvos. But you've bewitched my son, my Cesarino, the one who ought to be more jealous than I am of our dignity, of our name. If you had heard him, today! Yes, after listening to Salvucci, I wanted to hear from Cesarino this very day. I wanted to know from him if he was disposed to submit willingly to our shame, if he were disposed to sell himself. Not just disposed...no, he goes towards it as if it were a party. Don Cesarino, you understand? Don Cesarino who didn't dare look a woman in the face... who wanted to enter a monastery! Now he moons behind that daughter of Jews, of usurers, with whom he has never exchanged a word, whom he has only seen from his window, or in the streets. Because they have never seen each other close up, isn't that true? Have they ever been together? You aren't deceiving me? You haven't arranged for them to meet?"

"Oh, Donna Olimpia!" exclaimed the Monsignor, offended.

"By now, I don't trust anyone," the princess returned, "and you above all."

Having launched this last shot the elderly patrician stopped, choking on a knot of phlegm.

De Luchi suggested that she calm herself and hurried to get her a glass of water. "May I say something?" he asked.

Without saying a word she made an affirmative motion with her head.

"Well, princess," the priest began in his soft insinuating voice, "I understand your state of mind and I'm here to receive your thrashing...but hasn't it ever occurred to you that what you consider the work of the devil...?"

"Just so," muttered Donna Olimpia.

"On the other hand, hasn't it ever occurred to you that it is a grand design of Providence? Allow me...I am only an instrument. Allow me.... A little less than a year ago, when it was announced that the Bank of Italy had decided to realize its credit and every door was beaten on in an effort to avoid a financial catastrophe, do you think I knew Commendatore Moncalvo? And when, after every hope of a rich marriage had gone up in smoke, and Don Cesarino wanted to close himself in a monastery, do you think I knew that this Mariannina existed? It was only around that time, when the multi-millionaire family came to live in Rome opposite the Oroboni palace, that I developed a rapport with Commendatore Gabrio, with the help of the Count Ugolini-Ruschi. He immediately gave us five thousand lire for our refuge and presented me to his courteous, munificent ladies, always disposed to spend freely for our poor, always full of deference toward Catholicism, to the Church, to the Papacy...."

"And you think they are sincere?" interrupted the princess. "They have heresy in their blood."

"They have grown up in indifference," corrected the Monsignor, "like many of these Hebrew families of the West. They separated themselves from their religion and they haven't yet resolved to embrace ours. They mistakenly believe that they can live without religion but they are more prepared than people think to accept the truth of our faith."

At his princess's doubtful gesture, de Luchi spoke more fervidly: "Without this intimate, profound conviction, the plan that, with God's help, I'll carry out, would never have flashed through my mind. Notice, Donna Olimpia, notice the coincidences that can't depend only on chance. Don Cesarino sees this Signorina Moncalvo from the window, he who had a horror of the feminine observes her. He goes at night stealthily to the tower in the garden to try to see into her room, to try and catch her in the passage behind the window, behind the curtains. And, at the same time, the young girl is acutely curious about the secrets of this place, wants to visit the palace, wants to meet its inhabitants whom she hardly can make out from a distance in the midst of the trees. In the meantime, in agreement with her parents, she takes an interest in our pious work, participates in our beneficence, comes to our hospices, admires the powerful organizations of Catholic charity. Pay attention, Donna Olimpia, she influences her father to dispose him favorably to the financial operation that will save the Oroboni family from ruin."

"Oh, Monsignor, Don Paolo de Luchi!" exclaimed the princess. "You don't understand. That's natural...you can't understand." And in these words there was an allusion to the humble origins of the priest. "You can't understand how mortifying it is to me to know that our troubles were discussed in that house, that we'll get alms from those people."

"My dear princess," said Monsignor, "when the accounts are tallied the Orobonis will have given more alms than they receive. And consider whether I'm right to find in all this the hand of Providence? The first step towards a possible wedding was not made by me. It was the Signora Rachele Moncalvo...very timidly as if to test the ground.... I looked at her astonished. 'I know,' she said, 'the major obstacle is our religion. But if it were only that! It will be a blessed day when my daughter takes her baptism.' It is Providence."

"And you," retorted Donna Olimpia, "you immediately took the bait!"

"I..." responded the Monsignor with a certain haughtiness, "I had read for several days in the soul of that enriched bourgeois; I had no need to bite the bait.... Rather it was she who spontaneously took the path I had wanted her to enter. I am a priest, princess, and for many years I've been friend and devoted servant of the Oroboni house."

Donna Olimpia bent her head assenting.

"As a priest" continued the Monsignor, "I can't be indifferent to the salvation of a soul; as a friend and servant of this family I must do everything I am able to do to restore it to its ancient splendor."

A bitter smile flitted over the princess's lips.

De Luchi ignored it and, taking up the tone of humility that he had abandoned a short time before, he repeated the phrase he'd pronounced formerly. "I am only an instrument. It wasn't me who illuminated the heart of Signora Moncalvo, not me who disposed an experienced businessman like Commendatore Gabrio to take more than a million from his lucrative speculations to immobilize it in this palace, in the dilapidated villa of Porto Anzio and the unprofitable properties of Albano. But, above all, it wasn't me who has inflamed the blood of Don Cesarino, who has awakened his atrophied senses.... How many times have you said to me, sighing 'he's not like other men, he's torpid, frigid...he won't marry or, if he marries, he won't have children. Our poor house!' You said this to me after the collapse of various plans of marriage. And now the Lord has by means of this young girl who belongs to the race of reprobates...now all our hopes revive and again it's possible to count on a long line of descendants for the house Oroboni and perhaps one will be a defender of the realm, a champion of the faith."

"Ah, Monsignor," burst the elderly lady, "it's useless for you to gild the pill. Say that there is no escape, that rebelling against heaven's will is useless and don't say anything else. Quiet! Don't you hear it?"

"Yes," answered Monsignor raising his eyes to the ceiling, "Someone is walking up there."

"It's Cesarino's room. It's he who is walking."

"Perhaps he's about to come down?"

"There's no danger of that," replied Donna Olimpia.

"Now at night he has no peace. He gets up, goes to and from in his room like an animal locked up in his cage…because of her! And to think that three or four centuries ago if a woman of that race had disturbed, with her infamous spells, the mind of a Christian, of one of ours, the Church would have known how to liberate the victim with its exorcisms, and burn the witch at the stake. The Church no longer has arms, it can no longer redeem or punish."

"Calm yourself, princess," said de Luchi without exaggerating the importance of this offensive remark. "The Church has always the same power, but it will use the weapons adapted to the times."

"Marriage!" sneered Donna Olimpia.

"Why not? Marriage can also serve the Lord's glory. Don Cesarino will marry a baptized woman. I'll be responsible for the conversion."

"An apparent conversion," countered the elderly Oroboni.

"A sincere conversion," rejoined the priest. "I have already begun in secret to instruct the Signorina Moncalvo and I'm sure that my student will bring me honor…. Secrecy is necessary because the Moncalvos have many adherents in their community and don't want to cause an ill-timed scandal. It will be opportune if the bomb does not explode all at once, announcing the baptism and the marriage at the same time."

"God, God! What crossroads have I arrived at?" said the princess, twisting nervously the handkerchief in her fingers.

"You're in good faith, I admit. You think you're acting for the best. But you're compromised.... By now you are too interested in the success of your plan."

"You can consult with others," suggested Monsignor de Luchi coldly. "You have relatives and friends in the old Roman aristocracy...even in the Sacred College."

Donna Olimpia made a scornful gesture.

"No one has ever helped me neither with a lira nor a word. No one will help us now...if Pope Leo XIII were still alive, I would throw myself at his feet and beg him to enlighten my spirit."

"Go to Pio X. An Oroboni still must to be welcomed by his Holiness."

"This new Pope welcomes everybody now," said Donna Olimpia with an accent of patrician pride. "But he wouldn't understand... he's a Pope with democratic ideas...like you."

In the room above the pacing continued.

"Listen to him, listen to him, it never stops...he is feverish."

"He might do something crazy," the Monsignor insinuated. "He's twenty-five years old. He could make use of the power that the Law gives him."

"Monsignor de Luchi," exclaimed the princess wringing her hands, "have you become a revolutionary under your priestly tonsure? In our house no one has rebelled against the parental authority...and you think that Cesarino will do it?"

"I don't believe it. I was simply alluding to a possibility."

Donna Olimpia hid her face between her palms and stayed that way for a while, thoughtfully. In the room not even a fly moved. From the floor above came the usual noise of steps. Silently Monsignor de Luchi bent to lower the light.

With a profound sigh the princess began again:

"Then I must ascend to this Calvary. And we'll begin by receiving these ladies.... When?"

Monsignor de Luchi prudently hid the joy of his victory and was content to reply: "Whenever you wish...as soon as possible. You know it's a visit that we talked about some weeks ago."

"I was indisposed."

"Exactly and that was the reason for delay. Now..."

"Now," added Donna Olimpia, "it's better to make haste. Tomorrow, next week...you arrange it.... I will finally see this siren who has made my son lose his head. I know, you've showed her to me one day from the window of the tower. But I'm near-sighted.... What's going on?"

The priest withdrew his wallet and took out a small photograph which he presented to his interlocutor.

"Here it is, if you want to have an idea of her."

"Oh Don Paolo," she exclaimed in a tone between joking and scandalized, "what kind of priest are you? You go around with pictures of women in your pocket!"

"I took it to give to you," answered the priest with utmost seriousness. "No one could blame me for that."

Donna Olimpia looked at the photograph attentively, then put it down with a grimace on the small table.

"She is beautiful. But it's a sensual beauty, vulgar, brazen like her millions, like the gang she belongs to."

"She's more beautiful than her portrait," declared Monsignor. "You'll see her tomorrow...because I will accompany her tomorrow with her mother, a little before three. The days are so short in this season!"

"And will your Commendatore come too? I mean the father of the girl?"

"No, I don't think so...he's so busy. You'll have time to get to know him."

"I would be happy never to know him, never have heard him spoken of.... Ah, de Luchi, it is the Lord who castigates me! When I have confessed to you, you have listened to me...

but He...He doesn't absolve..."

"The Lord visits those He loves," replied the priest "and often the sorrows that he gives change into joys."

"In the afterlife."

"Not in the afterlife alone."

"But He can't want me to welcome this intruder like a daughter!" burst out Donna Olimpia.

Shrewd, discreet, de Luchi didn't insist. Most was accomplished and they'd arrived at the point where the rest would come by itself.

"God will inspire you," he said rising and kissing the hand the princess had extended to him. "Good night Donna Olimpia."

"Good night," she answered with a muffled voice. She shook the bell and ordered the old Plinio: "Accompany the Monsignor. And send me Adelaide. Until tomorrow, Don Paolo."

"Until tomorrow."

Chapter 8

Don Cesarino

The young prince who had offered his arm to Mariannina was accompanying her on a tour of the garden. "Yes," he said. "Yes, I often saw you behind the windows of that room opposite our little tower. I also saw you in the evenings... two times. You had opened the shutters and were looking out the window. I saw your profile in black against the lamplight."

While Don Cesarino was saying this, a gentle flush spread over his pallid cheeks and a nervous tic made his eyelids—over which he passed and repassed his white hand covered with rings—flutter. Used to long silences empty of thought, timid to the point of not knowing how to look a woman in the face, he was amazed by his own eloquence, amazed to find himself less awkward, less embarrassed than usual. Most of all, he marveled that he had dared to rebel against the authority of his mother who hadn't wanted him to be present at this first visit of the Moncalvo girl. But his mother had had to give in, faced by his preemptive statement: "If I can't receive them today in my house, I'll go tomorrow and look for them in theirs."

Don Cesarino turned a moment to show Mariannina the tower that rose at the corner of the enclosing wall whose base lost itself in a tangle of plants.

"We have a couple of little rooms up there."

"Now I understand," added the girl, "the light that I saw a few times behind the blinds."

"It was me."

A few steps ahead, Princess Olimpia, speaking with Monsignor de Luchi and Signora Rachele, evoked the time when a much larger garden had extended to where the street was now.

"When they ruined our Rome with their factories," she said, "they took a piece of our property as large as Via Nazionale. We had to rebuild the wall at the level of the tower that once stood alone in the midst of the park. Back then, we went up in the afternoon for the coolness of its air and all around was a wondrous green…palms, oaks, cypresses…and there was the fragrance of flowers, spreading outwards from our garden. The eyesores we see now didn't exist, and our ears weren't assailed by this racket of trams and cars. In the evenings there was a great silence broken only by the song of crickets."

Signora Rachele, although horrified at the idea of this mortuary, pretended to be ecstatic.

"Certainly it must have been more poetic…but inside this enclosure it's like being beyond the world."

"Never enough, never enough."

"Still, it's necessary to adjust to living in this nasty world," objected Monsignor.

"We know that you've adapted too much," said the princess between joke and severity.

Signora Rachele remembered some allusions of her husband's. It seemed that Monsignor de Luchi had some peccadillos on his conscience, some infraction of one of the vows pronounced in embracing the priesthood. But who is safe from calumny? Even the austere princess was thought to have had such weaknesses in her youth.

And Rachele Moncalvo was disposed to believe it, finding there an excuse for her recent escapades and concluding that in the "high life" everyone did the same. She deplored ever more that she wasn't a Catholic—able from time to time to adjust her accounts with the Lord.

"Don't you frequent society?" Mariannina asked Don

Cesarino, who had made mention of his monastic lifestyle.

"I frequented it a little," he said, "and now I never go."

"And still," the girl continued, "with your name and position everyone would make much of you."

He shook his head, "I don't think so."

It was a painful subject for Don Cesarino. Yes, he had mingled in society for two consecutive winters, when his mother was hoping that, like other Roman princes, he would secure a wife among the millionaires that America sent across the ocean to exchange their dollars for the titles of old Europe. In vain the enterprising misses had crowded around him, full of good will; but the boldness of their flirtation, instead of stimulating him, had disturbed him, and augmented his repugnance towards women in general.

It sharpened his desire not to meet on his path any of these fragile and perverse creatures. And he had gone through a period of religious exaltation, during which his mother and Monsignor de Luchi had their hands full stopping him from entering a monastery. Today he no longer recognized that man and, while he walked at the side of the beautiful Semite and felt the soft pressure of her arm under his, a passion spread though his blood that the superb Americans hadn't been able to communicate...a passion made of spasms and voluptuousness, that gave him—along with vague ascetic terrors—an unusual boldness, a new awareness of power and strength.

Seeing him preoccupied, Mariannina stopped talking.

"Why are you silent?" asked Cesarino. "I love listening to you! You have such a sweet voice.... You must sing beautifully."

"Oh no, really."

"But you know music?"

"I play the piano and I used to study singing."

"Have you stopped?"

"I studied a little when I was in Paris. Then we left and I

haven't taken it up again."

"But you will?"

"Maybe."

"Have you travelled much?"

"Yes. From the time I was a child, I've toured almost all of Europe and for many years I lived in Egypt."

"It must be beautiful to travel," sighed Don Cesarino. "I would love to go to the Holy Land."

"Oh, that would be my dream," exclaimed Mariannina with what seemed sincere enthusiasm.

But the young prince gazed wonderingly at her. What fascination could the Holy Land have for her, the reprobate, the descendent of Christ's crucifiers?

Then, reordering with an effort of memory and intelligence his basic understanding of sacred history, he thought that she, too, was tied to those places of the traditions of her ancestors, of the piety of her temple that had been destroyed and her people who had been dispersed.

In truth, Don Cesarino attributed to the emphatic exclamation of the rich heiress an absolutely imaginary significance. Her enthusiasm for Palestine had nothing to do with memories of the pavilions of Jacob or of the temple of Solomon. Hers was the worldly curiosity of a spoiled girl in search of new and diverse impressions. In Jerusalem she certainly wouldn't join the crowd of fanatics who sobbed every Friday on the ruins of the sanctuary; she would not, like the modern Zionists, study the ground plan for the capital of a new kingdom of Israel; instead, sitting at the round table of the New Grand Hotel, studiously hiding her origins, she would make reservations with the English Thomas Cook travel agents for the trips to Jericho, to the Jordan River, to the Dead Sea.

Still, Don Cesarino continued to read in the moist, luminous and deep almond eyes of Mariannina what wasn't true.

He read there, along with the mourning for past glories, the abasement of a condemned person who has not been pardoned, the ardent yearning to be lifted up to be redeemed. And he was exalted at the idea of raising with his hand that stricken angel, to rescue that soul whose wings had been clipped by her fathers' sins. Ah, to purify her with the baptismal water, teach her the truth of the faith and then to take her penitent, contrite to the tomb of Christ, to seal the conversion. What a magnificent dream, what new and unhoped for happiness. It seemed to Don Cesarino that a bundle of rays broke together through the gray sky of his life and opened his closed future.

The princess mother turned briskly towards her son and said, "It's cold. Let's go back to the house."

In the ground floor living room, occupied this winter afternoon by a discreet shadow, old Plinio served the chocolate and biscuits. His hands trembled, his inquiring gaze paused now on princess Olimpia, now on Cesarino, now on Monsignor de Luchi, and on the strange guests who dissimulated very badly their arrogance, hidden under humble and deferential behavior. And Plinio, who couldn't meet Moncalvo's carriage without a grimace that included in the same scorn the horses and the driver, the carriage and the people inside...he, Plinio, now had the mortifying experience of hearing lady Olimpia ask Signora Rachele if she wanted another piece of sugar and of seeing Don Cesarino in adoration before Mariannina as though she were a sacred image. What times were these? Was it possible that the Orobonis would humiliate themselves this way only because the Moncalvos were rich? Possible that they would sacrifice their dignity for money? And to think that he, completely broke as he was, had renounced his salary for several years in order not to abandon his ancient masters!

"Open the curtains covering the medallions," ordered the princess.

Then the portraits of the family appeared in the faded and dusty cornices. Monsignor de Luchi hurried to explain their significance. That lean old man with the red skullcap was the nobleman Andrea, a Venetian patrician (because the family originated there) and cardinal of the Church, a competitor of Camillo Borghese (who became Paolo V) for the Papacy and who was unsuccessful because of the situation in France. The man on his right, in the ample coat trimmed with ermine, was his brother Niccoló Alvise, knight and solicitor for the city of Venice, painted by a student of Tintoretto. Then, there were the two nephews, Don Antonio and Don Marco, and the great-grandchild cardinal Pietro, teacher at the Oroboni Academy. He, after breaking every tie to the Republic of Venice, recalled his father and uncle to Rome and established there a stable dwelling. Last in chronological order, the great-grandfather of Don Cesarino, secret manservant of Gregory XVI, who died of a heart attack the day of the flight of Pio IX to Gaeta. Alone among these men was a woman, the wife of Don Marco, pure Roman blood. Her name was Tarquinia of the Altieri princes: her superb small head, erect on its dazzling white neck and opulent shoulders, introduced a youthful note into the melancholy assembly of serious and wrinkled faces.

Don Cesarino bent towards Mariannina's ear.

"That painting resembles you."

"Resembles me?" asked the girl blushing intensely.

"Yes, in the arch of the brows and the cut of the mouth."

At a sign from the princess the curtains fell and the ancestors of Don Cesarino were spared the mortification of new comparisons.

"I don't dare invite you to us," Signora Rachele said timidly when they were saying goodbye. "It would be too great an honor."

"Thank you," replied the princess standing up "We don't

visit anyone." And with that "we" she included her son.

"But at least permit me to come from time to time to pay my respects…with Mariannina."

Donna Olimpia coldly assented.

"Come…but let me know in advance through Monsignor."

"I'm coming too," said the priest.

"And I'll accompany the ladies to the gate" announced Don Cesarino avoiding his mother's eyes.

Signora Rachele had barely reached the garden, sure that she couldn't be heard by anyone because her daughter and Don Cesarino had remained behind, when she couldn't restrain a little outburst with Monsignor de Luchi.

"Auff! There's no doubt she's a great lady from the tip of her fingernails to her hair…but my God, what coldness. Our queens, leaving aside their opinions, are infinitely more friendly."

De Luchi, facing the singular reservations of Signora Moncalvo, felt obligated to declare that he was completely devoted to the two queens (he didn't say to "our queens") The queen Margherita, above all, was a pious and holy woman with a strong affection for the Church. As for the Princess Olimpia, it was necessary to put yourself in her shoes. What was happening was something new to her and very far from the ideas she'd grown up with.

"But I want to know what the outcome of this visit was," insisted Signora Rachele. "There wasn't a word, or an allusion to the chain that should unite our families."

Monsignor de Luchi smiled.

"Have a little patience. Things are now at a point of no return. Where are the two youngsters?"

With the excuse of showing her an old oak that according to legend was planted in 1660, Don Cesarino had brought Mariannina along a path that also led to the entry but he succeeded in lengthening the path by a hundred steps. So for a moment the two young people were out of sight.

"Will we see each other soon?" Don Cesarino entreated her pressing her arm.

"Mah!" she exclaimed looking down at the ground. She seemed absorbed in the contemplation of a little stone the color of lapis lazuli. "It depends on your mother.... She doesn't seem enthusiastic about me, your mother."

"It's her character," he responded. "Mamma's had so many disappointments in her life.... But when she knows how much, how very much I want to see you...and to see you often... always...."

"Oh...always...that could be boring," said Mariannina toying with a pendant that hung from her watch chain.

"Yes, yes," the young man affirmed. "I'm not joking. And I need to talk with you at length. If I come to you, will you shut the door in my face?"

"No, as long as you come with the consent of your mamma."

Mariannina had understood very well that to better capture the heart of Don Cesarino, she had to act bashful and show deference to authority.

"Be quiet!" she said craning her neck. "They're calling me."

"Mariannina! Mariannina!" Signora Rachele, who had stopped near the doorway with Monsignor de Luchi, was in fact calling.

"Here I am, here I am! Come on...what are you doing?"

The girl's question was directed to the young prince who had grabbed her hand and was kissing it avidly.

"I love you so much," babbled the young man, his face inflamed.

"Tss," she said, bringing her finger to her mouth. And she freed herself in order to return to her mother.

While this was going on in the garden, in the first floor living room from which the guest had just exited, the servant

Plinio lingered to pick up the cups of chocolate and put them on the tray to return them to the kitchen. Evidently he would have liked to speak but didn't dare.

Donna Olimpia, who was sunk into an armchair immersed in her thoughts, shook herself at the clatter of the porcelain and admonished:

"Be careful…that's the last service of the old Saxony that's left…. What's that?" she added hearing what sounded like a repressed groan.

Plinio didn't answer. The princess, whose spirit was ulcerated, let some unjust, cruel words escape: "Who knows if in a little while you may recover your back wages."

At this offense, that included a vague confirmation of serious and feared events, the old servant staggered as if he had received a heavy blow on the head; he had barely the strength to put the tray loaded with cups on the little table (and if the tray didn't overturn, you have to believe that a God exists even for the porcelains of Saxony) and fled sobbing from the room into which Don Cesarino erupted with equal force and at almost the same time.

"Mamma, mamma," exclaimed the young prince, throwing himself at the feet of Donna Olimpia and squeezing her knees: "I want her, I want her."

Chapter 9

The Encounters of Brulati the Painter

A few days later, between one and two o'clock, the painter Brulati was coming back along via Merulana, from an excursion on foot right outside Porta San Giovanni, where he had invited two French friends of his to lunch at an inn whose owner was an acquaintance of his. His friends wanted to stop at the Lateran Museum; Brulati thought it more healthy to continue his walk and, with his head held high, his hands deep in the pockets of his overcoat, he drew in voluptuous breaths of that cold and limpid December afternoon, made precisely to dissipate the fumes of Frascati wine which he'd drunk in a greater quantity than necessary. And, truthfully, his ideas, which were a bit confused in the beginning, were reorganized gradually until, before arriving at Santa Maria Maggiore, he remembered among other things that he didn't have any more cigars. He entered a tobacconist's shop, refurnished his cigar box, bought four postcards and, in leaving the store, found himself face to face with Signora Rachele Moncalvo, who had just gotten off a tram.

The painter didn't know how to refrain from an "Oh" of amazement; the Signora, who found the encounter anything but pleasant, blushed under the veil that covered her face. With great self control, she drew her gloved hand out of the small marten muff and extended it to Brulati playfully.

"Well Brulati, you know what's amusing? You are looking at me as if I were a rare beast. Tell me the truth: you find it impossible that a woman who loves all her comforts, used to putting on a kilo after every meal, is out at such an hour and, instead of ordering her nicely closed and well-cushioned carriage comes here in a freezing tram? Well, I'm going to help a poor family who lives in this neighborhood and I don't like to arrive in a carriage."

Brulati approved this delicate thought and without thinking started walking beside Signora Moncalvo.

"Are you going that way?"

"Yes, the opposite direction from the way you were going. Goodbye, Brulati…don't go out of your way on my account."

"Oh, I can very well accompany you for a time," said the painter with an exquisite sense of opportunity.

Signora Rachele would have liked to eat him alive and, in fact, she showed him her still beautiful teeth but she showed them to him by forcing her mouth into a smile.

"Well then, I'll allow you to come with me until that street lamp."

Meanwhile she was thinking: "What an idiot! And they call him an artist of genius! He doesn't understand anything. But if he had understood it would be worse…if he tells everyone that he saw me here…"

And she continued in a strong voice: "There are acts which acquire additional merit the more secret they are. I really don't know why I've talked with you about them. Don't betray me, I beg you…Gabrio and Mariannina will tease me about it…they think we already spend too much in alms…."

"In fact," the painter observed, "the Moncalvos have the reputation of being generous."

"Certainly," added Signora Rachele, "my husband never refuses either his name or money…but hidden charity is the best. How much wretchedness would be overlooked if we didn't make an effort to look for it."

"Unfortunately, unfortunately," sighed Brulati while the Signora slowed her pace and, though pretending to be nonchalant, looked around her suspiciously.

All of a sudden she stopped in her tracks and said in a decisive tone, "Goodbye Brulati. We'll expect you tomorrow at dinner. And we agree, not a word of our encounter."

"Don't worry…better still…"

"What?" asked the Signora Rachele, restraining her impatience with difficulty.

"Here," said the artist drawing out his wallet, "since you have honored me with your confidence, I would like to participate in your good works and offer my small contribution to that poor family."

"What bizarre whims have possessed you? Don't even think of it. No, no…at any rate, it will be for another time. Thank you and goodbye."

But this blessed Brulati insisted so much that she, not seeing any other way to free herself, ended by accepting a twenty-five lire banknote that he insisted on putting into her hand and after a renewed thank you, she moved rapidly away. Whoever might have passed her in that moment would have noted a strange expression on her face and would have heard her complain: "Imbecile! What can I do now with this twenty five lire?"

Brulati, for his part, setting off again on his walk gave himself over to grave considerations. "Blessed women! Who will ever understand them? I wouldn't have thought that this Signora Moncalvo would have such a philanthropic spirit. Not that she's stingy, on the contrary, but she seemed to me more disposed to ostentatiousness than secret charity. And it's true that she had the air of wanting to berate me for surprising her. And the way she received my twenty-five lire! I know that's not much but I don't have her millions. Everyone does what he can."

At this point the excellent Brulati saw something that abruptly changed the course of his thoughts: a carriage, which the driver urged at the greatest speed permitted by the nag that was harnessed to it, hugged the sidewalk in order to avoid the tram; the carriage risked running over an old woman who was crossing the street holding a boy by the hand. The child cried out in fear, the old woman instead railed against the driver and the driver against her. In the meantime a fur clad man in the carriage gave manifest signs of impatience and shouted: "Go ahead! Let's not stay around chattering when nothing has happened."

In fact, the carriage returned to its course but not before Brulati had recognized Count Ugolini-Ruschi. It was doubtful if the Count recognized him, certainly they didn't greet each other. But the artist stayed a moment looking at the carriage which lost itself in the direction taken earlier by Signora Moncalvo. He couldn't help exclaiming: "Toh! So the Count also had some charitable work in these parts?"

Thinking about it, he remembered hearing rumors that he had dismissed. He remembered actions, words which he hadn't paid attention to but which now seemed clear and glaring proof of an intimacy between the Signora Moncalvo and the Count, and, we are sorry to say, he ended by awarding himself the same attributes given secretly to him by Signora Rachele: "Imbecile! Idiot!"

He walked quickly, gesticulating in a strange way and muttering unconnected phrases where the insults to himself alternated with those against the Signora Rachele Moncalvo.

"Ah an act of charity. Shameless! And I'm a fool! And I've given her 25 lire! Could anyone be stupider than that? But what a hypocrite! With that unction! With that air of a woman who is searching for hidden miseries! She didn't want anyone to know...of course! And yet I knew she was vain and excessively ambitious. But I didn't think she was corrupt. Ass! Why didn't I think she was corrupt? Why did I think she was any different from the women she runs around with? Ah, ah, ah! And she pants to be accepted, to enter the womb of the Church. Naturally…and the Knight of Malta will bring her in. When women give themselves to the arms of the Church you can expect the worst. The husband, of course, knows nothing, just as I didn't. If I had imagined I would have announced my candidacy.…Why not? She has always been an appetizing morsel and I would have made a better impression if I'd concluded something with her than I do with my platonic adoration of that flower of coquettes, her daughter. Am I in time? Should I try? It wouldn't be tactful, I understand, as a family friend…a friend of the Commendatore. But it's a cruel world and it's foolish to follow the rules. Poor Commendatore! In business he's a genius, at home he'll have the common fate…but what if it wasn't true? If it was only a coincidence? What if the rendezvous was just the outcome of my fantasy? Toh! Here I am beginning again with my naiveté. It's true, really true, super true. Imbecile! Cretin!"

In this bizarre mood, Brulati arrived at his studio on Piazza Esquilino where the model had been waiting for an hour and welcomed him in an unamiable fashion.

"I'm not really your servant," said the opulent-figured woman from Trastevere. "You told me to come at two and its half past three. I'm warning you, I have to be finished before four." She addressed him with "tu" not to assert a right over him but because that pronoun was more familiar to her and she used it with everyone.

"It's not true that it's past three," Brulati answered looking at the clock, "but I don't feel like working either and I'll let you free directly."

"Just a minute," resumed the woman of the people reattaching the buttons of her bodice. "You'll pay me my wage. It's not my fault that…"

"Of course I'll pay you," interrupted the artist. And he gave her five lire. "It's less than twenty five and it's better spent."

The model looked amazed.

"I know that you can't understand," added Brulati. And slapping her on the shoulders in a friendly fashion he asked: "Well then, you have to be free by four? Do you also have some charitable work? Don't you understand this either?"

"Your lordship is talking in a certain way," mumbled the woman reinstating a sense of social distance with that sibylline language.

"You're right.... Go with God."

"And for tomorrow?"

"Tomorrow at nine, without fail."

Brulati left shortly afterwards without either destination or goal, just to pass the time and, since he had walked more than necessary that morning, he took the first tram that came and got down at San Silvestro. The Corso, where he arrived in two steps, was full of movement as usual in winter afternoons. In front of Caffè Aragno someone called him:

"Brulati, Brulati!"

It was the Commendatore Gabrio Moncalvo. After the wife, the husband.

The Commendatore, standing on the sidewalk of the Caffè in the midst of a group of financial notables, signaled him to come closer.

"Bravo Brulati, now you can come with me to the Bank. No need for introductions… there's no one who doesn't know our Brulati, one of our most genial artists."

"Oh, please…"

Everyone bowed their heads condescendingly. They were all Commendatori; one with a German name was fat and ruddy with a grey top hat. He was a baron into the bargain.

"I must have one of your watercolors," this one said. "I bought it last April at the exhibition. It was very beautiful. I gave it to my wife. It represented…what did it represent? I think it was 'A Roman October'...very beautiful."

"Really," noted the painter with a smile, "at the last exhibition I had only one small piece 'A funeral in the country.'"

"'A Funeral in the country?' Yes, that's it. A jewel. I mixed up one painting with another."

"Thank you...but maybe the Signor Baron is mistaken. That watercolor is unsold. Perhaps the Signor Baron is confused.... He has really bought the 'Roman October' but it isn't mine, it is by Crunali, Mario Crunali."

The banker grimaced. "Crunali...Brulati...the names resemble each other.... I have so many things in my head, I..."

"So that's it, it will be for another time," said Moncalvo to cut short an embarrassing dialogue.

He took the painter's arm and said goodbye to his friends.

"Goodbye, my friends. You get into your carriages. I'll walk a few steps...the doctor has ordered me to exercise. Let's go Brulati. I can see that you have nothing to do this morning. The Bank isn't far...in Via del Plebiscito."

Affable by nature, Moncalvo was more expansive than usual. He too had eaten away from home between two sittings of two societies of which he was advisor, and the truffles washed down with a half bottle of Chateau Lafitte had put him in a good humor.

"Fine fellow, that Bernheim! He affects being a patron of the arts and mixes up the names of the artists and subjects of the paintings. All the same I'll make him buy the 'Funeral in the Country'."

"Forgive me," replied Brulati. "It's not for sale. I promised to give it...can you guess to whom?"

"How can I possibly guess?"

"I promised to give it to Signora Mariannina when she gets married."

"You don't say!" exclaimed the Commendatore. He regretted

to have kept secret from Brulati an event that was to take place in the family and that was already beginning to be talked about.

"Who knows if tomorrow at dinner you'll hear some important news," he began "because tomorrow we expect you. It's your day."

"An important piece of news?" said Brulati in a questioning tone.

Then Gabrio Moncalvo told him that he was on the point of drawing up a contract to acquire all the Orobonis' properties and that at the same time the promise of matrimony between Marianinna and Don Cesarino would be made firm.

"I can imagine the unkind comments that will be made," added the banker, anticipating objections. "I'm not talking of those from the friends of the Oroboni house; I'm talking of the comments of my so-called co-religionists, of the snobbish liberal intellectuals, of the pedants of the bourgeoisie. Unfortunately I will expect some form of excommunication even from my relatives. Imagine my brother and my nephew...the eminent professor and the aspiring professor as Rachele calls them...imbued with old prejudices and old formulas! And my sister, poor soul, an angel but frozen in the ideas of thirty years ago. I've noticed that sickly people find it hard to renew their intellectual baggage. That's right, they will consider us apostates, renegades... certainly, because Mariannina will have to convert. Of course! For now only she will convert...afterwards we'll see. What is it a question of after all? Four drops of water...and sooner or later one has to decide to cross the Rubicon. We are an anachronism but that doesn't mean that we have to disappear. On the contrary, with all that is sane and vigorous in our race, we must reinvigorate the enervated western aristocracy that has more reason to live because it has profound roots deep in the earth, in European history, while we are nomads. I say 'us' but you have nothing to do with it. Dear Brulati, these marriages have a providential character and can't help but have beneficial consequences. You understand that, in the beginning, this requires sacrifices on both sides. In this specific case, do you want me to ignore the fact that Mariannina pays for her title with a sacrifice? Leaving aside the money, Don Cesarino certainly isn't a young man who would turn a girl's head. He isn't handsome or cultivated, or witty, and on that side Mariannina deserved something better. But there'll be children. Oh, they'll come without a doubt...and the children will look like their mother and she will have the consolation of renewing the ancient lineage. You can't have everything in this world. That's how it is also for the Orobonis. The proud princess Olimpia would have liked a daughter-in-law from her caste with a genealogical tree that goes back to the crusades. But a patrician daughter-in-law would have been short of money and perhaps wouldn't have had children or would have had them lean and lymphatic. This one on the other hand will give her giants. And besides...and it isn't something to disregard...that she will cover their coat of arms with gold. Have you followed me, Brulati? You seem distracted. Or is this all a surprise? Didn't you suspect anything at all?"

The artist confessed that certain comments of Donna Rachele and the frequent visits of Monsignor de Luchi had prepared him for news of a conversion but not a marriage.

"Ah," countered Gabrio Moncalvo shrugging his shoulders, "conversion without marriage wouldn't make sense. You will hear, you'll hear tomorrow from my wife, because if the thing succeeds, it is in great part her doing."

"Really?" said Brulati, just to say something.

"Eh, yes" answered the banker. "It's been a delicate work of interaction between her and de Luchi. Honestly, I didn't believe her at first. I've always known her to be intelligent—but I didn't believe she was so astute, so tenacious in her proposals, so discreet above all. A little ambitious, certainly, but we'll restrain her…now she wants a title."

"Nothing easier," exclaimed the painter.

"Nothing easier I know—when it's a question of having one of the usual titles? But this blessed Ugolini has put it in her head to want a Roman title."

Brulati made an admiring gesture.

"You mean papal?"

"Yes, pontifical."

"And Count Ugolini-Ruschi…"

"…is a Knight of Malta and in the good graces of the Vatican. But this is all just talk. And they'll first have to discuss it with me. If they think that I will pass with arms and baggage into the papal camp…"

"That's exactly right. I don't understand politics but I've never gotten along with the priests—and the cannonballs of the 20th September 1870 are among the most beautiful memories of my adolescence."

"The temporal powers would have fallen even without that cannonade," added the conciliatory Moncalvo, "and at this point no one thinks seriously of reviving them. As far as priests go, there are good ones and bad ones. Monsignor de Luchi for example is a pearl. At any rate, Brulati, don't worry. I'm not the sort of man to tie myself to any party…. Here we are at the Bank door. Thanks for the company and goodbye until we see each other again for dinner at the usual time. In that regard, if my wife doesn't mention the marriage, don't you talk about it either. And quiet with everyone else, please, until after the signing."

Brulati's first impulse when he was alone was to repeat the injurious epithets with which he had vilified himself a few hours ago. Idiot and cretin who, living in intimacy with Moncalvos, wasn't aware of what was going on. Idiot and cretin who on the same day that he had let himself be made a fool of by Signora

Rachele and hadn't had the courage to reveal his true feelings about Mariannina's marriage and the family's politico-religious conversion. The thought comforted him, however, that there was someone more of an idiot and cretin than he was and that was Commendatore Gabrio Moncalvo in person, the knowledgeable financier, the genial speculator, the sought after advisor of infinite number of societies. Ah, that Roman title solicited for the Moncalvos by Ugolini Ruschi was the most farcical thing of all. The earldom! That was the least of the services that the Knight of Malta rendered to his dear friend—and the Commendatore Gabrio had plenty of reasons to hold him dear. What a world, what a world! And what would he, Brulati, do dining at the Moncalvo's tomorrow, to keep from laughing in the faces of both the spouses? Tomorrow also the bomb of the marriage would explode! It was strange. The news had produced a painful impression as of an absurdity, an ignoble contract, but it wasn't the blow that he might have expected considering that he was a fervent and devoted admirer of Mariannina. And observing the superficial character of his senile passion, he found himself in the position of one who becomes aware that he has only minor abrasions on his body after a fall in which he imagined that his bones would be broken.

These consoling reflections left Brulati less aware of fatigue as he went on wandering along the streets. He lingered in front of the brightly lit windows, resisting the temptation to pass a cheerful hour in a certain café near Campo de' Fiori where many young artists of his acquaintance were in the habit of meeting in the afternoon. The fact was that in the midst of those jovial fellows he feared that some word might escape him concerning the day's events. His throat was full of it and notwithstanding his promise to be discreet, they tugged at his tongue.

"Ah!" he exclaimed all of a sudden like someone who is in agony from a tooth ache.

It wasn't his teeth. The cry of pain was drawn out of him by the unexpected arrival of a person who in that moment couldn't be more inopportune. He tried to avoid him by stopping to look at the display of a jeweler, but the young Professor Moncalvo (it was he, the third Moncalvo to come his way in several hours) put his hand on Brulati's shoulder.

"Bravo Brulati, you pretend not to see me. How long has it been since you visited uncle and aunt?"

Chapter 10

The Eminent and Aspiring Professors

Coming home terribly upset, Giorgio asked the servant girl who opened the door for him: "Is my father in his study?"

"Yes, Signore, please notice that a letter came for you. I've put it on the bureau."

"Alright. I'll look at it afterwards," said the young man, giving the servant his coat and hat. And he rushed into the study at the same time that doctor Flacci, Professor Giacomo's assistant, was leaving.

He, the professor, was sitting in front of his desk with a pile of books and papers. A small oil lamp protected by a green shade, cast a circle of light on the books and on the bald head of the scientist who put down his glasses and raised his eyes towards his son to ask him, not without a certain anxiety, "What's happened?"

"Nothing has happened that you don't already know about," began the terribly agitated Giorgio. "It's impossible that you didn't know the secret...why did you want to keep me in the dark?"

"I don't understand you," replied the professor. "Explain and put a little order and calm in your speech. Take a chair."

Giorgio shook his head. "I prefer to stand. You want to make me believe that you are ignorant of what is going on in your brother's house. You who were there just yesterday?"

"I was there yesterday, after several days that I didn't visit. It was to see my sister who unfortunately isn't well."

"Yes, and I'm not allowed to visit...in obedience to the

paternal authority," said Giorgio with a touch of irony.

"Don't be upset," countered professor Giacomo, standing and coming closer to his son. "I didn't give you orders. I advised you for your own good. And now I beg you to come down from the clouds. What is the big secret that I must have been aware of?"

"Good God!" Exclaimed Giorgio with violence. "You spoke to Aunt Clara yesterday and she didn't tell you what someone outside the family, Brulati, told me now…and I noticed that he kept quiet about something else. I would swear that he had something else to tell me that I didn't succeed in prying from him."

"Alright then let's hear what you found out."

"That Mariannina will marry Prince Cesarino Oroboni; that she will have a million in dowry; that naturally before becoming a Roman princess she will purify herself like the pagan obelisk of Saint Peter in the baptismal water; and that, perhaps, Aunt Rachele will convert along with her or a little after. And you didn't know anything about this?"

"Nothing positive," answered the professor, "and I don't believe that things are at the point you say. But I'm not surprised at any of it. Gabrio, his wife, Mariannina—all are sick with ambition and vanity. They have a pathological impatience to escape from the bourgeoisie, to be forgiven for their origins."

"And Aunt Clara," interrupted Giorgio, "what does she think, what is she doing?"

"Aunt Clara, like me, has never had the confidences of her brother, of her sister-in-law, of her niece…she has merely a vague sense of what they are plotting. Maybe when she is better she'll go back with us…because, as you can imagine, she won't approve any more than I do."

This simple dissent, so tranquil, so measured, couldn't be enough for Giorgio; in fact, it irritated him further.

"Of course you don't approve! But do you think that's enough? It's a question of our name, our family. More than just not approving! It's necessary to do something."

Giacomo Moncalvo looked at his son with a stupor that was barely hidden.

"Are you raving, Giorgio? What right do you have to act? What rights do we have? Are we the custodians of all the Moncalvos? My brother has taken a path that isn't ours and he won't withdraw from it, because he found in it his heart's most gratifying satisfactions. And to do him justice, the position that he's conquered is owed to his cleverness, to his activity. And he is honest, though it is difficult for someone managing money to keep one's hands clean. He is honest and generous."

"Yes," Giorgio confirmed sarcastically, "he has all the virtues and he lends himself to an ignoble market and concedes the hand of his daughter to the cretinous offspring of an exhausted lineage."

"It is ignoble, I agree. But you can be sure that Mariannina isn't a victim. If this marriage is concluded that means that she is persuaded at least as much as her parents."

"No, papa, I can't accept that."

"And yet, you have to accept it. It's the great torment of your Aunt Clara, who adored this niece, who left our house to stay near her, who was confident that she had an influence on her, and yet day by day she saw her slip from her hands, grow different from what Clara had hoped: capricious, egotistical, impatient of every obstacle, not straight forward, not frank... more ambitious, more vain than her parents, though she knew how to hide it better."

"Oh, papa," said Giorgio, "You are pitiless against Mariannina! You hate her."

"I don't hate anyone. I don't know if she realizes the harm she does."

"Let's save her then," shouted the young man, interpreting his father's words in an opposite sense from what was meant.

"Ah, I don't allude to the harm she's done to herself," countered the professor. "That I don't have the means to impede. I mean the harm she does to others, that she does to you, my son." Giorgio was now sitting with his head bent, arms resting on his open knees. The professor caressed his son's hair with his hand and went on: "And yet you have to realize that even if your cousin was a perfect soul she couldn't be your life's companion."

Giorgio nodded his head in agreement.

"It's true. I would not adapt to her riches—nor could she to my poverty. I could be resigned to her having a reasonable marriage, even a patrician one...but not to this with Cesarino Oroboni, not to this comedy of a conversion. You are big-hearted, tolerant; your morality is above dogmas and rites. You have taught me to judge men according to the qualities of their souls and their talent, not by their religion. I don't much care what denomination they have, either another or none. What matters to me is the insincerity—I don't understand someone embracing a new faith because of the effect of a clause in a contract."

"Here you are totally right," declared the professor, "and these utilitarian conversions are one of the most disheartening and base spectacles of our times. But what do you propose to do about it?"

The easy acquiescence of his father continued to irritate Giorgio.

"No, no, it isn't right to wash our hands of it. We ought to make our voices heard. If it doesn't stop anything, patience. We won't have any regrets. And they can't make you keep quiet. I would like to give a lesson to that intriguing Monsignor de Luchi...and that Don Ceasarino—how I'd like to challenge him."

"Violence! A challenge!" said Giacomo Moncalvo, disturbed by the growing exaltation of Giorgio, who revealed the depth of the wound that Mariannina had opened in his heart. "You who are so mild and have such equanimity, you who are such a modern spirit—you know how much these famous chivalrous solutions are worth! Be aware that probably Cesarino Oroboni won't fight you, either so as not to cross swords with an infidel, or a plebian, or because of his religious principles...and even if you fight? Even if you kill him? Because I can't imagine the opposite outcome.... Will you be happier?"

"I've renounced happiness forever," Giorgio responded darkly.

"And you complain because I'm too severe with her?" exclaimed the professor. "With her who has ravaged your brain? Who has started you on a path with no exit? Who has distracted you from your research?"

"Papa, papa, I'm sorry," Giorgio began again, lifting his eyes imploringly towards his father. "But sometimes I think that if years ago I had accepted the counsel of my uncle, if I'd accepted the post that he offered me in Khartoum, things would have taken a different aspect. It was obvious that my uncle wanted to bring me into his business with a second purpose, seeing me as a possible husband of his daughter. And years ago Mariannina wasn't the way she is now. She was corrupted later on."

"Poor Giorgio! And you believe that you could have watched over her from Khartoum, while she, always more beautiful, always wealthier, moved from Cairo to Nice to Paris surrounded by a frivolous and cosmopolitan society, made drunk with homage and surrounded by luxury and pleasures? What disillusionment if she had been your fiancée, what disillusion would have waited for you the day in which you saw her again! No, no, my boy it wasn't a misfortune that you didn't accept the post in Khartoum; the real misfortune was that those people came to establish themselves in Rome. The error is that you came back from abroad; and it's partly my fault for making you return."

Until this point the scientist had succeeded in dominating his feelings. Now he could barely contain them. His voice trembled, and tears wet his lashes.

"I have only you," he said. "I was hoping to have you near to me. I didn't imagine that the sympathy you felt for your cousin when you were little more than a boy could, in greatly changed circumstances, become a violent passion. You never named her in your letters. I felt sure that you were indifferent to her."

"And I?" protested Giorgio "I had forgotten her. I swear, papa, the idea of seeing her in Rome didn't bother me. I knew that the distance between us had grown enormously...ten, twenty times a millionaire. I was also happy to come here, papa, to follow my scientific career here next to you. I was so content. Now I don't know what's the matter with me. I can't connect two ideas."

Springing from his seat, he resumed circling the room. After a pause, he returned to a phrase pronounced by his father.

"A violent passion? No, it isn't even that. I am even more convinced than you are that I ought to erase Mariannina from my mind and my heart. Look, if uncle Gabrio told me to marry her, and if she said 'marry me', I would say no—that's how absurd this marriage seems to me. Are you amazed? Do I seem to contradict myself? Oh papa, your poor son has lost his mind."

"It's a crisis, a crisis that will pass," responded the professor, trying to hide under his joking manner his own discomfort. "And if the events that were announced to you should really take place, we won't take part in it. I'll take a sabbatical of six months from the university, it will be the first leave that I've taken... we'll take a long trip outside of Italy, outside of Europe. Maybe we could even take my sister with us! If her health doesn't permit her to travel, we'll leave her here to put our house in order. I'm sure she won't stay with my brother. She'd feel too uneasy. At any rate, returning to Rome after six months passed in the midst of different people and cultures, we will have completely forgotten that famous Mariannina, even if she'll be a princess. All the more if she'll be a princess. Don't you think, young man?"

Giorgio shook his head with a sad smile. "You'd leave your routine, your professorship for me?"

"Certainly I'd leave it. Forever, if necessary. Luckily a short absence will be enough. Don't you like my plan?"

"We'll talk more about it, papa. Thanks for everything. You are so good."

Someone knocked timidly at the door.

"What is it?"

The servant announced that dinner was ready.

"We're coming," said the professor, who rose, giving his arm to his son.

Dinner was silent although Giacomo Moncalvo tried to bring into play the most varied topics. Only at the end did Giorgio became a little more animated, discussing Salvieni's lectures on physiology and the part of the course that the illustrious man had entrusted entirely to him, Giorgio. Eh, Salvieni didn't make his assistants sit around with their hands in their laps.

"Do you also have school tomorrow morning?" asked professor Giacomo.

"Yes, at nine. And by eight I have to be in the laboratory."

"You're not going out tonight?"

"No. I want to put my notes for the lesson in order."

"In that case, I won't go out either. I'll finish correcting the proofs of a memoir for the Lincei."

"Good night, papa."

"Are you going? I'm in no hurry."

"I'm sorry, papa," added Giorgio "I have a couple of hours of work to do. Tomorrow I'm going out very early."

That makes sense. It would be better if you went to bed right away."

"No, no. Immersing myself in my studies is good for me."

"Good night then, my son, and give some thought to my proposition."

"I'll think about it. We'll discuss it again."

"And," continued the professor taken with a sudden anxiety, "promise me that you won't take any step without consulting me."

"I promise you," replied Giorgio and sealed the promise with a kiss.

The letter that waited for him in his room and which he had completely forgotten came from Berlin and he immediately recognized in the address the narrow handwriting of Frida Raucher. Poor Frida! He had only written her twice from Rome and both times in October. Then he had limited himself to picture postcards. It's true that she didn't contact you either. Certainly she was angry and she was right to be angry. Or maybe she was sicker than usual? Giorgio ripped open the envelope with some trepidation.

Frida Raucher wrote in a fluent enough Italian, yet not without some uncertainties of spelling and grammar:

Dear friend,

I take the pen in secret from my father and against the doctor's orders who only since yesterday has allowed me to get up.

In the middle of October I had a serious relapse and believed that I had arrived at the ultimate. Can you say that in Italian? I am afraid not but my teacher will be indulgent. My father intended to let you know about my bad state but I myself told him to wait. Why trouble with useless worries the professor who is now in his own country, in his house among his occupations and who couldn't by any means come to Berlin to visit his little, sick friend? Naturally, we'll let him know later. But here I am still able to write him and thank him for the beautiful postcards by which I see that, though he is unable to find the time to write me a letter, he sometimes remembers Frida. Papa would like to take me to Italy this spring and I'd be happy to spend some weeks in Rome. You will be our guide, isn't that so? And will you show us the monuments that we admired in the photographs and the cards. But these are Luftschlösser, castles in the air. I know it isn't possible and perhaps by springtime I will not be in this world any longer. Poor, poor papa. Just for him I am sorry to die. I hope he will be consoled by his discoveries. Now he is doing certain studies which would make it necessary for him to go very far away. But he doesn't want to leave me. I am really a hindrance.

I have to stop because I am tired, very, very tired. Goodbye Signor Giorgio, live happy and save a place in your memory for your devoted, loving and *gar treu bis an das Grab*.

Frida Raucher

The last lines were confused, almost illegible whether Frida's hand trembled or a tear had fallen on the page. *Gar treu bis an das Grab*—faithful to the grave! Giorgio Moncalvo was crying too, conquered by pity for the gentle girl who took leave of life with such delicate abandon, chastely confessing her love, the only love of her brief youth. Already leaving her, he knew he wouldn't see her again—but now, hearing it announced by her hand, made him shiver in all his limbs and the tender farewell sounded like a reproach. It seemed to him that it would be his duty to run to the bed of the dying girl and receive her dying breath, to place a final kiss on her virginal forehead. How much better than fantasizing futilely about the other one who he would have wanted to despise and abhor but who nonetheless dominated his soul and his senses!

Chapter 11

Aunt Clara Also Takes Her Leave

The next morning a little after nine, Professor Giacomo Moncalvo was taking his coffee in his study when the maid came in with a note.

"Your brother the Commendatore sent this," she said. "And the carriage is waiting for you downstairs."

"The carriage?" exclaimed the professor, nervously tearing open the envelope.

"Has there been some disaster?" asked the woman, seeing him grow pale.

"My sister is ill," he mumbled. "I'll go right away. Has Giorgio gone out?"

"An hour ago."

"If he comes back when I'm not here..." began Giacomo Moncalvo, but he broke off as if it disgusted him to bring his son near Mariannina again. But he repented of his hesitation and began again: "If he comes back he should come too, there to the Gandi Palace on Via Nazionale."

He put his coat on hurriedly and rushed down the stairs while the servant leaning from the banister of the landing shouted behind him:

"Will you be home for lunch?"

"I don't know, I don't know..."

In the carriage he reread another time the note from Gabrio. There were only two lines scribbled down in a great rush: "Clara is gravely ill. There will be a consultation at eleven. The patient asks for you and Giorgio. Come immediately."

Nothing more than that. When and how had Clara taken a turn for the worse? It hadn't been forty-eight hours since he'd seen her—pallid yes, weak, suffering but certainly not in a condition to fear imminent danger. She herself said she was tired of being shut in her room, that the doctor imposed too many conditions, that a bit of air would do her good. What new complications had there been in such a brief time? The coachman wasn't able to give him any explanation. He too had heard that the Signorina Clara was very ill but he didn't know anything else. At any rate, there was no doubt that if Gabrio had sent the carriage the case must be urgent. Not apoplexy however: if Clara wasn't conscious she couldn't have asked for him and Giorgio. And there were no possible objections; Giorgio had a sacrosanct obligation to respond to the call of his aunt and neither his father nor anyone else in the world had the right to hold him back. Indeed it would be better to look for him right away, before it was too late. But meanwhile what seemed most urgent was to get there and to Giacomo Moncalvo it seemed that the carriage didn't go fast enough.

At the Gandi palace, the professor found everyone perturbed and anxious. Commendatore Gabrio wasn't the only one who loved his sister, Rachele and Mariannina were also accustomed to consider Clara an indispensable person, a judicious person, modest, ready to sacrifice herself for the others, just what was needed in a family of egotists.

"We can't imagine how this happened," Gabrio said. "That's the truth. After that unfortunate car trip...your son was there too."

Mariannina intervened.

"Where is Giorgio?"

"He has classes not far from here at the School of Hygiene on via Agostino De Pretis. We can get someone to go and call him."

"I'll do it," added the girl. Going into the hall where the telephone was, she rang the School of Hygiene.

"Is professor Giorgio Moncalvo there?"

"Yes; in the laboratory. Who wants him?"

"He must come to the phone immediately. It's urgent."

"But who is speaking?"

"It doesn't matter. It's urgent, urgent, urgent! Do you understand?"

After a brief silence another voice was heard on the phone, severe, agitated, almost aggressive, and he renewed the demand: "Who is this?"

"It's me, Mariannina Moncalvo! Am I speaking with Giorgio?"

The voice, which had sounded angry before, softened and he answered: "Yes, this is Giorgio...*you* are calling *me*, Mariannina?"

"Yes, me myself. You have to leave everything and hurry to us. Aunt Clara is very ill and wants to see you. Your father is here too."

"Oh God, is she very bad?"

"Very, very. Soon there will be a consultation. So we'll expect you."

"In fifteen minutes I'll be there."

"Alright. Goodbye."

Meanwhile, the Commendatore explained to his brother how Clara who, sadly, had never recovered from the bad cold she'd come down with after the ill-fated car trip, had developed difficulty breathing and a violent fever, how her condition had worsened in the night, how the doctor in charge had said it was pneumonia and had expressed the desire to consult with Marchiafava immediately.

"And now we wait for this consultation," concluded Gabrio Moncalvo looking at the clock. "It is set for 11 and it's only 10:15."

Signora Rachele, who was coming from the sick woman's room, turned to her brother-in-law: "She's calmer. If you want to see her…. But be careful not to let her talk too much."

The professor had difficulty hiding the pitiful impression made by the emaciated appearance of his sister. Just two days before she had seemed to be suffering from a cold; but what work of demolition the illness had accomplished in a few hours in her fragile organism. Her pale face, framed by two strips of gray hair, was sunk deeply into the pillows, her breast was heaving, her gaze was fixed; only a light tint of diffuse red on her prominent cheekbones revealed the destructive fire of her fever.

She signed to Giacomo to come nearer and whispered:

"Thank you for the visit. And Giorgio?"

"He's coming."

"He should hurry. I want to say goodbye to him."

She turned towards Giovanna, the housekeeper, who was caring for her, and begged her to lower the shade.

"Our talk the other day," she continued, drawing her slender, white hand outside the covers and extending it to her brother. "You remember? I was to come and live with you…."

Giacomo pretended to not understand the significance of these words.

"Well? You'll come back as soon as you are cured."

"At this point I won't be cured."

"Oh, Clara!"

"And perhaps it's better. I will avoid displeasing the people who have always been so good to me. And I won't see things that even seen from far off would displease me. Life is a sad comedy, dear Giacomo! You have your studies…you have your son…."

She had a bout of coughing and the professor, raising her a little, administered a few drops of the sedative that Giovanna held out to him.

"I'll leave you now" he added. "Don't tire yourself."

"And where are you going?"

"For the moment I'll be in the hallway."

"Ah," said Clara divining what he meant. "You're waiting for the consultation," and she gave a skeptical, sad smile. "If Giorgio comes, send him in."

In the hall, Giacomo found his brother who came towards him. "What impression did she make on you?"

"Who can tell!" sighed the professor "She has declined a great deal very rapidly."

"Sadly, sadly," replied Gabrio drying his eyes. "Poor Clara! I swear, I can't imagine this house without her. One day she declared her intention of leaving us to live with you again. But I hope that she'll reconsider. But why, why would she have to leave us?"

"Let's hope that she is cured," replied Giacomo. "The rest is secondary."

"You're right," added the Commendatore, happy to end his thoughts and the conversation on this common wish.

The two brothers came back together to the work room of Signora Rachele, who was conferring with the maid.

"You know that my sister-in-law has the keys, don't you? Maybe they're in her bureau. Now it isn't possible. You can look later after the consultation."

The Commendatore took out his watch again. "Ten thirty. They could at least be punctual. And Mariannina?"

"They called her to the telephone."

It was Miss Lizzie May, her American friend, who invited her to have tea at the Grand Hotel at 5, and Mariannina Moncalvo explained to her friend that it would be difficult to accept the invitation because of the grave condition of her aunt. Miss May was "very sorry indeed" about this. At this manifestation of sorrow, the American added a vague allusion to certain news that was going around about the grand marriage of Miss Moncalvo. She lamented that she had been left in the dark about an event of such importance. And Miss Moncalvo responded that the news was very premature and that when there was something positive the first to know about it would be her delightful Miss May. The delightful Miss May had already begun her brave response when, instead of the sound of known voices, the ears of the two interlocutors surprised a conversation lost in the labyrinth of the telephone circuits about a report of 500 Roman municipal bonds.

So, the dialogue ended this way and Mariannina, leaving the phone, saw the maid behind her who said: "Your cousin professor Giorgio has arrived. Should I take him to the Signora?"

"Heavens! He can come through here. Isn't he a member of the family?"

"Oh Giorgio, do we need the threat of a disaster to see you? You have forgotten us."

She spoke as though nothing had happened, as though nothing was coming, as though an insuperable barrier wasn't on the point of rising between her and this cousin, between her and all the past. And, in front of her, Giorgio was turning a deep crimson, amazed, confused, asking himself if he were dreaming, if this was really the Mariannina who in order to become a princess was sacrificing her sympathies, her dignity, her female ideals.

He babbled: "Aunt Clara?"

With a discouraged gesture, Mariannina answered: "I have little hope. We'll hear from the doctors soon. You know that at 11 there will be a consultation? Come."

"Where?"

"To her, to our aunt...for a moment."

She moved close to him and wrapped him in the caress of her gaze—she imagined that he would always be hers, no matter what happened.

And her satisfaction wasn't only pride. Because Giorgio pleased her. Because she had to confess that, near to him, she was more moved than with anyone else; and for exactly this reason she desired his company just the way the strong drinker wants the richest wine that excites him without making him drunk. She was quite certain that she wouldn't get drunk.

"How serious is it?" asked Giorgio marveling that his own question was so calm, that it didn't express a livelier anxiety, a more profound emotion.

"Very serious," sighed Mariannina. Avoiding the room where all the others were and from which came the sound of voices, she entered a corridor, turned, and opened a little door in the wall that led to an antechamber full of bureaus.

He followed her. She disappeared for a moment behind a door; then, raising a heavy curtain, motioned to Giorgio to come near.

"Here is Giorgio," she announced.

She brushed the sick woman's forehead with a kiss, exchanged a word with Giovanna, picked up a bunch of keys from the floor—the keys that the chambermaid was looking for—then exited on tiptoe, and it seemed to Giorgio that the little light brightening the room left with her.

"Giorgio!" called Aunt Clara in a voice he could barely hear.

He shook himself, ashamed, hearing a veiled reproof in her tone almost as if she wanted to ask him: "Did you come for her or for me?"

Drawing near the bed, he took the hand that greeted him and brought it avidly to his lips.

"Aunt Clara, Aunt Clara!"

"It would have made me very unhappy not to have seen you," she whispered. "And yet…maybe…"

She didn't finish the phrase but implored her nephew to arrange the pillows under her head. "That way. That's fine."

She made a sign to the nurse that she didn't need her help and said softly to Giorgio: "Don't think of her, Giorgio. Don't think of her."

She was exhausted and couldn't say anymore. Giorgio sat next to her in silence with his forehead bent towards the floor, holding back the tears that clouded his eyes.

Someone entered, touched him on the shoulder. It was his uncle Gabrio.

"Mariannina told me you were here. You were right to come. Now leave her... the doctors are coming upstairs."

And turning to his sister, whose eyelids were lowered and who seemed to sleep, he repeated. "See, Clara, the doctors are here."

She nodded weakly.

"You know Marchiafava, don't you?"

"Yes..."

The consultation lasted about forty-five minutes and ended with a distressing conclusion. The inflammation in the lungs was spreading rapidly, the heart was weak, they should prepare for the worst. In fact, all the remedies were in vain and a second consultation couldn't disagree that a disaster was imminent.

Signora Clara lived for two days more with the aid of oxygen and injections of camphor, pronouncing with difficulty some monosyllables but indicating that she understood what they were saying and that she recognized the people around her. Her veiled eyes lingered by preference on her two brothers, who were brought closer for a little while by her agony but who were irremediably divided by the vagaries of fortune and opposing inclinations. They stood before her as mature men but she saw them as boys, in their modest home, with their differing aspects, tastes and temperaments: Giacomo, pale, blond, tall, slender, with fine and delicate features, timid, patient, often silent, always studious; Gabriele stocky, hair and complexion dark, with a distinctively semitic profile, talkative, intrepid, rebellious in the family and at school and yet driven to be first and ready to supply with the quickness of his intellect any deficiencies of preparation. How they both loved her, how she succeeded in calming their little tantrums, in patching up their quarrels with narrow-minded parents, with grandparents so rigidly attached to the Jewish religion. Their parents and the grandparents had died early and she had remained, at eighteen years old, to direct the house and look after the brothers of whom, the eldest Giacomo, wasn't yet fifteen. Helping them become young men, she had let her own youth go by. And when each of them had made his way, she lived now with one, now the other, and she was always near to both of them in her thoughts. She had closed her world in the orbit of their worlds. It was she who brought them together, it was for love of her they forgot what was irreconcilable in their opinions and their characters. Now no more, no more...the thread was broken, Clara left never to return.

The morning she died, the two brothers, also wrapped in memories, threw their arms around each other's necks crying. They, too, remembered what Clara had been to them, and felt that she had abandoned them exactly at the time they needed her most.

The Commendatore was the more overcome of the two. He also would be, without a doubt, the first to forget. He would soon be desirous to return with his accustomed energy to his occupations, deaf to voices other than those of vanity, ambition, unbounded craving to add riches to riches. And yet, today, he begged his brother not to leave him, to protect him from bothersome people and help him take care of the tiresome obligations of these moments. Giorgio too could be useful.... Where was he?

Giacomo said that he had sent him to the university on a pressing errand.

"As long as that sainted creature is above ground you must stay with us," Gabrio continued. "Yes, yes, we can accommodate you for a couple of nights. For you there's the guest room that is always ready. We'll find a place for Giorgio too. And meanwhile it's necessary for us to see together if poor Clara left something written…I think she did…I think in one of her drawers there is a paper. Who will go and look for it? I can't, I can't…. And we will have to send out invitations to the funeral. Do me a favor, take care of it…and the transportation to the cemetery! My God, the transportation!"

Here they faced a great question. Clara, like the rest of her family, didn't practice any religion, yet she had never abjured the Jewish faith into which she was born. Indeed, it was known that she strongly disapproved of the coming conversion, now certain, of her niece and the probable conversion of her sister-in-law. So there wasn't a middle way: either she must have a civil funeral or a funeral according to the Jewish rites. And already a delegate of the Community had come to make arrangements.

But when secretary Fanoli gave the message to Gabrio Moncalvo, he became furious: "Here are the vultures who fall on corpses. It's not easy to get free of this torment, this shirt of Nessus. You can live thirty, forty years outside of the religion imposed by your parents and then, at the hour of death, it comes back to you in the guise of a funeral agency. Please tell them not to bother us."

Signora Rachele, arriving unexpectedly at this point, increased the pressure: "Yes, please, Fanoli, get that intruder out of here. Tell him we don't entertain any relationship with his Community."

"Let's stay calm," resumed Gabrio Moncalvo, called back by his wife's excessive language, "There is no reason to make a declaration of principles."

The professor intervened: "It seems to me that we can't decide anything without being assured first that Clara didn't make any specific provisions. I would tell this gentleman to come back later or, better still, that you will call him."

The suggestion was so reasonable that the Commendatore and Signora Rachele couldn't not welcome it.

Fanoli pointed out letters, telegrams, but Gabrio Moncalvo interrupted him.

"Do what you can…. Wait with the rest. And today I don't want to see anyone."

"By the way, the director of the International Bank came a little while ago in person. But he didn't insist on being announced and I didn't believe…"

"Very good. Thanks. And, we understand each other, dismiss that messenger for the Community. As the professor suggested, we'll telephone."

A servant tiptoed in and whispered something in the ear of Signora Moncalvo, who was prepared to go,

"What is it?" asked her husband.

She, distressed by the presence of her brother-in-law, answered hurriedly: "Nothing, nothing. An order to give." And she left.

Giacomo passed his brother a piece of paper on which he had put down a rough draft of the funeral announcement.

The Commendatore read in a low voice: "The brothers Gabrio and Giacomo Moncalvo, the sister-in-law Rachele, the nephew Giorgio and niece Mariannina announce with profound sorrow the death today of their beloved Clara—a woman of exemplary kindness and moral rectitude who lived fifty five years thinking the good, acting justly, always forgetting herself to do good to others."

"True, true. It reads very well…but you are the elder brother…your name ought to go first."

"But she died in your house and it seemed to me…"

"Whatever you think," added Gabrio who predicted the

objections of his wife if the order were inverted. "And you didn't mention our titles?

"Your commendation. The professorships of my son and I? They could be added but they seem so out of place in a funeral announcement."

"You're right. What's needed is a mention of the day, the hour and the method of transportation."

"I know, and it's precisely for this reason that we have to authorize that search of our sister's papers."

With an effort the Commendatore got up.

"Will you come with me?"

"Yes. Do you have the keys?"

"My wife has them. She said she'd be right back."

"It wouldn't be bad if she were present."

Signora Rachele entered at that moment. "No, no," she declared to her brother-in-law who invited her to follow them. "I don't trust my nerves. These are the keys. The one to the desk is the smallest, I'll wait for you here."

She pressed the button of the electric bell.

"And the Signorina?"

"She's still in her studio with her friends."

How invasive those Americans girls are, thought the mother to herself, and she made a mental comparison between them and Monsignor de Luchi and the Count Ugolini-Ruschi who had come a little while ago to bring her a good word. They had remained standing and had insisted on not disturbing anyone, neither the Signor Commendatore nor Mariannina.

Signora Rachele had wanted to know the opinion of Monsignor about the funeral and he had answered in these exact words: "It's natural that funerals are done according to the deceased's religion. It can't be done otherwise. A civil funeral would be worse, much worse. It would make a terrible impression on the Orobonis too."

The two brothers had no difficulty finding what they were looking for and now Gabrio reentered his wife's room holding a little sealed envelope on which was written "The last wishes of Clara Moncalvo." He was pale and undone, as if he had a vision of death before his eyes. He put the envelope silently on the table and sat with a fixed look, a look which didn't see the things that were in front of him.

Perturbed, Signora Rachele came near him.

"Do you want to open the window? Do you want a glass of Marsala?

He refused with a gesture.

"And Giacomo?" asked his wife.

"He's coming. He was delayed down there. You know that Brulati's in the room. He offered spontaneously to do a sketch before the features change. A true friend, Brulati."

"Monsignor de Luchi was here also," said the Signora Rachele.

"He was here? Did you see him?"

"Yes, when the servant called me. He didn't even want to sit down…he only wanted to leave his condolences and the condolences of all the Orobonis."

"And imagine that exactly now we ought to draw up the contract," sighed the Commendatore.

"He said as much. He said that you would draw up a contract after the funeral. Whenever you think it best…. Incidentally, his opinion…quiet! Here's your brother."

"And there's also Mariannina. Finally. Where were you?"

"With Miss May and her aunt."

The professor, quite calm, said, "The sketch will turn out well. If you could see, Rachele, what serenity breathes from her face. She has all the beauty of her goodness." He took the envelope and asked Gabrio, "Shall I open it?"

"Open it."

Mariannina turned towards her uncle. "Aren't you waiting for Giorgio?"

"It's not necessary. I'll represent him." The will was from two years previous and was very short. Aunt Clara had kind words for everyone in the two families with whom she had lived alternately. She left each one of them a souvenir; she left small bequests to the servants and instituted as the residual heir of her modest fortune a second cousin, widowed and extremely poor, who lived in Ferrara, and of whom Giacomo and Gabrio had lost every trace. Only Signora Rachele remembered that one day, when she was walking, she met her sister-in-law entering the postal office to insure a letter. She perceived the address of that letter, which certainly contained a consignment of money, and it seemed to her that it corresponded to the name of the person mentioned in the will.

"It must be a daughter of our grandfather's brother, whom we hardly knew."

"Or maybe the daughter of a son," added Gabrio. "If she was so poor, why didn't she apply to me?"

"She didn't dare."

"Clara could."

"She would have preferred to give it herself in secret," replied the professor. "She was one of those who didn't show off, and she did well to aid a relative so badly off."

"What does this famous inheritance come to?" asked Signora Rachele.

"The amount can be figured out quickly," answered her husband who, in talking about business, could find his pulse again. At the death of her parents, Clara had a part equal to what went to Giacomo and me. Twenty-five thousand lira. She hasn't touched it, but she hasn't increased it; after taxes perhaps twenty thousand lire remain. For the relative who has nothing it is a providence."

"Yes, yes," muttered Signora Rachele with the condescension of a millionaire. "And not a word about the funeral?"

"Nothing."

"So we know as much as we did before. What shall we do?"

"Eh," answered Giacomo, "there is nothing to do except to telephone the Community as if it were understood. In the absence of concrete instructions I think we should proceed the customary way. Our sister was very open-minded, but we can't know that in the intimacy of her heart she didn't feel tied in some way to the religion of her infancy."

The Commendatore shrugged his shoulders: "You counsel me this way.... You who have declared so many times that you want a civil funeral?"

"I decide for myself, not for others."

"A civil funeral—certainly not," protested Signora Rachel energetically.

"It's so ugly!" said Mariannina.

"You see," Giacomo began again, "your wife and daughter share my opinion."

"Yes, even if they are fiercer than I am against the Mosaic rites."

"Excuse me, but these are prejudices," the professor said. "The rites of all religions have their profound significance in times of faith. And even when there is no faith, they are worthy of respect. What's more, you can't intend to have a Catholic funeral for our poor Clara."

"I know it isn't possible," Signora Rachele answered scornfully, "but this is the last time that those Satraps from the Community climb our stairs. It's time to end this humiliation."

"Dear sister-in-law," said Giacomo. "I wish you never have a greater humiliation."

Gabrio signaled his wife to keep quiet and, having decided to get it over with, called for his secretary. He had already risen from his downcast state, recovered his strength, his activity.

"So for the funeral, go ahead and telephone. They must understand that we want a first class funeral."

"Remember," insinuated Giorgio, "that Clara had extremely simple tastes."

"Excuse me," the Commendatore replied promptly, "this isn't a question of her tastes, but of my obligations." And he asked Fanoli, "Will it be tomorrow?"

"No, Signor Commendatore. It will be the day after. Tomorrow is Saturday."

"Ah there's the holiday. Well, telephone and let us know the precise time so that we can insert it in the announcement that needs to be printed and sent off today. My nephew will help you with the addresses. Do you think Giorgio will say no?" Gabrio asked his brother.

"He'll help, no doubt. He had such affection for his aunt."

"Here, Fanoli," the banker recommenced. "Take this note, complete it as soon as you have come to an agreement with those people and then send it to the printer. Have them print a thousand copies. Do you have errand boys at your disposal?"

"The International Bank has as many as you could want."

"And now," added Gabrio Moncalvo after dismissing Fanoli, "now let's think of a way of worthily honoring our sister. I would like a list of donations in her name to appear in the newspaper tomorrow morning for a total of, let's say, twenty thousand lira. Clara doesn't deserve less. The essential is to spend them well. Let's think together."

This form of sumptuous charity displeased professor Giacomo, as it would have displeased Clara; all the same he was content to be evasive.

"It's you who is spending the money. You do it."

The Commendatore concealed an impatient gesture. "I am in business and have been able to accumulate a fine patrimony.

It's natural that I spend it. But my intention would be to make this offer in both our names."

"Don't even dream of it," the professor said firmly.

"I know you're proud, I know."

"It would be strange if I spoke otherwise."

"I recommend the Charity of Sant'Antonio," interjected Signora Rachele.

Marianinna approached her father sweetly.

"I hope you won't forget my destitute women…some of them are so lovely."

"What destitute women?'"

"Those of the pious works that mamma and I visited in the company of Monsignor de Luchi."

Professor Giacomo couldn't help abandoning his neutrality.

"I said that I wasn't going to participate. It seems to me however that in these charities you ought to conform to the probable desires of our dear deceased. And I don't think that she would have thought either of the Charity of Sant'Antonio or of the destitute women of Monsignor de Luchi."

"Why, why?" shouted with one voice Rachele and Mariannina.

But the Commendatore recognized that Giacomo was right.

"We'll consider the Charity of Sant'Antonio and the destitute women another day," he said in a conciliatory voice. "Today let's consider the institutions that Clara as well would have loved."

The professor thanked him with a look.

Chapter 12

A Strange Appointment

Giorgio Moncalvo turned to the florist's boy who was following him. "Here, here" he said. "On this chest where there is still room."

And the boy put in the indicated spot a beautiful evergreen wreath from which hung a silk ribbon with these words embroidered in silver: "To my dear aunt, her nephew Giorgio."

While the professor felt around in his pocket for a tip to the boy, a side entrance opened and Mariannina Moncalvo appeared next to the American heiress, Miss May. Dressed all in black, Mariannina's black eyes sparkled under her long, curved lashes; the marmoreal whiteness of her forehead stood out under the opulent mass of her dark hair; and under the heavy fabric of her belted dress, most elegant in its severity, the form of the person that Phidias wouldn't have disdained to take as a model could be clearly seen.

"Oh Giorgio," she exclaimed holding with her glance her cousin who was trying to sneak away, "you too brought a garland for our poor aunt. Look at how many wreaths have come."

In fact there were every size and kind so as to almost cover the walls: the most grand and beautiful was that of Miss May.

"Now I'll present you to my friend," added Mariannina. "Professor Giorgio Moncalvo, my cousin; Miss Lizzie May. He's a little bit of a solitary bear but he can be tamed. *Address him in English my dear. He can speak very well.*"[16]

"*Oh indeed?*" said Miss May. And she exchanged some words with the young professor, who had an embarrassed, confused air, and hardly noticed her, absorbed as he was in the contemplation of the other, so much more beautiful and fascinating.

In the proud security of her millions, the American didn't experience either vexation or envy; she let the conversation with Giorgio die and took leave verbosely from Mariannina.

"Tomorrow I am very afraid that I won't be able to be present at the funeral...if I could follow the funeral in a car? *What do you think of that?* That wouldn't be suitable? Eh no, I too am aware that it wouldn't be proper. And so I'm afraid we won't see each other before Monday...tomorrow I won't even have the time to breathe. Mass, the sermon...two lectures, a concert... *the five o'clock at the Grand Hotel* where there will be our celebrated novelist Vannoni...and then, at eight, dinner at the American Embassy. The ambassadress wants to show us the Christmas tree that she is preparing for the children of the colony.... My dear, this Rome will kill me.... But Monday early I'll call you.... No, no, don't call me. It is useless...my car must be waiting for me downstairs. *Goodbye darling. How beautiful you are in black. Goodbye sir.... Very pleased to have made your acquaintance.*"

Giorgio, who was at the other corner of the room, bent over a garland of unknown provenance, shook himself with a jump, came near, and mechanically took the jeweled hand that Miss May extended to him.

Mariannina accompanied her friend to the first floor; Giorgio turned back to the attraction of the mysterious garland. It was much smaller than the others, all of violets, without a ribbon.

"Who sent this?" the professor asked his cousin who, after a final goodbye to Miss May, closed the door again.

"Which one?"

"This...the only one without the name of the donor."

Mariannina frowned. "What does it matter to you who the donor was?"

"Is it a secret?"

"No," answered the girl haughtily. "Don Cesarino Oroboni sent it."

Giorgio Moncalvo grew pale, his face portrayed acute suffering and for an instant words failed him.

Mariannina, impassive, dominated him with her eyes.

Meanwhile, a final ray of sun entered obliquely through the large glass, crept across the evergreens, across the chrysanthemums, across the orchids, and the long silk ribbon woven in silver or gold.

Giorgio made a supreme effort.

"I have to talk to you," he said.

Mariannina didn't show any surprise at his brusque request.

"Talk."

"Not now."

"I know... it's impossible."

"When?"

She collected herself for a moment, then went on. "Tonight. Papa has asked you to oversee the return of the visiting cards to those who gave their condolences. You will be in the mezzanine with Fanoli and the two scribes from the International Bank. By midnight the work will be finished and in any case towards midnight you'll dismiss everybody...they will be happy to go. As soon as I am sure they are gone, I'll come."

"You'll...come?" He asked, stupefied by the rapidity with which she agreed to his demand and, more than that, by the hour and the place she chose for the meeting.

"I'll come...ought I to be afraid?" She added with a scornful gesture.

The sun had disappeared, the brief winter day ended almost without twilight.

Mariannina drew near to a wall, turned a key and, as by enchantment, five electric lights shone at the center and the corners of the room, raining their cold light on the garlands, throwing into relief the tall figure of the young woman who in the scanty dark dress in the midst of those flowers of death had the air of a beautiful mythical creature set to guard the entry of a cemetery.

"Mariannina!" babbled Giorgio.

She put her index finger to her mouth.

"Quiet. Someone might hear us. Till tonight." And she left him alone, alarmed at the idea of the meeting that he had desired before. Why had he wished it? What would he say to Mariannina? What would she say to him that he didn't know or imagine already? At any rate, even if he wanted to, it wouldn't be possible to withdraw.

Almost as if he had consulted with his daughter, uncle Gabrio called him a little while later and said: "Have patience poor Giorgio.... I was hoping to free you from annoyance, but it didn't work. Tonight you will do me the favor of taking the place of that wretched Fanoli who hasn't had a moment of respite since the day before yesterday. The two employees of the International Bank will be at your disposal. Get them to do as much work as they can and when you've dismissed them close the mezzanine and take the key. You can give it to me tomorrow before the ceremony. I'll go to bed early in order to have the necessary strength to follow the carriage. We'll all go to bed early tonight, we're all exhausted...my wife, Mariannina, your father.... He has more reason than the others...he is no longer young and has wanted to do too much. Imagine, he wanted to put her in the coffin himself, didn't you know? Yes, yes at three... with the help of Brulati. Oh, I wouldn't have been able to... enough, again tomorrow."

And under the broken, disconnected phrases of Gabrio Moncalvo, one could discern a kind of intolerance at the spectacle of sadness and death that had afflicted the family for several days, a sort of impatience for it all to be finished and for life to take back its rights and its force. Already for him, life began to take them back and, before dinner, he wanted to take a look at the last letters and telegrams that had arrived, and he called Fanoli to remind him of a certain deposit of bonds that he had to make Monday at the Treasury general. Then with Fanoli, who was invited to dine, he spoke of a Union that he had in mind to promote—to push up the price of the bonds and facilitate the conversion. At table he was almost the only one to talk, comforted by the approving monosyllables of the secretary. He spoke of finance, of politics and even of the Roman construction industry as if wanting to distract his mind from bothersome thoughts, and his ears from unpleasant sounds. In fact, there was in him a horror of death, which had now entered his house and was so close to him.

Before the fruit was served, Signora Rachele, who had only drunk a smaller-than-usual broth and eaten a chicken wing, complained of dizziness and a strange nausea and indicated she was leaving. Mariannina followed her after having wished them all a good night. It seemed to Giorgio that she said good night to him in a special way, that her eyes were fixed on his to remind him of their appointment. And the color rose in his face.

A little later, professor Giacomo got up.

"Does your head hurt?" his brother asked lovingly.

He indicated that it was nothing.

"Good night."

"Good night."

"I'll go with papa," said Giorgio.

"Yes, go with him," responded his uncle, "and afterwards come back here."

"It isn't necessary," murmured Giacomo leaning on his son's arm.

They passed in front of Clara's room. The door was simply closed. Giacomo Moncalvo pushed it and entered.

The bed was unmade, without covers or sheets or mattresses, naked as a skeleton. Resting on two solid trestles, the bier, covered with a black drape with silver fringes, held the center of the room. Four long candles burnt at the sides, spreading a smoky yellow light, more or less intense according to whether the air, flowing in from the half-closed shutters, was more or less lively and crisp. The mirrored bureau was almost entirely hidden by an enormous garland of green leaves and lustrous black berries with a large ribbon on which could be read: "To the angel of the house." Two coarse looking women, neither old nor young, sat near a little table with their legs wrapped in two large woolen shawls; in front of them they had a tray, and on the tray a flask and two glasses. The expressions on their faces revealed the supreme indifference acquired in the professional fulfillment of an unhappy office.

At the appearance of Giacomo and Giorgio, the two women rose and obsequiously offered their seats.

Giacomo Moncalvo signaled that it wasn't necessary and, with a finger on his lips, imposed silence. They stood for several minutes, father and son, with their eyes fixed on the coffin where she lay, who rightly was called the angel of the house. Then, quietly as they had come, they dispersed without paying attention to the women who, leaning against the table, bowed deeply, hiding perhaps from a sense of modesty the flask and glasses, the companions of their vigil.

Giorgio, meanwhile, remembered the last words that he received from the mouth of the dying woman "Don't think of her." A futile admonition. He had never thought of her so intensely as he did now.

Chapter 13

The Sphinx

In the mezzanine, precisely in the room occupied by secretary Fanoli, two portable electric lamps lit the desk behind which the two employees of the International Bank attended to their labor. Giorgio Moncalvo sat at a little table cluttered with papers and lit, as the other was, with an Edison lamp.

Fanoli, before leaving, had given him the necessary instructions.

"There, in that tray to the left are the cards already returned, I have checked them. On this side, there are those yet to be answered. Over there is a heap of telegrams that have been answered. I will respond to the others under the paperweight without haste. There on the desk, there is a reserve of our own cards in groups of a hundred. And, also on the desk, there are also thirty or forty funeral announcements which are late but which will be sent tonight. Spinati is one of the two employees who lives in the neighborhood of San Silvestro. When he leaves, he will have the kindness to take everything that's ready to the central post office."

Now Giorgio Moncalvo was asking himself what the job of inspector that had been given him entailed. The two young men intent on writing didn't demonstrate any need of his guidance, rather he was certain that they knew how to do the addresses better than he did, since they had a magnificent script and he had a terrible one. In addition in the state of feverish restlessness in which he found himself, he wasn't in shape to exercise any efficacious supervision and it was already a lot to hide his agitation and stay seated at his post. In front of him, the wall clock with its uniform tick-tock reminded him of the passage of time and Giorgio followed with his eyes the movement of the hand on the clock face. How long the minutes were! Until eleven and three quarters, eleven thirty at the earliest, he couldn't be left alone...and it was only ten!

The one of the two employees—Fanoli had called him Spinati—said to him: "Here, Signor Professor, if you like you can examine these hundred already-written envelopes, comparing them with the cards which we need to answer and have conserved here."

Giorgio Moncalvo shook himself.

"Compare? But that seems completely useless. Why don't you let me help in something I know how to do? Let me attach the stamps."

"Oh Signor Professor, you want to take the trouble?'

"What's strange about that?"

"And then," added Spinati maliciously, "you don't have experience."

"What?'

"Certainly. You would use old methods." And Spinati showed a little machine, very simple and practical, with which you moisten the stamp without touching it with your lips.

"You're right. It's easier and more practical. But I could learn it too."

"I believe it. And you'll learn quickly...but it isn't worth the effort."

"Then," the professor went on, "Pass me the packet of those thank-you notes. I'll put them in the envelopes and then I'll pass them on you and your companion so that you can write the addresses."

Spinati obeyed with a resigned air.

Giorgio Moncalvo set conscientiously to work but couldn't last long. Those envelopes rimmed with black, exhaling an acid odor of ink and stamps, all the same dimension, all with the identical script—"The Moncalvo family thanks you"—irritated his nerves and produced a painful sensation in his eyes, his head, his fingers. And then the continual immobility was intolerable to him. "I admire you," he exclaimed rising brusquely.

The two young men looked at him in amazement.

"Yes," repeated the professor, "I admire your patience, your calm. You are indefatigable."

"These aren't fatiguing occupations," observed Spinati. And the other, who had been quiet till now, added, putting down his pen for a moment: "It must have happened sometimes to you as well—to have to stay nailed to your seat to finish work that can't be put off until tomorrow?"

Had it happened to him? Yes, certainly, and how many times! How many days had he risen at dawn only to have evening surprise him in his study or in a laboratory, absorbed in his books, intent on scrutinizing with the lens of the microscope the secrets of living beings, to investigate in the beaker and in the retort the transformation of matter! But all that seemed so far away. It seemed to him now that he'd lost every faculty of attention and exploration; a thick veil had fallen between him and the world of his thought; he felt himself incapable of resolving the simplest problem or to repeat the most common formula. Oh, pride of science and intellect! In this moment, the two young men who tranquilly wrote addresses with the security that they were free of mistakes were by far superior to him. And maybe they too had some pretty girl on their mind but their Dulcinea wasn't one of those that drive you crazy.

Giorgio drew near the desk where the few leftover announcements were. He opened one mechanically and read the sincere and moving words dictated by his father: "The brothers Gabrio and Giacomo Moncalvo, the sister-in-law Rachele, the nephew Giorgio and niece Mariannina announce with profound sorrow the death today of their beloved Clara—a woman of exemplary kindness and moral rectitude who lived fifty five years thinking the good, acting justly, always forgetting herself to do good to others."

How true that was! How true! And how Aunt Clara was worthy of being remembered and loved! And yet she was still above ground and he had almost forgotten her, and his heart was filled with nothing but Mariannina who was worth so much less than his Clara!

When the clock signaled 11:40, Giorgio Moncalvo said to the two young men: "Most everything is done. You can go. It seems to me that secretary Fanoli had asked one of you to take it all to the central post office."

"Oh," said Spinati, "we'll both go by the central post office, that way we'll share the weight."

"In fact," Giorgio agreed, "one alone would be uncomfortable."

"Oh, I said it in jest. In winter, with an overcoat, there are so many pockets available."

"Be sure not to forget anything."

"Don't worry. Good night Signor Professor.

"Good night."

Giorgio was alone and waited for her anxiously. Mariannina had only told him the hour, she hadn't given him any more precise instructions but certainly she would have come down on the small internal stairs that led precisely to Fanoli's room. Giorgio opened the little door, illuminating that way a piece of the winding staircase.

At midnight, he heard a slight noise from above and the blood stirred up in his veins, She was coming.

"Who is it?" he asked.

She was already in front of him.

"It's me," she answered with her usual enigmatic smile. "Didn't you ask for a meeting? Hadn't I promised to come?"

And she planted herself in front of him, interlacing her hands and leaning with her elbows on the back of a chair.

"Why are you standing?"

"I'm not tired. Talk, come on…"

He, so eloquent on his podium, was no longer able to find ideas or words.

"I'll help you," she went on with her proud calm. "You asked for a meeting about the garland of violets."

"From Prince Cesare Oroboni?"

"Exactly."

"Your fiancé?"

"Probably."

"But you, are you willing to marry him?"

"Yes."

"You're frank at least," Giorgio declared with great bitterness. "And you love him?"

"Not for now. Nothing's to stop me loving him later."

"And you'll change religion because of this marriage?"

"For that, too."

"So you believe in the Church?"

"Look, for the moment there is little faith but Monsignor de Luchi instructs me with such patience, he'll end by convincing me."

"Oh Mariannina, Mariannina!" exclaimed Giorgio Moncalvo raising both his arms. "You marry without love, convert without faith, aren't you ashamed?

"What should I be ashamed of? How many girls are there who marry with love and how many of them seriously believe the religion they practice? I can guess at what you want to say. Not believing in a religion you were born into isn't the same thing as entering into a new religion in which you believe even less. But who knows if I won't believe tomorrow? At any rate, the ceremonies of Catholicism please me. And in truth you ought to be the last to be scandalized. It doesn't seem to me that you have ever shown a great tenderness for the so called faith of our fathers."

"And what does this mean?" replied Giorgio. "I haven't abandoned one superstition to embrace another. My father's conduct was always rational, and he taught me with his example that the upright life, the spirit of sacrifice, the love of one's neighbor don't have to rest on the dogma of any Church."

Mariannina shrugged her shoulders.

"Those are utopias. The world will always need a religion. The religion that was ours is coming undone everywhere. Let's take the other one. Let's take the religion of the majority."

"Not the major part of humanity in any case..."

"Oh what do I care? The majority of these countries... If I were in Turkey I'd become a Turk."

"How you talk Mariannina! How positive, utilitarian at your age, when your mind ought to be open to all the currents of the future. And you instead turn to the past."

"Who knows if the future isn't just what you call the past."

"Ah no," Giorgio Moncalvo protested energetically. "The past won't return. And you, you who are ambitious..."

Mariannina's eyes sparkled.

"You are ambitious," Giorgio repeated. "How you've mistaken your path! If matrimony for you is only a means to shine, to be an admired, powerful woman, look for your companion in the crowd of those who throw themselves into public life. There are intelligent people, titled people, who will become ambassadors, ministers.... How many among them would be happy to give you their name! You are so beautiful! You are so rich!"

"I know," responded the girl, "that I could have married in that way. But it was too easy. I have had so many of those suitors you allude to, and I've left them for my friends. In fact, there is one who is now Secretary of the Embassy at Petersburg, another is Deputy and at the next crisis he will move up a grade. Her husband chatters in the Parliament, works in the institutional offices (notice how aware I am of the technical language) and he will soon get his nice government portfolio. What an achievement! To be minister in a country where the cabinet only lasts a few months and where the first scoundrel who arrives can cover him with a load of insults."

"But that's life, that's the struggle," shouted Giorgio.

"It's an open field to all the intriguers," retorted Mariannina "I want to triumph where few triumph."

"So you'll attach yourself to a cadaver?"

"A cadaver that isn't afraid of decomposing. But think...I, who am of a race that those people despise and abominate, I will rise to the rank of Roman princess! I will overcome all the antipathies, all the prejudices."

"You won't overcome them," Giorgio Moncalvo interrupted violently. "You will always be the reprobate."

"Oh, I'll overcome!" she answered, "I'll know how to impose myself! You don't know me."

Saying this, she fixed on his face her superb eyes which seemed to enclose in themselves all that woman can promise or threaten.

And again he experienced before her what he had experienced at other times, a strange sentiment made of contrary feelings of attraction and repugnance, audacity and cowardliness, a need to grab her and to flee her, to tell her he hated her and to fall at her feet adoring her.

"It's true, I don't know you," he declared gravely, looking into her face with concern, with a fervent expression. "We have passed too much time without seeing each other. Seven years ago you were very different. Not as beautiful as you are today... but kinder...."

"Seven years ago, seven years ago," repeated Mariannina. And there was in her voice a regret for the irrevocable past. And the flash of her dominatrix's pupils was veiled by a shadow of sadness. But she chased that shadow away with a rapid movement of the little head and asked, smiling: "I was less beautiful? I was little more than a girl. And still there were those I pleased."

Giorgio blushed deeply. And he saw Mariannina in that long ago past, he saw her again by his side in the streets and among the monuments of Rome, disposed to accept the superiority of her older cousin, happy to draw from him a word of praise or approval. Today, at the distance of seven years, telling him "I pleased some"—that was the truth, no doubt. But she deceived herself if she thought that back then she had inspired a passion.... Seven years ago he was a student, serious and austere, infatuated by his science, averse to anything that could distract him from his dreams of glory, decided to open his way in the world, to compensate with a good result all the care his father had given him. How much wiser then than now! It was for this reason he had blushed today at Mariannina's allusion, because he loved her now when he should have cancelled her from his mind, now that she was so much less worthy of love. But he also felt, from the way she spoke, that in that now distant time it had been she who had loved him. He sensed that maybe back then, if he had wished, if he had accepted the offers of his uncle, she would have ended up being his. Would he have been happy? No, no, he still had enough clairvoyance to understand that there was too much difference between their characters, their tastes, their aspirations for a union between them to be happy. It didn't matter. She had given him an hour of intoxication and he, the rigid scientist, buffeted by the wind of madness, asked himself whether to have that hour it was necessary to sacrifice his life.

"Mariannina," he said, drawing near to her, his voice deep and agitated, "Mariannina, if years ago our souls were so close, if then circumstances have divided us, have erected a barrier between us, do you think that barrier might be broken down?"

She shrugged her shoulders. "You are raving."

Giorgio pressed on: "Maybe I am offering you a life raft. You are at a terrible crossroads in your life. You are about to throw yourself into an abyss of cowardice and lies. You are about to buy a miserable coat of arms with the price of your body and soul. And yet you are intelligent and have a heart that beats, a heart that needs to love. Break the malevolent spell…obey your heart…your heart which is also mine."

"My heart isn't anyone's," she replied with hauteur while Giorgio himself, marveling at the phrases that had escaped him, became aware that he was at that extreme limit beyond which reason and will no longer govern man's acts.

Facing him, Mariannina, entirely controlled, continued calm and placid with her voice that was music.

"Poor Giorgio! You would like to save me. And you don't understand that I am the one who saves you? You don't understand that if I listened to you, tomorrow you would be the most miserable of mortals. Don't you see that the force of things pushes us in opposed directions? What novel of knightly times you are creating in our positive century! Not seven years, we should have met a hundred years ago, more than that we should have grown next to each other in the city where our family originated, in the old enclosure that restricted the people of our race, in the shadow of our old synagogues, isolated in a hostile world, restricted in ambition and ideas, faithful only to the mission of our people. Then we might have married and been happy. Today it's impossible. The death of Aunt Clara reunited us for an instant. We won't see each other ever again. Let's separate without rancor."

"And you will become Princess Oroboni!" shouted Giorgio.

"I hope so."

"Oh Mariannina, what a sphinx you are! What a mix of contradictions! You drown in cynicism whatever in you is good and high. You are full of talent and you latch onto dead and putrid things."

She stopped him with a gesture.

"Enough Giorgio, I am what I am, and it doesn't matter because we aren't going to live together. Don't deny me at least the merit of having been frank with you. What right did you have to ask me for explanations? What obligation did I have to give them to you? Does it seem to you that I am a woman disposed to explain her affairs?

Giorgio's lips shaped a bitter smile. "You have accorded me a sad preference. You wanted to thrust the knife into my breast yourself. Don't fear having missed the blow. The wound is mortal."

What did Mariannina feel in her heart now? Was it the vain wish to heal the wound or cruel desire to exacerbate it?

The fact was that she moved violently away from the chair she had been leaning on during their talk and, with a lightening quick movement of her flexible figure, threw herself on her cousin and kissed him on the mouth. But when he, leaping like an animal under the burning of that kiss, tried to draw her to his breast, she unwound herself with a vigorous movement and with the agility of a squirrel she reached the threshold of the winding stair and slammed the door in his face.

"Don't you dare follow me! Goodbye forever!"

In an instant she was at the top of the stairs. She pushed the other door that led into the apartment above and that she had only left ajar, and closed it behind her.

From below, with his eyes fixed on the dark where she had disappeared, where the air was still impregnated by her perfume, Giorgio called uselessly "Mariannina, Mariannina!" Then, staggering, he reentered the study. A chair, the chair that

Mariannina had pushed away, was overturned on the hemp sofa; a pack of envelopes that she had knocked against in her passage was scattered on the floor. Those envelopes bordered in black, those envelopes that recorded the family's mourning and the presence of a corpse in the house, seemed to throw a lugubrious shadow on the rapid scene taking place shortly before. Poor dead one! Poor Aunt Clara! She wasn't yet buried and already there was hardly a small place for her in the memory of her nephew.

Mariannina, Marianinna! "Goodbye forever," she had said to Giorgio. But she was in his blood, in his soul; she was on his lips where she had impressed her burning kiss, she was in his veins where she had infused a feverous ardor. And he had let her slide from his arms and hadn't known how to show her—he, young and strong—that you don't play with fire, that you don't raise with impunity the tempest of the senses.

Giorgio felt suffocated. He had an overwhelming desire for air and space, a need to run, to tire himself, to tame with physical fatigue his body and spirit. Instead of re-entering the house by the internal stairs, he went out the door which led to the landing, shut it with the key, and a little bit by feel, a little by helping himself with matches he descended to the vestibule, lit by a feeble lamplight flanked by evergreens, sad ornaments for the ceremony tomorrow. He opened the door which that night wasn't even latched and found himself in the street, wrapped in a cold, fine fog. In the fog, at long intervals, the few curved lamps spread a whitish light, reflected here and there in the puddles left by the recent rain; mysterious, grim and inhospitable, the massive wall of the Oroboni garden rose in front and, almost as if the night itself was its reign, seemed to dominate the sleeping way.

"Cursed! Cursed!" screamed Giorgio, squeezing his fists towards the cyclopean structure, symbol of a past that the agile modern life didn't manage to remove. "Cursed!" he repeated, livid with hatred against that medieval fortress where Mariannina was about to bury her youth. As he hurled himself ahead on the deserted street, the sense of his own impotence gnawed at him ever more angrily and acutely. Why hadn't he known how to be cynical and brutal with Mariannina, whose reckless challenge didn't merit another response? That way he was certain he wouldn't have found a way to strike the invisible enemy who triumphed by the sole virtue of the antiquity of his race. With what arms to combat him? To what war call him? What provocation, what insult sling at him? A provocation? An insult? How? When? To one whom you never met. To one with whom you have nothing in common, neither habits of life, nor connections or friendships. Because friends serve (oh how well they serve) as intermediaries of offensive actions, nothing is more difficult than to injure a person with whom you have no point of contact. The idea of a duel came into Giorgio's mind again. But he remembered what his father had said: "Probably Cesarino Oroboni wouldn't fight, either so as not to cross swords with an infidel commoner or so as not to go against his religious principles." Yes, but he might accept. And then what joy! To kill him or be killed... A joy? Maybe death would be a joy. But to kill? Nature and education, everything there was in Giorgio Moncalvo, whether inborn or acquired, rebelled against this savage voluptuousness of the blood, against this blind and mad way of resolving one's own contests. Even in the midst of his exaltation, he was aware of the profound difference between him and Don Cesarino. He would not be made ridiculous either by refusing to fight in the name of his prejudices or accepting the challenge in the name of the knightly traditions; the ridiculous one would be him, Giorgio, the man of meditations and study: he would be ridiculous either way, whether his antagonist threw him out the door or gave him the honor of single combat. Ah, where were the times when he had passed tranquil days between the walls of the laboratory absorbed in his research under the loving guidance of the illustrious physiologist he had considered a second father and who resembled his actual father in brilliance, in the cult of science, and in the purity and simplicity of his character? Then too, even in the silent laboratory, he had experienced profound anxiety and emotions; he had trembled before his retort and his beaker in the course of an experiment that might reveal a new secret of matter, a new law of the physical world. Even then, among the pestiferous gasses and poisonous cultures, he had seen death close up. But he hadn't trembled, or ever lost the serenity of his spirit.... Today instead...

The fog dissolved into rain, a fine rain that penetrated the bones. Giorgio paid no attention to it; he proceeded rapidly on his walk, biting his fists, agitating his arms, mumbling broken and incomprehensible phrases, looked at with a diffident curiosity by the rare night walkers who took him for mad or drunk.

His legs had taken him in the direction of his house but perhaps he didn't think of it; he thought of it only when, after via Tomacelli, he entered Cavour Bridge. And then he stopped, perplexed, confused.... What was he going to do at his place, where no one expected him, where he wouldn't even find his room prepared and the single maid would be soundly asleep knowing that the gentlemen were sleeping in Gandi palace? Yes, he was lodged under the same roof as Mariannina, the future Princess Oroboni! No, in truth he wouldn't be staying that night in Gandi palace because, in closing the door, he had forgotten that he didn't have the key. Until dawn (and, in the heart of December, dawn comes so late) he was a vagabond who the police could have asked to show his papers!

There wasn't a living soul on the bridge; some light dispersed on the banks and the surrounding hills broke the profound shadows with difficulty; under the arches, against the piles, the water gurgled with a dull roar. Giorgio Moncalvo drew near the side, looked down, and felt for an instant the terrible attraction of the abyss—to throw oneself head first, to be swallowed by the vortex, to lose memory and consciousness after a few seconds, to become an inert thing that dissolves... And meanwhile, in a few hours, at the funeral of Aunt Clara, they would expect him in vain. Where is he? Where did he sleep? Who saw him leave the mezzanine? Who was the last to talk to him? Ah, certainly Mariannina wouldn't betray herself! But was it possible that she didn't experience a vague disturbance, that she didn't have a vague suspicion, that she didn't say, "If there is an accident, it's my fault?"

No, no, she wouldn't say this. Instead she'd say: "He was crazy. He was destined for a bad end."

Sometimes, in the thickest dark of a tempest, the shadows split open for an instant and in the space between two clouds the sun's eye appears, returning form and color to the objects. Thus for an improvised and fleeting moment Giorgio Moncalvo had a clear vision of what there was of the grotesque, the absurd in his propositions of suicide. To die for Mariannina! For her, to immerse his father in mourning! His father, the respected and upright scientist, for whom he was now the only joy and object of affection. To renounce for her the fever of exploration, the hope of glory, the sacred ambition to add some particle of truth to the patrimony of humanity?

The young man withdrew briskly from the side of the bridge and took up his nighttime pilgrimage under the rain that, even when it stopped falling was dispersed in the air, wrapping things in a damp and heavy atmosphere. He went by way of via Ripetta to Piazza del Popolo, from Piazza del Popolo to via del Babuino and to Piazza di Spagna, where a cabby seated in a box under an umbrella made a sign: "Do you want a ride?"

Why not? Giorgio was tired, drenched; the carriage would offer him a refuge until morning.

"Where?" asked the coachman who had gotten down to open the carriage door and to take off the oilcloth that covered his horse.

"Oh, where you like. Even nowhere. Even standing still."

And since the other looked at him in amazement, he added an explanation: "I've forgotten my house key and it was useless to knock. I only need to be covered. I'll take you by the hour and I'll pay you right away."

He put a ten lire note in the hands of the cabby, whose suspicions vanished by magic.

"Staying still is not allowed," he said. "We will circle around here."

Giorgio Moncalvo huddled in a corner and closed his eyes, hoping that the movement of the carriage, which went at a walking pace, would have brought him sleep. He didn't sleep. He fell into a sort of lethargy during which the tempting image of Mariannina persecuted him insistently. There she bent over him, kissed him on the mouth...and laughed. Shaking himself with a start, he held his arms out towards the Siren, towards the Sphinx. And, at each of these awakenings, he woke feeling worse than before, with his limbs aching, bones battered, and his temples bound in an iron circle.

When he returned to consciousness, it was still night but already the city was waking and the less silent and deserted streets announced the approach of day. With an effort, Giorgio Moncalvo lowered the window and gave the cab driver the address of Palazzo Gandi.

Chapter 14

The Funeral

The entrance hall, the stairs, the mezzanine, the entrance of the main building weren't enough to hold all people who had come to be present at the transport to the cemetery of Clara Moncalvo's body. To tell the truth, there were only a few who had come for her—simple, good, modest as she had been; they looked for each other and they exchanged a word and a handshake, uselessly forcing themselves to come together in a corner, to flee from the swollen crowd that pushed them, tossed them here and there in the effort to be seen, to arrive at one of the tables where, on the appropriate sheets of paper bordered with black, each one wrote his signature indicating the house, the institute or the society that he represented. More indiscreet and meddling than anyone else, four or five reporters who wrote the local section of newspapers stuck their noses into everything, interviewed this one and that one, taking notes as if they were at a ball or a meeting of Parliament. "What a funeral! What a funeral!" they repeated. It was in fact a great funeral that brought together the most disparate classes of Roman society. There was the conspicuous personage of the Minister of Foreign Affairs; there was his secretary Cherasco, a pair of senators and a pinch of deputies; there were, you understand, the big wigs of high finance, presidents and administrators of the banking institutes, annoyed to be inconvenienced without the comfort of a formal recognition of their presence but hiding their boredom under the faultless correctness of form. And they, cosmopolitan citizens of the world, superior to religious and political quarrels, served as a cushion between the diverse groups that observed each other in a hostile manner: in one group there were many of the acquaintances that the Moncalvos had made among the papal aristocracy, thanks to Monsignor de Luchi and Count Ugolini-Ruschi; on the other, the orthodox of the Israelite community who, like birds of prey, had fallen on Commendatore Gabrio as soon as he had arrived in Rome and who today seemed to have gotten a place in this house from which they had first been driven away. Today, because of the death, they had entered again and, coming there with their emblems and their rites, affirmed once more the indomitable vitality of their God and their race.

Secretary Fanoli and the painter Brulati, intimates of the family, received the condolences—and thanked everyone in the name of the Commendatore, who would have shaken everyone's hands but had to save his strength to accompany the body to the cemetery.

"And how is the Commendatore? And the Signora? And the Signorina?" they fought to ask, pretending great solicitude.

"Well! You can imagine...after the torture of those days.... Not that Aunt Clara enjoyed good health. On the contrary. But perhaps, just for this reason, one was used to her indisposition and no one expected such a sudden catastrophe."

A young man, white as a ghost, made a brief appearance on the threshold of one of the rooms leading into the reception hall.

"Who's that? Who's that?" asked those (the most part) who didn't know him.

"He's the nephew of the Commendatore," responded the well informed. "He's the son of the university professor."

Someone seemed surprised

"The Commendatore has a brother?"

"Certainly, a brother who was also in Rome quite a bit before him."

"No one ever heard him mentioned."

"And yet he's a fine man…a member of the Academy of the Lincei…. He keeps to himself."

"He must be a solitary man…and his son?"

"He lived several years in Germany. For the last few months he has been an assistant of Salvieni."

"He's also a teacher by profession. He probably cannot afford meat."

"He certainly looks as if he's always eaten sparely and he's not going to have a long life."

"In fact he seems to be just recovering from an illness. But where's his father?"

"He must be with the rest of the family. We'll see him soon in back of the coffin."

"And is it true," asked one of them sottovoce, "that in a few days the bomb of the marriage and the conversion will explode?"

"Who knows?" answered the person being interrogated. Squinting his eyes, he pointed out Count Ugolini-Ruschi standing a short distance away. "You'd have to ask the man over there."

"Or the painter Brulati…"

"No, no, the Count would certainly know much more about it."

Some words spoken in a low voice and received avidly provoked malicious little smiles, coughs, and throat clearings.

"Come on, those are calumnies," admonished a benevolent person.

And another one, impatient, looked at his watch.

"The invitation was for nine thirty. And it is nine forty five. There should be a little punctuality. The priests of all religions take their time."

"But the Rabbis are already here."

"Yes."

"No."

"Without a doubt they have come...quiet!"

A door was thrown open. The crowd swayed. A weak light of candles, a mumbling of prayers in an incomprehensible language, the coffin covered with a black drape passed. Three or four men raised their hats.

"No, you have to keep it on."

"What?"

"Yes, of course! Haven't you ever been at an Israelite funeral?"

"Here is the Commendatore."

"And that's his brother on the arm of his son.

"Ah, that one there! He's older..."

"I think so."

"He doesn't resemble him."

"Not much. But you can tell they have the same origins."

Fanoli and Brulati linked arms to regulate the crowd. "A moment, a moment. Let the women go ahead."

There were about twenty women, among them the millionaire Miss May, who had decided to come and had ordered the driver to wait with the car in front of the steps of the Exposition. Her aunt, indisposed, had remained at home.

"Now," said Fanoli, "those who will hold the funeral drape, please come in."

Truthfully, being a woman's funeral, this office should have belonged to the women—but Commendatore Gabrio had preferred to see around the coffin of his sister the big bonnets of finance.

Now, called by name by Fanoli, all the commendatori, working their elbows, panting and snorting, opened the way with difficulty. The shining top hats, the furs of otter and marten, the diamond pins on their neckties, the rich watch chains gave to these highly regarded personages a certain air of family.

"If they were scrambled together, what a precious frittata

there would be!" murmured the reporter for the *Tribuna* into the ear of a companion.

Despite all their efforts, at the turn of the great staircase on the ground floor there was a jam. No one could go either forward or back.

And meanwhile, Hebrew prayers—a language unknown to most—heavy, slow, nasal, rose up from the entry hall. They were in the same singsong that had echoed on the paths of Zion and along the rivers of Babylon, the same that in the painful exiles had comforted the mourning of the wandering families. There wasn't an angle of the world where they hadn't carried an echo of the Orient, confused by the shuddering of the seas, the shout of all the winds. They had invoked peace to Israel's dead in all the dispersed cemeteries from Warsaw to Paris, from Frankfurt to Seville, from Venice to Amsterdam, from London to New York, from Calcutta to Lisbon. Handed down from generation to generation, from century to century, they had conserved like precious oils the faith, the hope, the illusions of a people, who, no matter how fallen, continued to have faith in its own resurgence.

Today the funeral melodies elicited neither emotions nor affections; the drawn out guttural notes rose and fell back like the spurting of a fountain which no longer quenches anyone's thirst.

"*The grace of the Eternal be on us,*" sang the officiator in the unknown language. "*You prepare for us the reward of our actions and you dispose the actions themselves in a way that we can merit it. Who lives in the secret place of the highest dwells in the shadow of the Omnipotent. I say to the Lord: You are my refuge and my fortress: in you my God I trust.*"

The prayers ceased.

"Go ahead!" screamed those who were at the top of the stair.

And from the bottom, they answered:

"In a minute. Have a bit of patience."

"Go ahead! We're suffocating," insisted the first. In this manner, from the top to the bottom, they exchanged irascible words, irritable exclamations until, when God willed, there was a little space in the entry hall and the human mass, squeezed and crushed between the walls, was able to move again and join the procession ahead. The first class funeral carriage that carried the coffin was quite a ways ahead when the last people came out of the palace. The congested faces shone with the ineffable joy of liberation. The sun, erupting triumphantly after the night and the rainy morning, swept away, along with the clouds, the images of death. The funeral itself became a spectacle. After putting down the mask of sorrow which many had believed necessary to wear on their faces in the first part of the ceremony, the participants, especially those furthest from the cart, chatted gaily among themselves, eyed the girls, strutted under the curious glances of the passengers on the electric trams, who were constrained to stop or at least slow down.

Among the businessmen, the conversation took on a technical character.

"These stock markets are always in a good mood, eh?"

"Definitely, yesterday Paris rose half a point."

"And in Genoa, the Terni stocks, have you seen?"

"Oh, they'll grow even more if they create a trust," said Baron Bernheim polishing with his cuff the ubiquitous white top hat whose fur was curled like that of a frightened cat.

"Fertilizer has a great future," pontificated a broker. And he announced the coming formation of a new company of chemical fertilizers capitalized with ten million lire.

But already many were sneaking away, persuaded that they had sacrificed enough time to social convention. Thus, for example, Miss May, who had walked from the Palazzo dell'Esposizione, left the group of women in the lurch with

American nonchalance. Quick as a wink, she climbed the stairs, and grabbed the camera which she had held slung across her shoulder under her otter fur coat. She turned it on the crowd, attempting to fix in an instant the picturesque scene which unfolded in front of her. Then she descended tranquilly and got into the car that was waiting for her.

Nonetheless, the desertions didn't stop the still-numerous procession from arriving at the Piazza delle Terme. Only family members pushed on after that, along with secretary Fanoli, the painter Brulati, Count Ugolini-Ruschi, the director of the International Bank, two professors, friends of Giacomo Moncalvo, the young and extremely timid doctor Flacci, who was Giacomo's assistant, and a few others.

Under the sparkling air and the sun, Commendatore Gabrio cheered little by little, as he discussed business with the director of the bank and Fanoli. He criticized the government and the Parliament which were enslaved by old formulas, incapable of following the miraculous economic reawakening of the nation. It was absolutely necessary to change everything, with new men, new programs.

Giacomo Moncalvo left his brother to draw near to Giorgio, worried by his son's mortal pallor and, more than pallor, his dark silence and profound sadness.

"I kept a vigil all night. I'm tired," said Giorgio in justification.

"I know. Instead of resting, you went out. You didn't return to the house until morning. It was crazy. All the more reason why you should rest now. It's not necessary for you to come to the cemetery,"

But Giorgio gave a dry, resolved refusal to his urgings, only consenting to lean on his father's arm.

And professor Giacomo sensed the effort he made not to burden him with all his weight in order to hold himself up on collapsing legs.

"But you aren't well. You can't get as far as the Verano cemetery. Do you want us to go back together? Or would you like to get into one of those carriages that follow slowly behind us?'

"No, no, it's better that I walk. I beg you, papa, don't insist. We'll go back in a carriage together after the funeral. I'll go home and get into bed after I've seen the aunt who loved me so much descend into the earth."

Yes, she had loved her nephew dearly and Giorgio had loved her too; but Giacomo, though he wasn't aware of that night's strange adventure, sensed that his son wasn't telling the truth, that he wasn't in this state only from his emotions at having lost his aunt. Clara, the good Clara, could only leave a gentle memory. Something, or someone, had disturbed his peace—someone blooming with health and life who had distilled her poison in his blood.

Giorgio was quiet, avoiding the disturbed paternal gaze, holding his eyes down, absorbed in his visions of pain and voluptuousness, from time to time pressing a handkerchief to his mouth that was still burning with the flame of that last kiss.

The thinned out procession drew near the destination. After Porta San Lorenzo, following via Tiburtina flanked by the stores of the stone cutters and florists shops and taverns to console the survivors, leaving on the left the church of San Lorenzo, passing the entrance door of the Israelite section, the procession passed between two walls towards an open gate facing the mortuary chapel.

While the coffin was taken from the cart, the officiator intoned again the funeral prayers.

Praised be the Lord our God, King of the Universe who has created us in his justice, who nurtured us and conserved us in an act of his justice and in his justice has made us die. He knows the number of those who sleep in this dust and He will make all rise up again one day through an act of his justice. Be blessed, O Lord, who raises the dead.

He continued in the mortuary chapel: *The works of the Omnipotent are perfect. He is just in all his ways. His acts are all love and truth, neither can there be defects in them. Who would dare to ask him: What are you doing?*

He governs the universe; at his will he makes us live or die. He makes the corpse descend into the tomb but recalls the immortal soul to Himself.

In his haste to finish, the Rabbi muttered some other prayers in a low voice. But from a corner of the chapel arose a beautiful bass voice: *Pardon, O Lord, the sins of our sister whose body we lower into the sepulcher.*

Everyone turned in the direction the beautiful voice came from. Even though in an unknown language, everyone felt vibrating in it an accent of unusual conviction and faith.

The officiator, disconcerted for a moment, began again. *Have mercy on her for the merit of our fathers.*

And the other, that one who no one remembered seeing in the procession, went on to the next verse: *May her body rest in peace and her soul fly to the heavens to enjoy eternal happiness. Amen!*

From mouth to mouth the question came:

"Who is that?"

"It's a German, he's Doctor Löwe," answered someone who, in the exotic figure, had recognized the fervent apostle of Zionism.

And, as they were leaving the mortuary chapel, the doctor drew near to Gabrio Moncalvo to tell him that he had arrived that morning from Poland, that in the train he had read the sad news and, learning the time of the funeral, had been brought right away to the cemetery.

The garlands were removed, along with the black drape

bordered with silver, and the coffin was put on a little cart drawn by hand to the burial place at the foot of an empty columbarium that waited for it.

In lugubrious silence, the people joined in the last part of the ceremony. Already the open mouth had devoured its prey; already the stonemasons were intent on closing the space with bricks and mortar. The final prayers resounded: *Merciful God, pardon the sin and don't destroy the sinner. Use your greatest forgiveness to suppress your rage. Dust to dust, as it was in the beginning, and the spirit returns to God who gave it.*

Gabrio Moncalvo said to his brother "They're putting her there for the time being. I have the intention of erecting a little monument to her."

Giacomo shook his head: "Poor Clara! We won't see her again."

"Poor Clara," repeated the Commendatore, "I wouldn't have believed that we'd lose her so soon. Ah, misery if we weren't able to dull our senses with work! Unfortunately, there's nothing else to do. Let's go!"

He couldn't wait to leave that sad enclosure and re-enter life, to take up his habits, to forget these painful days. But first he had to exchange more handshakes, put up with new condolences and squander new thanks.

"Thanks from all of us, also from my wife and daughter. Certainly we won't ever forget these demonstrations! Giacomo, Giorgio won't you get into my carriage?"

"Excuse us," the professor answered "we're in a hurry to return home. I am exhausted and Giorgio is in a worse condition than I am."

"It's true…I've also noticed that this morning he has a terrible color. What's the matter?"

"I hope it's nothing more than a little fatigue." The Commendatore extended his hand to his nephew.

"Take heart, young man. At your age, illnesses pass quickly. So, if you insist on getting back quickly, take one of these carriages. Fanoli, you see which are available. There ought to be some extras. Be patient. Fanoli, arrange everything and later we can meet up back home. You can have lunch with me. Brulati too, if he likes."

The painter excused himself. He had another engagement.

Before getting into the carriage of the Sovereign Order of Malta, Count Ugolini-Ruschi asked Gabrio Moncalvo: "Do you think I can pay my respects to the ladies sometime today?"

"Try later. They were in bed with little desire to get up today...especially Mariannina. But try anyway."

The Commendatore turned to the director of the International Bank:

"You come with me...we have to talk. That's right...and now let's go."

Sticking his head out the little door, the Commendatore ordered the driver to make the horses trot.

He no longer seemed the man he had been earlier that day, beaten down, exhausted under the weight of his sorrow. And yet that sorrow had been as sincere as was his affection for his lost sister. But in him the impressions were lively yet not enduring, and he had the happy ability to see the good side of things. Also in this disaster, this great disaster, there was what one might call the other side of the coin.

It was known that Clara wouldn't have approved of the coming domestic events but until now she had remained silent out of prudence. Would she have continued to hold her tongue when the bomb exploded? And wouldn't the inevitable discussions risk creating an incurable quarrel? It was enough that the quarrel was with the other branch of the family. At least Clara died in peace with everyone, taking with her the security of knowing that she left a void in the home where she had been a welcome and precious guest for so many years. With her gone, the Commendatore felt more free and already his thoughts hurried towards the meeting that he had fixed for three in the afternoon with the notary and Monsignor de Luchi—a meeting which was to be a prelude to the official request of Don Cesarino and to the stipulations of the two contracts: the contract for the deed of sale of the Oroboni palace and the villa of Porto Anzio, and the contract of marriage. Now was time to move from the preparatory period and cross the Rubicon. *Alea jacta est.*

In itself, the affair was less than mediocre. Gabrio Moncalvo knew that very well and that the sum that he tied up in the palace and the farm would have had more value if it had remained in his hands. But from the commercial point of view, the speculation could finish well if it could facilitate for him and his bank the conquest of new clients in the Catholic world. At any rate, it was necessary to see things in their entirety, to think about the great significance of Mariannina's marriage, of her solemn entry into the most closed, most aristocratic society of Rome. Oh Mariannina had good reason not to care for that which everyone could have. Wife of a deputy, of a senator, of a general? For a girl who brought a million lire of dowry there were great expectations….for dozens of generals, of deputies, of senators. But to be wife of Prince Oroboni, of one of the most genuine representatives of religious and political intransigence: that was a victory that Mariannina, neither noble nor Catholic, had a right to be proud of. There was to be sure the formality of the conversion, and the prospect of the inevitable ceremony troubled Gabrio Moncalvo slightly. This was even the reason he had insisted that his wife rein in for the moment her ardor as a catechumen. It wasn't proper to make too much noise at one time or to compromise her relationship with the house of Rothschild. Maybe later quietly, without publicity…

These thoughts that sped through his mind didn't stop

Gabrio Moncalvo from talking about politics and finance with the director of the International Bank. And when this man turned the discussion to the conversion of the assets, the Commendatore gave a response that accounted both for the religious conscience of his wife and for his financial interests:

"No, for now the conversation will not take place."

Meanwhile, in the carriage he'd entered with Giorgio and doctor Flacci, professor Giacomo was absorbed by extremely different worries and he didn't take his eyes off his son, who was crouched in a corner with his head sunk in the cushions and his legs wrapped in a plaid.

He hardly responded to the anxious paternal interrogations.

"Yes, I think I have a fever but it will go away."

"Flacci," said the professor when they were getting down from the carriage, "would you do me the favor of passing by the pharmacy in via Cicerone and asking them to call Rangoni, our doctor?"

"I'll go immediately"

"Oh papa, what's the rush?" spluttered Giorgio. But he didn't oppose it. Instead, he thanked Flacci with a movement of his head.

Held up by his father and the doorkeeper, who was a muscular and robust man, Giorgio came up the stairs. The maid, who had come to open the door, couldn't hold back an exclamation: "Mother of God, what's happened?" and she turned towards the professor.

"Quiet, quiet," he replied. "Don't make a fuss. It was the fatigue, the emotions; a couple of hours in bed will be the best remedy. Go and prepare the room."

Chapter 15

The Two Brothers

This was the first evening for more than two months that Giacomo Moncalvo spent in his study. The pale face of the scientist, where the signs of anxiety were merely quieted rather than dissipated, expressed the pleasure of the man habituated to finding himself in the midst of dear and familiar objects, taking up again the thread of his interrupted thoughts.

It was raining outside and it was cold. In the study, there was a gentle heat from the stove and a faint, gentle odor of violets that recalled images of spring.

"Ah, Flacci, Flacci!" said Moncalvo, turning to the young and timid assistant who sat across from him.,"you even bring me flowers...you treat me like the lady of your heart."

Flacci blushed.

"I don't have one, a sweetheart," he said, and added: "I know that violets please you and I've taken the liberty of adorning your study with them on the day when you come back with a tranquil spirit."

"Thank you, Flacci. Thanks for this as well as for all the other attentions that you've offered us. Eh, we'll always be in your debt. But do not believe that I have a tranquil spirit."

"Oh Professor, why? The doctor..."

Giacomo Moncalvo shook his head. "The doctor maintains that the crisis is over, that recovery is assured...perhaps. But I don't dare hope that Giorgio returns to what he was before. His stubborn silence in regard to the things and people he talked about in his delirium disquiets and disturbs me. Now I almost wish that his convalescence were put off, that it shouldn't occur at the same time as certain events that he can't ignore and that will have repercussions on his state of mind."

Doctor Flacci asked submissively, "Don't you intend to take him far away?"

"It depends if he wants to go. He's not a child. And then a trip only amounts to a few months of absence. It's the air of Rome that isn't good for my son. How much better if he had never moved from Berlin! Now I have sad news to tell him from there too. Enough. Let's talk about our affairs. Monday I hope to take up the lectures at the point where you left them."

"What a pleasure it will be for the students to see you returned to the podium," exclaimed Flacci.

"The students are very courteous and I have no doubt that they'll welcome me. But as far as the teaching, they won't notice a difference."

"Professor, you astonish me," stuttered Flacci. And his cheeks blushed deep red again.

"I'm not used to paying compliments," replied Moncalvo. "By the way, Flacci, will you stay to have dinner with me? Yes, yes, without ceremonies. I'm alone. And you are such a modest eater that it's always possible to ask you at the last moment. Anyway, wait until we hear what time it will be ready."

And he prepared to ring but at that point there was a peal of bells at the entry.

"Who could it be?"

"Do you want me to go and see?" asked doctor Flacci.

"It's not necessary. If it's someone who asks for me, we'll find out. For the rest, I haven't yet taken away the instructions."

After having knocked at the door, the maid appeared on the threshold. She was perplexed and confused.

"Well?"

"Your brother is down there, the Commendatore. I told him that the Signor Professor wasn't receiving but he insisted and..."

"Let him come in," ordered Giacomo Moncalvo after an instant of hesitation.

"I'll withdraw," declared his assistant.

"No," answered the professor, "Don't hurry. You can go later if it's necessary." And he got up to meet his brother.

"Finally!" exclaimed the Commendatore advancing with open arms. "You've removed the chains of your door!"

"I wasn't planning on seeing anyone, besides this young man for office duties. My assistant, doctor Flacci."

The Commendatore bent his head without saying anything. The presence of a stranger disturbed him.

Flacci, who was already on pins and needles, slipped away in silence.

"I thought he was a student," Gabrio noted, "he's so young."

"He is very young, and he looks even younger than he is."

"Well, then," resumed the Commendatore, "I have kept informed every day about Giorgio's condition."

"I know. Thank you."

"I've asked innumerable times if I might come."

"You will have to excuse me...I didn't have the strength."

"Believe me it weighed heavily on me to say no to your demand."

A blush rose on the face of Giacomo Moncalvo. "My request was absurd," he replied hurriedly, headlong as if the words burnt his tongue. "I lost my head. Giorgio always had that name on his lips. 'She alone can cure me,' he kept repeating. 'It would be enough to see her for a minute at my bedside...it's you who is keeping her away' and he called her, he called her. It was torture; the doctors didn't have any hope. It was then I asked, 'Should I try to beg her?' 'Try,' the doctors said to me. And I wrote to you. But I understand, your refusal was inevitable."

"You're not still angry then?"

Giacomo made a negative sign with his head. "If Giorgio

had died I would never have forgiven you."

"Instead, thank heaven he will recover."

"I hope so."

"But yes, yes, there's no question. I myself talked with your doctor today. It was then that I thought, since you are free of this anguish, you would receive me'."

Giacomo sighed, "It will be some time before I'm free of anguish. For the rest, it's true you aren't to blame."

"No one is to blame," Gabrio insisted, "It was fate."

The professor was silent.

"She couldn't have led him on," the other insisted. "She treated him with intimacy like a brother. I know her, she has no haughtiness."

"She surely must have had it on this occasion," Giacomo interrupted. "She ought to have been aware of the harm she was doing. But for heaven's sake, let us not stay on this burning ground. Giorgio will regain his reason either here or elsewhere."

"Giorgio will leave Rome?" exclaimed the Commendatore. "He'll leave the positions, the career on which he'd set out?"

"If he can't save himself otherwise... The essential thing is that he lives. And that he'll be a man."

"And you?"

"I?" said the professor. "I've been alone so many years, I'll stay that way. In a desperate situation, I'll liquidate. I would ask to receive my pension and follow my son." But he repented of this weakness and added, "No, no...I wouldn't follow him...old people are a hindrance."

"You are a stoic," muttered Gabrio Moncalvo.

"I bend to the inevitable," replied his brother.

Gabrio screwed up his courage. "And haven't you ever thought of the economic question? Giorgio's sickness must have brought heavy sacrifices."

"None that I can't deal with. In the worst case, I will save on my only expensive luxury, my library."

"And it didn't occur to you," insisted the banker, "that I am rich, very rich, and I would think myself fortunate if you were to permit me to help you."

"Your offer doesn't astonish me. You've always been so generous. But I think that every man, as long as he is healthy in body and spirit, should be self-sufficient."

"Then you refuse?"

"I thank you, but I do refuse."

"You're proud, proud. It offends you to owe something to your brother."

"If there's nothing I need? If I don't feel poor?"

"Because you are used to depriving yourself of everything."

"You are deceiving yourself, Gabrio. I assure you that none of my privations weigh on me. When I am confronted with so many who lack even the necessities of daily life, it seems to me that I'm swimming in excess. Did you see that young man who left here?"

"Your assistant?"

"Yes, Doctor Flacci, a boy who will become a great mathematician. Well, for years and years, as long as he's been a student, he lived in an attic and suffered from cold and hunger. Today, with a stipend of a thousand two hundred lire plus the fruit of three or four lessons a month, he maintains not only himself but also his widowed mother. It seems to me that he deserves to be commiserated more than I do."

"What does this mean?" responded the Commendatore. "However badly off one is, it's possible to find someone worse off."

"And yet Doctor Flacci is content."

But Gabrio Moncalvo protested this humble conception of life. "Yes, certainly that's admirable, but you all are missing a great stimulus and a great satisfaction. You, your son, Doctor Flacci…you are all scientists, you are persuaded that your discoveries and your teachings are useful to humanity. But don't deny that there are some goods that one can only effect with money—and that the best intentions in the world aren't enough if one doesn't have the means to carry them out."

"Everyone operates within the limits of his own strength," objected the professor.

"Naturally. But it must be a great pain. But, why do I say 'must be'? I experienced it myself at the beginning of my career. It is a great humiliation to hear at every moment: 'Stop there. You can't go on.' One doesn't pass because there is no money; it's as if to say: Today one can't assist a friend, tomorrow one can't protect an artist, the day after tomorrow one can't participate in an enterprise that will be a fountain of prosperity and work; and neither today nor tomorrow nor ever can one indulge a caprice, or satisfy the pleasure of his wife, of his children, of someone dear to them. Ah, go on, you can keep on declaring your crusade against the rich, you can keep insisting that we have soiled our hands counting our gold and bank notes. I affirm that one of our grubby hands spreads more benefits around it than a thousand of your clean hands."

Giacomo smiled. "Now you are the one to put us ruined poor on trial."

The Commendatore shrugged his shoulders. "It's a tactic of war. To defend oneself effectively it's necessary to carry the attack to the enemy's camp."

"And you attack deeply…. You even crush us."

"This doesn't concern you," responded Gabrio. "You have a kind of richness that we honor."

"But that doesn't figure in the lists of the stock market," Giacomo finished.

"It could figure when it is transformed to applied science."

"You see that isn't the case for me," said the professor. "I haven't created any single application."

"It doesn't matter. There isn't a truth that can't ultimately be applied. When the seed is good, sooner or later it will bear fruit."

"Let's hope so," added Giacomo Moncalvo who wasn't in the mood for discussion. And he glanced mechanically at the clock hanging from the wall, which reminded his interlocutor of the other reason for his visit.

"Listen," began Gabrio in an unassuming voice of someone who is about to approach a difficult topic. "Mariannina will get married Saturday."

"Ah," Giacomo said without losing his composure. "I knew she was engaged…not from you."

"How could I tell you if you were invisible? And furthermore…well, you understand…you won't be present at the ceremony?"

The professor didn't answer but the expression on his face clearly showed that he was amazed by the question.

"I mean, I mean…" Gabrio Moncalvo went on, "I understand you can't come. You disapprove of everything…the conversion, the marriage…"

"How many of you will convert?" asked Giacomo.

"Only Mariannina, for now. Rachel later."

"And you?"

"Oh for me there's no rush. I foresee that I'll convert also. But there's no hurry."

"In fact," said Giacomo ironically, "it would be better to let several years go by from the time when you were fiercely anticlerical."

"Who hasn't had the experience of changing his opinion?" argued the Commendatore.

"The terrible thing," his brother responded promptly, "is that your opinions are enslaved by your interests. At least to what you think of as your interests. Your convictions of today don't accord with those of seven years ago."

"What do you know about it? Seven years ago I learned at my expense what the demagogues were worth."

"And today you want to learn what the reactionaries are worth?"

"At any rate," Gabrio began again, "why have they rejected me? Wouldn't I be a better congressman than so many others? Haven't I given sufficient proof of intelligence, of energy, of innovative spirit?"

"No one denies that," agreed the scientist. "But your very words confirm that your change depends in great part on wounded pride."

"And if it does? Who doesn't react against injustice? I am ambitious. Except for poor Clara, we all have been ambitious in the family. Even you, with your modest appearance. You want to say that your ambition and character is nobler than mine. It doesn't matter. You wanted to be one of the first mathematicians of Italy and you have succeeded."

"You've succeeded in becoming one of the richest men in Italy," said the professor.

"It's not enough," Gabrio Moncalvo exclaimed impetuously. "I want for myself, for my wife and daughter a social position that is outside the fluctuations of wealth. That's the reason why I approve of the marriage and conversion of Mariannina, that's why sooner or later Rachele and I will embrace the religion of the majority. Rachele will also do it for faith."

"Really?"

"Yes. Monsignor de Luchi, who has given her lessons, affirms that he has never found better prepared terrain. You laugh?"

"Not at all. And if it's that way, I recognize that your wife is superior to you."

Gabrio raised his eyes questioningly.

"Certainly," returned Giacomo, "because to do it for a serious reason would be a serious thing."

Gabrio shook his head. "It isn't serious now. She leaves a religion she doesn't believe in…"

"…To enter in another that she believes in even less?" said Giacomo, finishing his sentence. "I know, Gabrio, that this is the phrase with which one justifies fashionable conversions. But I prefer the old ways when there was a little more idealism and enthusiasm."

"You're funny, you, with your scruples. What is your faith?"

"Ah, I'm a heretic; I'm a positivist, a materialist. Everyone says so, and that's fine with me. Nonetheless, I preserve respect for the things which thousands and thousands of men believe and hope. One can fight religions in the name of a higher and purer truth; but it isn't right to treat them as a suit one wears or discards at one's pleasure."

Before the Commendatore could reply, Giacomo stood up and added. "But that's enough. Let's not take leave with quarrelsome words. You came to make me a generous offer and, again, thank you; you came to announce the wedding of your daughter: may she be happy."

"And," babbled Gabrio, rising to leave, "you won't come to see us even when Mariannina isn't there?"

"If you have need of me," said the professor, "I'll always be at your disposal. But you, so rich and influential, what need could you have of a poor teacher of mathematics who lives outside the world, closed in his formulae?"

"What pride, what irony there is in your modesty," exclaimed the banker as he made for the exit. But on the point of crossing the threshold and while Giacomo was about to ring the bell, he turned suddenly and took both his brother's hands.

"Do you really think that I'll never have need of anything?

Do you really think that I'm happy?"

And Gabrio Moncalvo no longer seemed the same man who, a quarter of an hour earlier, magnified the condition of the millionaires.

"Money!" he went on. "Certainly you swim in it while things go well. But do you think that I don't know the other side of having riches? Do you think that I'm not dismayed to have to be always going strong, always on the lookout so that no good opportunity escapes me, so that no danger catches me unprepared?"

"Who stops you from liquidating, from finding peace for yourself?" asked Giacomo.

Gabrio smiled bitterly.

"It's so clear that you have no acquaintance with these things! As if it's easy to liquidate wealth like mine! A wealth invested in hundreds of different businesses, represented by hundreds of titles exposed to all the oscillations of the Stock Market, by hundreds of partnerships, partial interests that will keep me busy for years and years. And after I have liquidated, reduced everything to the same denomination, do I myself know how much will be left? Maybe thirty, maybe twenty million..."

"And that seems little to you?" interrupted the professor.

"Eh, my dear, the day in which you withdraw from the businesses and invest the money at three, three and a half percent, you won't have much to celebrate."

And noticing his brother's astonished face, Gabrio explained his idea: "I say 'you won't have' as a manner of speaking.... One knows that for you eight or nine hundred thousand lire of income would be an enormity, but everything depends on habit."

"As boys," objected Giacomo, "they kept us on short rations."

"Ah, those habits," interrupted the banker. "I lost them quite a while ago."

"How much do you spend, for God's sake?"

"I'll leave you curious so as not to scandalize you…and now imagine if I don't have to fill the needs of the Oroboni couple."

"Aren't you giving a million lire of dowry to your daughter?"

"A million and the palace that I bought just to give it to them as a gift."

"And are you afraid that the couple will die of hunger?'

"I'm certain that the fruit of this million will be enough for a trimester. Princes are expensive; and Mariannina feels the dignity of her new state. And add to that the demands of my wife, which grow every day."

"To think that it's going to be just the two of you left in the house."

"Rachele costs like a thousand people. It wasn't like this once, I admit, but now she's in gear and there is no remedy. In their world, you see, those who are born with little manage with little. We others don't ever stop paying the entrance tax…and if all paid could be paid in coin!"

Gabrio Moncalvo made the motion of swallowing a bitter mouthful and then went on lowering his eyes and his voice: "Rachele married me for love and, notwithstanding her defects, she has always been a good wife, far from gallantries. And who knows if she's betraying me now?"

"Eh, what an idea!"

Gabrio rolled his shoulders with affected indifference.

"Maybe it's not true. There are always so many rumors. It's curious…until a few years ago I wouldn't have doubted Rachele for all the gold in the world, as she wouldn't have had reason to doubt me. Now, at the sunset, this reciprocal faith no longer exists. *Les Dieux s'en vont.*[17] You remember how our grandparents magnified married faithfulness among the virtues of the race? This too is a legend, one more sign that the race is degenerating."

"We are like the others in quality and defects, observed Giacomo. "It's not possible to leave the race, even with the help of baptismal water."

"Very true. But after some time I'll forget and I'll make everyone forget that I ever belonged to it."

"What a gain!" exclaimed the professor. "Is this worth the effort to commit an act of cowardice?"

"You're not fair," answered Gabrio Moncalvo, deciding finally to go. "You consider things from the point of view of an incorruptible man, completely dedicated to science, superior to our little miseries. If you were in my shoes...*Fata trahunt*, they taught us in the lyceum. We're slaves of our destiny. Yours is to isolate yourself in the world of your thought to discover the eternal verities that will grow the intellectual patrimony of humanity. Mine is to throw myself into the chaos of economic interests to augment the material riches of the country—and mine. You only depend on your genius, you're not afraid of rivals, you don't have to rely on the approval of allies, of friends...I depend on everyone. If the machine of your brain stops, the work that you've done remains; if mine stops, what a debacle! Yes, yes, of the two of us I am the weaker; I am the one who might need to come and ask the other to invite him to dinner."

"If in the meantime you want to ask me to invite you for dinner?" the professor said in a playful voice while he pressed with his finger the button of the bell.

"Thank you, but not today. I have an invitation and I have to hurry and get dressed."

Then Gabrio repeated as if to unburden his conscience, "You know... it's on Saturday...at nine in the morning. Afterwards, at two, the married couple will leave."

"To where?"

"They're going to the Holy Land."

"Oh," exclaimed Giacomo. "In homage to the Old or the

New Testament? But I'm indiscreet…excuse me. And good night."

"Good night!" replied Gabrio, getting into the fur coat that the maid held open before him. "Greet Giorgio, if you think that won't displease him."

The professor mumbled a phrase of thanks. Then, after he accompanied his brother to the door of the stairs, he turned to the maid.

"Doctor Flacci?"

"He's with the Signorino."

"That's fine. I'll go and call him. And you can serve the dinner."

"There isn't much to bring to the table," declared the brief and witty maid.

"Why?"

"Because everything is burnt," was the lugubrious response. "The visit would never end!"

Giacomo accepted the news philosophically.

"We must be patient. But it would have been better not to let us know. Probably we wouldn't have noticed, neither Flacci nor I."

The maid lifted her arms to the heavens to invoke mercy of the Lord on the imperfect beings that had no palate, and she rushed off towards the kitchen.

Chapter 16

Baptism and Marriage

That Saturday morning, the news of a double ceremony had attracted to the Basilica of San Giovanni Laterano the local loafers, who saw ten or twelve festive carriages arrive on the piazza and stop one after another a few steps away from the large bronze doors of the Baptistry. Thirty or more personages, VIPs, ladies, knights, and priests descended from the carriages and, with the help of servants in livery, opened a way in the midst of the crowd and disappeared behind the heavy door where two municipal guards forbade entry to the profane.

The public, forced to content themselves with a fleeting and confused vision, vented their anger in unpleasant comments.

"Of course, because they're rich, they drive us away like dogs."

"That Jewess isn't such a beauty after all."

"As far as being beautiful, she is beautiful," said one who had an impartial spirit. "But she must make her wretched husband suffer a lot!"

"Is he that blond, pallid wimp, who seems an hour short of death?"

"Exactly. And certainly he won't have a long life. It would be better for him if he became a priest.... But they wanted an heir to pass on the family name."

"Umm," went a skeptic. "He doesn't look like the type to have an heir."

"Another, even more skeptical, rejoined quickly: "Oh she'll know how to fix that problem."

"Is it true that she is bringing a dowry of five million?"

"No, no, she's bringing only one. When her father dies there will be more."

"Was her father that dumpy, ruddy fellow who gave her his arm?"

"Yes. He is filthy rich."

"And will he be baptized too?"

"No, I don't think so."

A car that arrived suddenly with a great noise drew their attention.

"Make way, make way!"

Two extremely elegant ladies descended from the car and, with a free and decided pace, headed to the bronze doors whose double panels opened and closed at their passage as if by magic.

"Did you see what airs?"

"The one in front seems like the Empress of the Grand Mogul."

"It's the American who can spend a million lire a day," said a shop assistant who wasn't afraid to exaggerate.

"Eh! What a fortune! Three hundred and sixty-five million a year."

"And three hundred sixty-six in leap years."

"Who are you kidding?"

"But it *is* that way!" repeated the shop assistant, relying on the authority of the undercook at the American embassy.

While those outside almost quarreled over the millions of Miss May (the reader will have understood that it was she), in the center of the Baptistery, between the eight porphyry columns that Sixtus III had raised there, in the circular enclosure that a railing protected, Mariannina Moncalvo descended by way of a few marble steps. She was dressed all in white. Her forehead freed from the veil, she received the baptism and pronounced the abjuration. One by one, responding to the questions of the priest, she repudiated her errors. The priest, who was our good friend Monsignor de Luchi, after having poured the purifying water on her head and sprinkled several grains of salt on her tongue and anointed her ear lightly with oil, welcomed her into the lap of the Church with the consecrated formula: "In the name of God, I baptize you."

In the meantime, the godmother, an elderly woman from the papal aristocracy, Lady Cornelia Flamini, standing close to the neophyte, kept her hands on her shoulder and repeated with her in a low voice the words of the Creed pronounced in a loud voice by Monsignor. Other soft voices echoed among the crowd of those present, almost all kneeling in front of the altar set for the Mass.

This essential part of the rite completed, Monsignor de Luchi, in the midst of a great silence turned towards the little sheep who entered the fold of Christ and explained to her how she had been wrapped till now in a profound night through no fault of her own; but now the shadows were ripped open and her eyes were enabled to support all the light of the truth. "What joy in heaven," continued Don Paolo "for this victory of the faith! For this return to the Lord of the descendants of those that persecuted, derided and crucified him! And how the paternal heart of God will rejoice when, after everyone's repentance, he can abandon his rage and cancel the mark of infamy on the forehead of the rejected, returning a country to the dispersed."

With a muffled groan, Signora Rachele Moncalvo betrayed her impatience with the regenerating baptism, but her Commendatore husband held back only with difficulty the gesture of an annoyed man. This Monsignor de Luchi, usually so measured and discreet, today was overstepping all bounds. How did those sonorous words resonate before Gabrio Moncalvo, who hadn't yet declared explicitly a wish to leave the crowd of reprobates! And wasn't there time to finish it with this speech about persecutors and crucifiers? Oh, hadn't nineteen centuries of judgment against them been enough?

Quite other thoughts agitated the mind of Don Cesarino Oroboni during the various phases of the ceremony. Alone in a corner, with his knees on the bare pavement, he had tried to immerse himself in prayer, to put aside every profane thought. But from time to time a force more powerful than his will pushed him to raise his eyes towards the fascinating woman who in a short while would be his. Here, it wasn't a dream; the inseparable barrier that had divided her from him had fallen; a Catholic priest had proffered the liberating words that unlocked the fountain of health. There, a bishop who had waited apart praying in silence drew near, grave and solemn, to the new recruit of the faith. He confirmed her and offered her the mystic bread.

And now Don Cesarino was prostrate next to her before the altar—he in a black suit, she wrapped in a cloud of white veils; they exchanged the blest rings. From the pale lips of the Roman patrician, from the swollen lips of the Semite girl issued the ultimate "si" that united the couple unto death and after death. Opening his arms, Monsignor Don Paolo de Luchi invoked the grace of heaven on the young couple. Then there were a quantity of handshakes and kisses and that gay restlessness and abundant chatter that follows long and forced meetings. Everyone wanted to approach the bride. Everyone wanted a glance from her, a word, a smile. The parents, the relatives, the friends embraced her with smiles and damp eyes. The simple acquaintances added to the congratulations some compliments on her beauty, on her elegance, her regal air. She showed pleasure at the homage and motioned to Don Cesarino, who was anxious to give her his arm, not to hurry. Weren't they going to spend their whole lives together? But Don Paolo de Luchi intervened.

"Yes, yes, the married couple together arm in arm. From here...oh, the people from the Municipality are waiting. Come on, come behind me. I'll clear a path."

And the Monsignor, leaving the Baptistery first, preceded the group through the internal doors of the Basilica up to the Sacristy where magnificent refreshments had been prepared.

"Oh Monsignor," poor Commendatore Moncalvo said in a tone of mild reproof slapping his shoulder in a friendly manner, "With this lavish reception you make war on my lunch."

"Our Commendatore wants to joke," responded de Luchi. And helped by two servants of the Basilica, distributed tea, chocolate, liquors and pastry."

"Ah, Count," sighed Donna Rachele, accepting a small pastry from the Knight of Malta, "What a ceremony! It's only the Catholic Church that has rites like these...I hope that blessed day will come in which I too will be welcomed into the communion of the faithful. I swear I am already there with my heart."

"And the heart is the most important," answered Count Ugolini-Ruschi, just to say something.

Separated as much as possible from the worldly crowd, together with Lady Cornelia Flamini and another two or three of the purest, Princess Oroboni devoured in silence her humiliation. Her eyes didn't have tears, her lips had no laments, but her face betrayed the struggle between untamed pride and the rage and pain that wanted to break out. There was a freezing atmosphere around her: those who wanted to approach her were stopped in their tracks, those who wanted to exchange a banal compliment felt the words go dry in their throats. From time to time, she raised her hostile gaze towards Mariannina, towards the enemy who had bewitched her son, who had drawn that weak soul to herself, who triumphing with her sensuality and her gold, had dragged the illustrious name of Oroboni in the mud. All the prejudices sucked in at the breast, all the hate of the race passed on from generation to generation, the jealousy of all daughters-in-law by all mothers-in-law united in that look—

which Mariannina endured without batting an eye, with the calm and tranquil smile of one who didn't doubt her strength.

From the gesture with which the princess had refused a cup of chocolate that he himself had come to offer her, DeLuchi understood that for a certain time at least the old patrician wouldn't pardon the part he'd had in that marriage and that he ought to resign himself to hear all sorts of rebukes—which didn't make a big impression on him because he was used to them. But *non est hic locus*, this is not the place. And, to avoid in such an inopportune moment the menaced discharge of electricity, he withdrew prudently. Collecting around himself Miss May, her aunt and other ladies, de Luchi showed them the chalice given him upon this solemn occasion by the family of the bride.

"A beauty, a real beauty…pure Renaissance."

And assuring himself that none of the Moncalvos could hear him, Don Paolo de Luchi added softly: "The Commendatore procured it from one of his co-religionists. But still! Two thirds of the treasures of our church pass into the hands of those people. And who knows at what cut prices? Thank goodness that some objects return to the right path."

Since Brulati was one of the witnesses to the civil marriage, he let Gabrio Moncalvo know that there wasn't time to lose. They should already be at City Hall.

"Yes, yes," said the Commendatore, who in the last days had made every effort in vain to have the civil rite precede the religious one. The Orobonis had been inflexible and Donna Rachele, burning with mystic zeal and a great despiser of the formulas that were pronounced at the city hall, had been just as inflexible. "First in church, first in church…we can go to the city hall afterwards, and only because the law demands it."

Aided by Brulati, Commendatore Gabrio gathered people together. "Come on ladies and gentlemen. If you are coming to City Hall, please have the courtesy to hurry."

Only a few responded. Others melted away in silence; still others, overcoming their discomfort, gathered around countess Oroboni who had made a terrific effort to get to the church and couldn't wait to bury herself again in the old palace—alas no longer belonging to her but which she continued to regard as hers.

The nuptial procession, considerably reduced, rapidly crossed the Basilica and, by way of the majestic stairs, descended to the immense piazza of Porta San Giovanni that sloped slowly down to the church of Santa Croce in Jerusalem. From there, beyond the remains of the old aqueduct, beyond the roofs of the new factories that disfigure the landscape, the voluminous shape of the Alban hills could still be seen. There, the crew and the car of Miss May awaited, surrounded by urchins. A swarm of beggars, itinerant venders and the simply curious, all badly reined in by the few municipal guards, pressed the noble group who, disliking contact with any plebeians, hastened to get into their carriages and ordered the drivers to whip the horses.

"I'll go ahead," shouted Miss May cutting through the crowd with her superb Mercedes, raising a cloud of dust behind her, while a dozen ragged boys—ill content with the alms they'd received—unleashed a string of expressive epithets taken from the Roman lexicon.

Others, for the same reason, followed for awhile the carriage of the bride and groom shouting, "The Jewess, the Jewess," which drew a sigh from the breast of Donna Rachele: "Even after the baptism! When will they stop?"

"What do you expect?" asked Count Ugolini-Ruschi. "They're ignorant."

At City Hall the function was brief, all the more as the mayor and clerks, annoyed by the long wait, couldn't wait to go for lunch. In fact, the mayor rushed through the speech he had prepared and limited himself to two words of best wishes.

Signora Rachele triumphed. And, not content with unburdening herself with Ugolini-Ruschi, she turned almost with an air of challenge to that unrepentant painter Brulati.

"What a difference from the ceremony in church! You don't want to deny that?

But Brulati, who was in a bad mood, answered: "Well, yes in church there is more pomp—but that's all appearances, this is the substance. And in order to become Princess Oroboni it's necessary to pass through here. By the way," continued the painter, liberating himself at last from the matter that had weighed on him for so long, "what news do you have of that poor family?"

Signora Rachele at first didn't understand.

"What family?"

"Don't you remember? The one on via Merulana."

"Ah," murmured Donna Rachel blushing. "What a memory you have!"

"The thing is," went on Brulati, impassive, "on this happy occasion, I would renew willingly my offer…"

"Thank you, thank you," interrupted brusquely the Signora. "It's not necessary…conditions have improved…"

"Have they won the lottery?"

"Oh well…"

"What rare good fortune!"

"He has days that he's insufferable," mumbled Signora Rachele. And leaving her petulant interlocutor in the lurch, she accepted the arm of an important official of Foreign Affairs, the one who had the habit of falling asleep in her parlor.

"Maybe I compromise myself," said the diplomat. "Now that the Moncalvos have entered the field of the enemy. Thank goodness that His Excellency the Prime Minister doesn't want to antagonize the Vatican."

"Ah Commendatore," Signora Rachele exclaimed, "the

statesman who reconciles Italy with the Church will be more deserving of honor than Cavour. His Excellency should aspire to that glory."

"These are delicate questions, dear Signora, questions that time will resolve. But look, everyone has put their signatures and we can go."

"Will you come to lunch with us?" asked Signora Rachele.

"Thanks. It is impossible. They are expecting me at the Senate."

The public on the piazza of the Campidoglio was composed in part of foreigners who came to visit the museums and was more restrained than that of San Giovanni Laterano. Here, nobody knew or cared about the recent baptism; here, no one shouted impolitely at the Jewess; instead, a spontaneous murmur of appreciation welcomed the new bride who, on the arm of her husband, exited the municipal office and got back in the carriage.

A Frenchman who had heard the words "a princely marriage," said with a convinced air: "You can tell she is a princess."

A cloud veiled the proud beauty of Marianinna Moncalvo. Now that she had proffered the "yes" considered valid in law, now that an indissoluble knot tied her to Don Cesarino, for the first time she asked herself whether she had been the victim of a vain illusion, whether giving herself wholly wasn't too high a price for the conquest of a name and a title. Yes, certainly she could and would dominate her spouse, but meanwhile at least for some time she would not be able to refuse his caresses or to flee a contact that repulsed her.

Another image that she wanted to drive away returned insistently to persecute her: the image of the cousin whose passion she had amused herself by fanning, the cousin who was on the point of dying for her. She didn't love him, no; she was too in control of herself, too guarded against the assaults of passion, but still...she felt on her mouth the burning of that kiss that he had given in exchange for the one she had offered provocatively. And she wondered: "Shall I see him again?"

With her face turned obstinately towards the little window, she barely answered the questions of her husband.

"You are a little pale. What's the matter? Don't you feel well?"

"I have a headache...too many flowers."

The carriage slowed and stopped in front of Palazzo Gandi and Mariannina leapt to the ground in a flurry of white. She crossed the entrance swarming with people, ascended the great staircase and, separating herself from Don Cesarino who didn't dare follow her, entered her girlhood room for the last time. In a flash she took off her nuptial clothes and put on a traveling suit. She looked, from above the street, across at the high, dark, massive wall of the Orobonis and her heart swelled with pride at the idea that she had forced open that inviolable rock where, up to now, no one of her race had dared to set their feet. Today it was she who was the Princess Oroboni. What difference did the proud disdain of her intractable mother-in-law make to her? What grief could that pallid larva, destined to perish so soon, give her?

Away, away from her mind these sentimental fixations! Mariannina Moncalvo was now an Oroboni, and she had to wear her title like a queen. When she went down among the guests, her eyes sparkled and her cheeks had recovered their usual color.

"How beautiful you are! How beautiful you are!" exclaimed Don Cesarino. "And your headache?"

She shrugged her shoulders: "It disappeared. My indispositions never last long."

Don Cesarino bent his head, humiliated. Ill since birth, would this splendid creature blooming with health, exuberant with life, bear with him?

Gabrio Moncalvo embraced his daughter enthusiastically. "You are more princess than all the princesses."

The Commendatore had been uneasy in the church and uncomfortable at City Hall—because of the haste and the unwillingness of the mayor—but here, in his own house, in his ambience, he had recovered his aptitude and his spirit. He was careful not to say it but, contrary to his wife who was humiliated and irritated by the almost complete absence of the heraldic aristocracy, he was relieved not to see the grim Princess Olimpia or lady Cornelia Flamini, or many of the other old mummies who had been present at the ceremony in San Giovanni in Laterano. Now the crowd that surrounded him and that did honor to his sumptuous buffet were mostly from the aristocracy of bankers to which he belonged and where he was revered like an absolute monarch. Yes, yes, this was his kingdom. Fine if they made him a papal Count; but he would always be a banker tied by a double thread to the other financiers without distinction of country, descent, or faith; therefore, he was also linked to his old Semitic brothers that the increasingly fanatical Signora Rachele would have liked to exclude from the present domestic solemnity but which he had invited in spite of her.

"They won't come," she said to support their exclusion.

"Let them decide," was the immediate response of Gabrio Moncalvo. "I won't commit such rudeness. Anyway I think they'll come."

Not only had they come but some of them had sent the bride splendid gifts that now figured among the most beautiful shown in the dedicated room where the visitors were allowed, in turn, and where a trusted servant kept guard discreetly. There were so many people...you never knew. There were extremely expensive items—like a pearl necklace with a diamond pendent, a gift of Miss May of which it was said that the jeweler had some time ago refused sixty thousand lire.

Two or three reporters, like those at poor Clara's funeral, stuck their noses into everything, besieging the intimate friends of the family with questions. They took notes in their notebooks, sometimes interrupting their work to make some profound philosophical reflections.

"Well! The affairs of this world! It hasn't been three months since we were here for a funeral." "*Les morts passent vite.*"[18]

One of the reporters, less discreet than the others, bumped his neighbor with his elbow to point out an ostentatious prayer book, bound in leather with studs of gilded silver, offered to the bride by Monsignor de Luchi. The reporter muttered: "The teacher didn't want the scholar to forget his lessons."

"I don't know! She doesn't seem a woman to recite psalms."

"Eh, who knows? The neophytes are the most fervent."

"Ah, if the old Moncalvos could witness this!"

"Quiet. There's the prince."

Since Mariannina was captured by her friends, and particularly by the invasive Miss May, Don Cesarino appeared lost in this society new to him. Leaning on the arm of Count Ugolini-Ruschi, who at least was of the same caste, he went here and there through the rooms. From him, who was a Knight of Malta and had been in Palestine, the prince obtained information about the voyage, the convents of Jerusalem, the Mount of Olives, Golgotha, Nazareth, the distances to traverse—in short, all the difficulties one must sustain to know all the places that heard the words of Jesus. And Ugolini-Ruschi, who boasted considerable connections in every quarter of the earth, besides providing the requested information, promised letters of reference for this and that, for an important official of the Orders (and his fellow disciple), for the Superior of the Franciscans who is his friend, for the Austrian consul who is the son of a cousin of his mother, for the husband of the niece of a Hohenstein baron of Monaco who he'd met years before at his relatives, the Wartenburgs of Berlin.

But little by little, with new congratulations and best wishes, the guests withdrew. Only the close friends of the family stayed for lunch. Among them, it was understood, the most important were Miss May, Count Ugolini-Ruschi, the painter Brulati, Mr. Fanoli and Monsignor de Luchi who had arrived at the last moment when everybody had lost hope of seeing him. Also present, though he wasn't one of the intimates, was the Baron Bernheim, who had invited himself.

The Monsignor, most amiably excusing himself for being late, offered his arm to Signora Rachele and accompanied her to the table. He took the seat to her right; on the left sat Count Ugolini-Ruschi, whereby she found herself between today's sweet sin and what would soon be an easy penitence. With what anxiety she imagined the day in which she would have to prostrate herself at the feet of the worthy prelate, confess her sin and obtain absolution!

The champagne overflowed, foaming from the chalices; the toasts and the *vivas* to the couple mingled. But everyone grew silent when Monsignor de Luchi rose to speak.

The Monsignor opened a sheet folded like a telegram and began with a solemn voice: "I have a surprise, a precious surprise for the happy couple. Right now I've received from his Eminence, the Cardinal Secretary of State, the following dispatch: *His Holiness sends benedictions and best wishes to his most precious children, Cesarino and Mariannina Oroboni.*"

"Oh Monsignor!" exclaimed Signora Rachele. And being unable to say anything else, she exhibited a ready disposition to faint, uncertain only if she should fall on the side of Don Paolo or that of Ugolini-Ruschi. But the two of them held her up and refreshed her and she regained control of herself, calming with signs and smiles the fearful solicitude of her fellow diners. "It's nothing. It's over," she assured them. "The effect of the commotion...such a special favor...so unexpected. And I owe it to you, Monsignor. Mariannina, dearest son-in-law, haven't you thanked Don Paolo?"

And she took the hand of the priest and covered it with kisses. The young spouses wanted to do the same but the Monsignor defended himself, declaring that, if there was any merit, it wasn't his alone. There was also Count Ugolini-Ruschi with his influence and his connections. Modest and dignified, the Count shook his head.

"Yes, yes, I feel that you were responsible too," Signora Rachele protested with emphasis, blushing at not having thought of it sooner. And she squeezed the right hand of her incomparable friend effusively and incited her husband with a glance to manifest his own gratitude.

"Thank you, thank you," babbled the Commendatore with moderate enthusiasm. It happened that he, too, had a surprise for his daughter in reserve and he was sorry to see its effect spoiled by this dramatic turn of events.

"How interesting!" exclaimed Miss May reading the dispatch from the Vatican over the shoulder of the Monsignor while the waiters opened other bottles of champagne and refilled the chalices.

"Quiet! The Monsignor has something to add."

"I propose," he said, "a toast to our Pope Pious X."

There was a moment of hesitation and Baron Bernheim, who was expecting a new Italian commission, couldn't restrain an expressive "uhm, uhm!"

"I'm toasting the Pastor of souls and not the Sovereign," explained Monsignor. And at that point everyone rose to their feet applauding; only the painter Brulati, with the excuse of picking up the napkin sliding down from his knee found the way to get out of the touching demonstration and grumbled frowning: "After the comedy, there's the farce."

"I hope that the echo of this applause arrives as far as His Holiness," resumed De Luchi as soon as the tinkling of the glasses was silent.

And since the fumes of the wine tended to go to his head, he let two or three imprudent phrases escape him. "Yes, this applause has a great significance. It is one of so many signs of the reconquest of Rome that is the truest, the most desirable. 'My reign is not of this world.' Ruling souls—that is what interests me. And if the souls return to us and to the Church, it won't be a great disgrace to have lost four leagues of ground."

"Bravo, Don Paolo," the Commendatore jumped up laughing. "You renounce the temporal power. What if your friends heard you!"

"I renounce nothing," replied Monsignore, aware of having gone too far. "The Church has its rights and will always protest against violence committed against it. But I speak as a private person. And for me the essential is that the Church reconquers souls. For the rest, I accept the friendly warning of our illustrious Commendatore...and keep my mouth shut by drinking water!"

To seal his words, Monsignor de Luchi brought the glass to his lips. This roused the hilarity of those present who noted that there was wine in the glass, not water.

"Well, my children," said the Commendatore looking at his watch, "if you don't want to arrive too late in Naples it would be good if you prepare to leave. The car is ready and it's not the usual car. It's a fifty horsepower Fiat that I add to Mariannina's dowry."

"Ah, papa!" screamed the new princess, throwing her arms around the neck of the author of her days with a burst of filial affection that could only be understood by those who have a millionaire father.

Gabrio Moncalvo was happy. His surprise had a greater success than the other one; the auto checkmated the benediction.

Caressingly, Mariannina asked: "And how fast can it go?"

"Calm, calm," interrupted the banker. "The chauffeur has orders not to go above fifty kilometers an hour. For today I'm in command. I hope that your husband won't be offended."

"Please, don't worry!"

Don Cesarino thought with heartfelt tenderness of the old family coach, of the old coachman, of the two old horses that used to take twenty-five minutes to bring them from his house to Saint Peter, and he instinctively closed his eyes, disturbed by the vision of the headless auto race that awaited him. But when he reopened them, he discovered an ironic smile on Mariannina's lips and he was ashamed of himself. "Tell the truth, are you afraid?" asked the young bride.

He reddened and babbled:

"With you? With you I'd go around the world."

Months before, she had heard the identical phrase from that other one.... Yes, certainly both would be ready to make the tour of the world with her; but that other one wouldn't have been afraid.

Chapter 17

Sad Convalescence

Giorgio Moncalvo, who had been up and about for two days, was nevertheless still weak and pale. He sat on a couch next to the window. "Flacci," he asked, "would you please ring that bell for me?"

"If you want anything, I'm ready," the obliging young mathematician responded, leaping to his feet.

"Thank you but it's enough if you ring," replied the convalescent.

When the maid quickly answered his call, he directed her to send immediately for the *Giornale d'Italia* and the *Tribuna* of the night before and the *Popolo Romano* and the morning edition of the *Messaggero*.

The maid consulted the assistant with a glance and he, in turn, risked a timid "But..."

"This is going to happen no matter what," said Giorgio. "If you raise obstacles, I'll go in person though the doctor forbids it. I can already stand very well."

The threat had its effect. Doctor Flacci held his tongue and the maid left to execute Giorgio's commission.

Giorgio Moncalvo brought his hand to his mouth to suppress a yawn. "I know, I know, dear Flacci, there is a plot between you and papa and you take turns watching me."

Flacci made a vigorous gesture of denial.

"I understand it's to a good end," the other continued without getting agitated. "You're afraid I'll do something crazy and you want to keep me under a glass bell, far from emotions. If I'd asked you to get the newspapers for me you would have brought a thousand difficulties into play. This is why I preferred to give the order directly. There is going to be a description of my cousin's marriage in the papers. Come on, don't act innocent. No matter how much you are accustomed to living in the clouds, you can't have failed to hear that yesterday the daughter of the most illustrious Commendatore Gabrio Moncalvo, my uncle, was married to Prince Cesarino Oroboni after—it is understood—having been baptized with all the proper formalities. The news has come to me notwithstanding all your precautions. And you pretend not to know about it...."

"I knew about it, but..."

"But the thing didn't mean anything to you? That's natural. You're not a relative of the bride. But I am her cousin, her first cousin, and this indifference would be unpardonable. It is true that my father and I are disgusted by it. My father didn't even want to go to the wedding. But it doesn't really matter. The relation will always be there. Do you have cousins?"

"No," admitted Flacci.

"That's better. They are the cause of much trouble and gossip. The least that can happen is to hear it said that you were in love with her. They said it of me. And it isn't true. Imagine if I could fall in love with a multi-millionaire cousin! As for approving of the marriage that she made...that, no. Neither the marriage nor the conversion. Neither my father nor I could digest those things. Decide for yourself, Flacci."

"Truly, I..."

"Stop with that diplomatic air. If you had a cousin would you be pleased to see her going through this comedy because she wants to be a Roman princess? You are laughing."

"The idea of a Roman princess in my family seems so funny."

Giorgio Moncalvo became annoyed.

"That's no answer. Would it please you?"

"No, certainly not."

"Thank God. It's so absurd! In our days, to enter the reactionary camp with flag unfurled! To wear the mask of bigotry in order to be welcomed by fanatics!"

Giorgio, who hadn't been so talkative in a while, continued for another five minutes in this vein, only interrupting himself from time to time to marvel that the servant hadn't brought the papers yet.

Finally the papers came and the professor took two of them, and gave the other two to Flacci.

"You take a look in the *Popolo Romano* and the *Messaggero*. Look at the gossip column, the wedding section. It should be on the third page...God, what a man! Outside of his mathematics he's utterly confused. Here, I have already seen that the *Tribuna* and the *Giornale d'Italia* have only three lines...the announcement, naked and crude, of the ceremony and a sentence of praise for the beauty of the bride. They are important papers. They can't give too much space to such trivialities. Well?"

"Here there seems to be something."

"Ah, in the *Messaggero?*" said Giorgio snatching the paper from the hand of his assistant. "Certainly, there's a column. They call this knowing how to be a journalist!"

And he began to read avidly, accompanying his reading with ironic remarks "Of course, it begins with a description of the baptism...truly touching...the bride was an apparition. The journalist becomes ecstatic...regrets not having the pen of D'Annunzio to exalt her beauty worthily. Idiot! Let's go on. Here's the list of the principal gifts: diamonds, pearls, emeralds, rubies.... Aren't you dazzled Flacci?"

"I'm not competent. I'm afraid I couldn't distinguish a diamond from a piece of common glass."

"Bravo. Gifts follow...magnificent silver service, magnificent Japanese porcelain...all magnificent. Let's go on. Oh, oh, this is the most magnificent of all: 'At the champagne'—they are talking of the sumptuous reception at my uncle's house—'At the champagne, Monsignor Paolo de Luchi, who had officiated at the religious ceremony, brought the Pope's benediction.' Aren't you even impressed by that, Flacci? Are you as unmoved by this as you were by the jewels?"

"Basically, it doesn't affect me."

"I, on the other hand, am moved to tears. Think: until yesterday my cousin was a reprobate; my uncle and aunt are still outside the community of the faithful; they will enter, it seems, but for the moment they are outside. And, that notwithstanding, the Holy Father bestows his apostolic blessing on a house polluted by heresy. And perhaps he wouldn't bestow it on you, dear Flacci, who, orthodox or not, were born and grew up in the lap of the Church. I would protest if I were you."

"You must be joking, Professor."

"Not at all. I am so aware of the honor that has been conferred on the Moncalvo name and in which I have a part. See, this is the good fortune that comes to someone who has a beautiful cousin sought after by Roman princes."

Giorgio glanced at the newspaper again. "Listen, listen. 'The couple left at three in the afternoon for Naples in a splendid Fiat with fifty horsepower given by Commendatore Moncalvo. In a few days they set sail for the Holy Land.' Can you imagine my cousin making a pilgrimage to the tomb of Christ?"

"I have not had the honor of making her acquaintance," objected Doctor Flacci.

"It's true you don't know anything…apart from your formulas. Blessed you! That way you have no distraction, and may reach celebrity in a straight line. My father always says that you will wake up famous when you least expect it."

"The professor is too kind to me."

"No, no, my father is only right. However, I'm sorry that you lose an excellent occasion to laugh behind the back of the new Princess Oroboni prostrate at the foot of the Holy Sepulcher. And, excuse me, isn't there anything in the *Popolo Romano*?"

"Nothing, or so it seems to me."

"Give it to me.... It's true, nothing. Merely the announcement. What a paper! Enough! I'll re-read the *Messaggero* before I go to bed. It will be good for me. Today I've really spent an amusing hour."

Giorgio Moncalvo got up from the sofa, rubbing his hands and whistling through his teeth the nuptial march from *Lohengrin*.

In this state of excitement, Professor Giacomo found him a little later and had new confirmation of what he already knew. Sick or convalescent, taciturn or loquacious, his son was fixed by a single thought: his constant preoccupation with Mariannina. It was as if the rest of the world didn't exist for him; he never made an allusion to his beloved studies, never uttered a word about his friends in Berlin. And it was such a word that his father was waiting upon before he deemed it proper to give Giorgio some news—and deliver a letter that arrived when he wasn't yet out of danger.

But why wait any longer? With the indifference that Giorgio showed for everything around him, there was no fear that the sad news would bring too violent a shock. And, at any rate, even if there were a shock, couldn't he derive more benefit than harm from it?

In this way, the professor decided not to delay any longer and that very evening he turned the talk to the Rauchers. At the name, Giorgio made a disconsolate gesture. "The Rauchers," he said, "poor family! That last letter from Frida was so sad, so discouraged. Now I remember. She was afraid of not living until the spring. And I didn't answer. But it wasn't my fault. I was sick right afterwards. I'll write to her and excuse myself."

Giacomo Moncalvo put a hand on his son's shoulder. "Respond to her father."

"What?" exclaimed Giorgio, becoming agitated. "To her father? And not to Frida?"

The Professor inclined his head.

"Why don't you say anything? I want you to tell me the truth."

"You know there was no hope of saving her."

"Dead, then? And since when? How did you find out?'

"The invitation to the funeral arrived along with a letter for you."

"When? When?" insisted Giorgio.

"About three weeks ago...you were still very sick."

"And why did you continue not telling me after I got better? Why did you wait three weeks to give me that letter? Where is it?"

"You were still weak," the professor excused himself taking an envelope rimmed in black from his pocket.

Giorgio recognized the handwriting of doctor Raucher. He took the letter and turned it around between his slender fingers. "Three weeks!" he repeated. "What will they think of me when I haven't written a word?"

"I wrote for you," added Giacomo Moncalvo. "I told the professor of your illness. There is also a book."

"What book?"

"I don't know. It's still wrapped. The letter will explain. Do you want me to open it, to read it?"

"No. My eyes are enough."

Giorgio moved closer to the lamp to read the funeral message, then to Doctor Raucher's sad letter:

My Frida ceased to suffer the other night, and I am fulfilling a precise request of my blessed one by informing you, who have known and appreciated that angel. "Write him yourself," she said. "Write in my name and assure him that I have never forgotten his goodness to me and that I die convinced that he hasn't forgotten me even though he hasn't written me lately. I imagine how absorbed he must be in his studies."

You will also receive a book in the mail that my daughter begged me to send you. It is the volume of Carducci's poetry that you gave her and that you read together a year ago. Frida was so fond of that volume! Keep it, Moncalvo, conserve it in memory of the gentle creature who left me alone in the world.

I won't talk to you about myself. You can imagine my state. I just lived for my daughter, towards whom it seemed my duty to expiate the grave sin of bringing her to life. How much that poor saint suffered! I don't believe that in her twenty years there was a day in which she didn't suffer, and she never had a complaint or reproof.... Enough of this. My Frida gone, I feel the vanity of everything. I don't know how I will be able to re-enter my study where, though my dear daughter rarely visited, I could sometimes hear the sound of her voice through the walls.... But then, why study, why meditate? If I weren't broken in soul and body, I might search to offer my life for some grand cause. At my age one isn't good for anything. It's up to you now, up to those who like you have the future ahead of them. May you find in science the consolations that are denied me forever. Let me know that you have received the book, remember me to your father and believe me,

Yours,
Wilhelm Raucher

Giorgio Moncalvo put the open letter on the little table and remained silent with his face hidden in his hands. His mind was flooded with memories of his residence in Berlin, memories of the austere laboratory where he was taught the scrupulous severity of the research, memories of the hospitable house that the delicate Frida filled with her smile and her suffering. And to think of that house without her; to think of the illustrious man without his beloved daughter who, for twenty years, had given him ineffable tenderness; and to think of his unquiet and anxious care. Giorgio was suddenly ashamed of himself, ashamed for the agitations in which the fevers of his fantasy put him, so small and vain compared to real miseries.

Professor Giacomo, who had left quietly, returned with something in his hand and came near to Giorgio. "Here is the parcel arrived for you from Berlin," he said.

"Yes, yes," responded the young man. "It is the volume of Carducci's poetry. I gave it to Frida Raucher last year. It was her wish that it was sent back to me…" And Giorgio gave his father the letter of the German scientist. "Read it if you like."

In the meantime he had torn the wrapping enclosing the book and turned the pages, many of which were annotated by Frida in her minute and subtle handwriting. Giorgio remembered many of those notes very well, as they were dictated by him; but others Frida had added later after he left Berlin; a word here and there, a date, a day of the week. One page was folded, that one contained the short, exquisite ode.

Or che le nevi premono,
Lenzuol funereo, le terre e gli animi,
E de la vita il fremito
Fioco per l'aura vernal disperdesi,
Tu passi, o dolce spirito…[19]

At the bottom, Frida had written, and her writing seemed more uncertain, more trembling than usual: "*Letzer Gruss.*" Last greeting! And certainly the greeting was for him, for Giorgio, and the little phrase was the last that Frida's tired hand had penned. Dear good girl who had given him her heart without asking anything in exchange and in the solemn hour of her death had absolved him of the two faults most difficult to forgive: indifference and oblivion.

Moving away from the evocative poetry of Carducci, the young man's eyes saw behind a veil of tears the Northern city buried in snow, the snow falling in large flakes on the roofs, on the streets, the parks, on the cemetery where Frida slept. He felt a lump in his throat and burst into tears.

His father bent affectionately over him.

"Giorgio, when you are stronger and the season is milder, would you like us to go to Berlin and visit Doctor Raucher? I'm convinced that it would give him great pleasure to see you. You were so dear, so dear to his daughter."

With an energetic movement of his head, Giorgio rejected the paternal suggestion.

"Go to Berlin? Present myself to Doctor Raucher? After the cowardly negligence with which I treated poor Frida in her last months?"

"One understands from the letter that he preserves no rancor against you."

"What does that matter? It's I who can't pardon myself."

"Confessing your fault will ease your remorse. Consider Giorgio, you have need of a change of air, a change of city to give another direction to your thoughts. In Berlin you were happy. Do you want to go back? Do you want to ask Professor Raucher if he would consent to have you back with him? Today he is broken by sorrow, he thinks he isn't good for anything. But a push might be enough to get him back to work. And it would be fortunate for science. I speak against my own interest. What would I want for myself if not that you remain here at my side in this house, which your presence reanimated and revived? Instead, I realize that's not possible. At least for a few years, you can't remain here in Rome."

"No, papa," answered Giorgio. "To leave would be cowardly. Let me stay here next to you, let me learn from you how to be strong. As soon as the doctor permits, I'll begin my lectures again. I'll try to distract myself working, the way you did in the midst of the disappointments of fortune. No, going to Berlin wouldn't be the remedy."

"Let's go somewhere else if you prefer," said the Professor. "Let's go to France, to England for three or six months as I proposed in the past. Do you remember? The evening in which my poor sister worsened? You can't, you shouldn't live in Rome for now."

Giorgio sketched a smile.

"I can't? You think me so weak? Have patience and I'll know how to demonstrate the opposite."

But immediately afterward, with a different tone and manifest incoherence, he added: "Doctor Raucher is right. What is needed in certain cases is a noble cause to which one can offer your life. Ah, why wasn't I born two generations before when one fought for Italy and Garibaldi gathered around himself the flower of youth and there was a magnificent fervor of generous ideals—a robust faith in the future of the country? Ah, I assure you, papa, had I been born at that time, I wouldn't be here today struggling with confusion."

"The heroic periods of a people's history don't recur so often," objected the professor. "The country can also be served in quiet times."

Giorgio Moncalvo made a violent movement.

"The country of the Moncalvo commendatori and the

Oroboni princesses? The country of adventurers and snobs who, through vanity, draw near our eternal enemies and make toasts to the Pope, safe for the rest to change their jackets when it profits them? Ah no, by God, this country one doesn't serve or want to serve."

"How agitated you are, Giorgio! Even you must see that you're neither calm nor strong."

"No wonder! There are spectacles that make you sick."

"Another reason to get away from them. You will see baseness and cowardice everywhere unfortunately, since the world is made that way. But get away for a certain time from the spectacle of those that most irritate your nerves. No, I don't ask you to answer right away. Let's sleep on it. The night will bring counsel. You'll answer me when you're ready. And you'll write to Doctor Raucher?"

"Yes. Tomorrow I'll write to him. Not yet to announce our visit."

"Do as you think best."

Giacomo Moncalvo kissed his son's forehead and withdrew, having decided that he would also correspond with the German scientist.

Chapter 18

Towards Exile

Without telling Giorgio, Giacomo wrote Doctor Raucher the next day, not hiding anything from him. He received a prompt reply.

"Don't imagine," said the letter of Doctor Raucher to Giacomo Moncalvo "that my pain keeps me from understanding yours or fear that I will be offended by what you are expressing with such noble frankness. The fraternal affection which your Giorgio gave to my Frida was all that the poor invalid could ask for and she died recognizing the benefit unaware— and that was better—of the tempest that recently overwhelmed her friend. I, too, think that Giorgio must distance himself from everything that can feed his unhappy passion. If I saw the possibility of going back to my usual life I would ask him to return to me but I have the absolute need at least for some time to change habits. How? When? I don't know. A hundred diverse projects, a hundred ideas agitate my mind. If any of them takes a concrete form that would permit me to turn to my old assistant I will hasten to tell you. Have a little patience. In two or three months at the most I'll be able to tell you if I'm still useful to others or whether I'm a finished man."

Giacomo Moncalvo waited.

Meanwhile Giorgio wanted to resume his lectures. But he resumed them without warmth, without enthusiasm. He was no longer the man he was before. Professor Salvieni, who had given him a part of his course, praising him to the students as a brilliantly promising scientist, began to feel he'd been deceived. Giorgio's rivals, the imitators, maligned him: his reputation had been puffed up. He was one of those who infiltrate the University through their father's glory. "Today he is only an assistant but at the first competition he'll know how to get himself a full professorship. That way we'll have the dynasty of the Moncalvos. As if there aren't enough University dynasties already."

Giorgio felt himself losing ground in the esteem of others and himself and every day he made heroic proposals for the next day. "Tomorrow I'll recover my energy. Tomorrow I'll take up my work seriously."

Despite that, tomorrow was similar to today and any continued and intense application was impossible. His favorite books bored him, his old manuscripts, his notes in Italian and German documented an intellectual activity that even he marveled at. They spoke a language which now he struggled to understand. How? How many ideas had he had! How much research had he started! Is it in this way that he had sketched out the design of so many splendid structures? Devised how many edifices of glory? Poor architect who now didn't know how to put two bricks together.

Disposed by temperament to benevolence, he nevertheless became little by little quarrelsome and sarcastic. Since the spring of his energy was broken, it seemed to aggravate him that others weren't as inert as he—nor did he spare even his father from his censure. Couldn't he manage to take it easy? Couldn't he have been content with the fame he'd achieved? What more did he want? He was ferocious even with Flacci and missed no opportunity to sting him. "You don't have blood in your veins," he said sometimes. "It's mathematics in a liquid state. You aren't a man, you are a factory of theories. I'm amazed that you don't ask for the patent. Come on, let's hear how many memories a week you release for the Academy of the Lincei or for any other Academy?"

Now Giorgio often saw Brulati. After the wedding of Mariannina the bizarre artist went less to the Gandi palace and drew near to him whom he called improperly the cadet branch of the Moncalvo family—sharing the mistaken belief of many people who thought Gabrio to be the older of the two brothers.

No one dared to think that Brulati, also angry with the Princess Oroboni, made at this moment the most desirable companion for Giorgio Moncalvo. Certainly professor Giacomo didn't. But how to close the door in the face of a man whom everyone loved and esteemed and who, to make himself more acceptable, had offered the new friends a precious gift: a copy of the most beautiful portrait made of poor Clara on her deathbed? But the Professor, welcoming him with open cordiality, had said to him, between serious and playful: "Be careful. Here we don't talk of my brother or my sister-in-law or my niece or of marriages and conversions."

And in the house the request was respected well enough. But outside things were different and when Giorgio gave a flying visit to Brulati's studio or met him in the café of old Rome that was a hang out of artists, the painter willingly let himself be drawn into conversation.

Mariannina? The princess? Certainly, like a good daughter she wrote every once in awhile to her parents—and Signora Rachele proudly showed Brulati the letters full of praise for Don Cesarino's virtue and tact, and full of enthusiasm for the holy land where the new bride, blessed woman, had set her foot. Signora Rachele had dissolved in tears of tenderness. To him, Brulati, the skeptic, the reprobate, she said with a triumphant air: "Did you see, Signor prophet of ill omen? Have you seen that those two were born to understand each other? To complement each other? My daughter has the beauty, the intelligence, the money; my son-in-law has the race, the blood, a patrimony of beliefs, of convictions that the men of today are lacking."

A point that Brulati loved to spread around was the religious ardor of Rachele the neophyte of the Moncalvo. She wasn't yet baptized but frequented church functions. She was already the patroness of several Catholic foundations, enrolled in the Society of San Vincenzo of Paola, vice president of the Institute for the destitute women, councilor of the pious works of the Bread of San Antonio, promoter of collections for the missionaries, etc., etc.

"Why does she hesitate to take the big step?" Giorgio asked.

"Who knows?" Brulati said, admitting that he didn't know precisely the reason for the delay. According to some people it was the Commendatore himself that created every sort of obstacle; according to others who were probably right it depended on an incident touching Monsignor de Luchi, the spiritual director of Signora Rachele. Monsignor de Luchi—this seemed impossible—was for the moment in disgrace with his superiors and had been forced to withdraw for two weeks to a convent of Franciscans to do penance. They had not forgiven his discourse pronounced at Mariannina's wedding with an ambiguous phrase about temporal power. Open you heavens. Nothing more was needed to let loose the anger of the Curia. And yes, the unctuous priest had proposed a toast to the Pope and predicted the reconquest of Rome by the Church. And unfortunately, added the painter, unfortunately the prediction threatened to come true.

In his walks with Giorgio Moncalvo through the streets of the capital, Brulati often returned to this bugaboo of reconquering Rome on the part of the Vatican, and commented bitterly on the phrases of de Luchi, showing his companion now the new buildings bought or constructed by religious corporations. Now the priests, the brothers, the monks of every kind and color were popping out on all sides.

"As if we didn't have enough of our own," protested the artist, "the ones that France has swept away have rained on us. They open convents, hospices, schools, even hotels; every weapon is good to take possession of souls and bodies. A fine generation that they prepare for us of bigoted women and sacristans.... And to think: not only do they meet no resistance, but they find help where you least would imagine it; because it's the fashion to make love with the clerics... people throw away every human regard and proclaim themselves on the side of the clerics. Look at your ineffable aunt, dear professor mine," went on Brulati with the cordial assent of Giorgio, "and have patience. I've always believed that anti-Semitism is a barbaric and idiotic thing, but if the Jews themselves join with the priests I don't promise that I, too, won't become a ferocious anti-Semite."

Another incentive to Brulati's tantrums was the destruction that—on Commendatore Moncalvo's orders—was being visited on the Oroboni palace and gardens. Mariannina, now proprietress of the place, had given carte blanche to her father, and the Commendatore had put himself in the hands of an engineer. Within a few months, the small 16th century palace had changed into one of the most vulgar houses of this century of merchants.

"Not that this little palace was a masterpiece, not that there weren't more beautiful gardens in Rome, but it was a complex harmony of blended colors. You'll see, you'll see next year.... Now the work of destruction is barely started and one isn't aware of anything from the outside. It's necessary to look out the window of Gandi palace. You don't go there anymore?"

No, Giorgio didn't go there and wouldn't go again. Still, at time, he gave in to the attraction of the place where Mariannina had lived until two months ago and the places that would welcome her in a near future. At such times, he passed by that street, often raised his eyes towards his uncle's habitation and the massive walls in front that hid the small Oroboni house.

"The wall is also destined to fall," said Brulati one morning. "Already they want to substitute an 'artistic' railing. Imagine, the wall was naked, unadorned, and yet the eye was accustomed to it and its dark inhospitable aspect that corresponded so well to the temperament of the reactionary and antediluvian people who lived there. It was one of the many contrasts between old Rome and the new. No sir they'll throw it down. These millionaires don't know anything. All that matters to them is to show off their riches."

"And what does the old princess do?" asked Giorgio.

"Donna Olimpia," replied the painter "has taken refuge in her room and never comes out and doesn't receive anyone. She has said that while she lives she won't let anyone in, neither engineers, nor master builders or workers. I think that they are resigned to wait for her death before finishing the restorations."

"And how will they house the married couple when they return? Do they think of delaying their absence forever?"

"On the contrary. They'll come back in a few weeks. But for the time being they'll live in a small villa on via Ludovisi, rented for them by their respective father and father-in-law. Commendatore Gabrio told me that yesterday evening."

"Ah, they'll come back," muttered Giorgio, to whom the news, though so natural produced a disturbance that he tried to hide.

"Yes," Brulati said looking his interlocutor in the face. "I'm curious to see what kind of attitude the new princess will have with her old friends. In order to ingratiate herself with the black Aristocracy she will have to break off all her old connections. But with Mariannina one is never sure of anything."

"On my part," said Giorgio, "I consider her dead."

Brulati agreed with a movement of his head "You're right. She's a dangerous creature."

"Dangerous for you too, then?" added the professor with a forced smile.

"Oh, I run no risk. At my age you don't get certain ills."

"You think so?"

"But yes, it's like the whooping cough."

'Ah, you can still catch that and watch out, it's more serious in adults."

That morning Giorgio and Brulati separated somewhat haughtily as if there were a hidden rivalry between them.

At home Professor Giacomo Moncalvo waited for his son impatiently. When he heard him come in he called him into his study. He was pale, stirred.

"What's the matter?" asked Giorgio anxiously, "are you ill?"

"I'm fine. Sit down."

"Bad news?"

"Bad, I don't think so. You judge for yourself."

Giorgio took a letter bordered in black from his father's hands.

"Is it from Doctor Raucher?"

"Yes. The letter for you was open inside."

There was a brief silence.

"Then you know the tone of the letter?" Giorgio went on.

"I know it. Doctor Raucher proposes to take you to India with him and another young German scientist to study the bacillus of the plague. He has a large subsidy from his government and from the Society of Physiology of Berlin and has the authority to hire two assistants of his choice. You will be one of the two."

Giorgio began reading aloud from the letter:

It's a question of staying away from Europe for at least a year in inhospitable countries, in the midst of spectacles of misery and death, exposed to the risk of contagion, exposed to danger from superstitious and ignorant populations. I offer you this post, the one that seems to me, old and disconsolate, the best way to ennoble the last years of life. You are young, you have a long future ahead of you. Before accepting my offer, before endangering everything in the name of a humanitarian and scientific ideal, think about it. I will await your response until the 20th of this month. If you accept we will meet the morning of the 25th at Brindisi to take sail that afternoon on the steamer the Peninsulare.

Keeping the page unfolded Giorgio raised his eyes to his father.

"What do you advise me?"

The professor's lips contracted forcibly.

"Go," he said. And seeming to him that this counsel from his mouth surprised his son he added, "Oh Giorgio, Giorgio, you can be certain that I wouldn't talk this way if I thought you were cured of your madness. Be frank and sincere. Can you swear to me that when your cousin returns…and she is about to return… that you won't try to see her, approach her. Can you swear to me that the mere fact of knowing that she is in the same city a few steps away from you won't be enough to take away the quiet and serenity you need for your studies?"

"You're right," declared Giorgio with a firm voice and resolved tone. I'm not cured and without a powerful shock I won't heal. Perhaps my salvation is in the remedy proposed by Doctor Raucher. Admirable man! At sixty years old he has the energy and the self-confidence of a young man. Accompanying him on his dangerous voyage I will pay back a part of the debt I owe to him and to the memory of poor Frida. Also with you, my father, I hope to resolve my debt if I live. Up until now I've given you few joys."

"Oh, how mistaken you are!" exclaimed professor Giacomo, swallowing the tears that made a knot in his throat. "You have always been my consolation and my pride. I am proud of your character, your talent, and the esteem in which you are held by renowned scientists like Raucher; I saw in you—and do still—a future famous Italian. And I don't want, do not want this hope to be disappointed.... Pay me back you say? No it isn't that. You have to pay yourself back. You have to find yourself. You are lost in I don't know what labyrinth. You have to get out of it at all costs. And it was to get you out that I had recourse to the help of Doctor Raucher."

"You, papa?"

"Yes; from Raucher who respects you and wishes you well, also in the memory of the love that his daughter had for you. You remember the desolate letter he wrote you after his disaster? There was a phrase that remains sculpted here inside: 'If I weren't prostrate in soul and body I'd offer my life for some great cause.' It was more or less the same vow I heard from you. And I begged Raucher, if upon recovering his strength he persisted in his proposal, if he saw a cause worth fighting for, I begged him not to forget you, to choose you if he had need of a companion. He promised me and now he maintains his promise, and with what affectionate, flattering words. If you read the letter that he sent me you will see. Doctor Raucher has a heart similar to his mind. And knowing that you, whom he considers like a son, will be with him I will suffer less from you being at such a distance; I will be consoled for not being able to share your risks. Because I've thought of following you.... But what would I do? I'm only a mathematician. What help could I bring you in your studies? Upon such an expedition anyone who isn't useful will be an encumbrance. It's better that I stay here without moving to await your return."

The professor had taken Giorgio's hands in his and continued to look at him and question him with look and word.

"Because you'll return, you'll win your test. You've always

been robust and you're not feeling the effects of your sickness anymore (I am speaking of your physical malady). Isn't that true?"

"No" said Giorgio. "I've recovered faster than I thought I would."

"And I too," resumed professor Giacomo. "I still have a well-functioning body. You'll find me waiting for you."

"Oh father mine!" exclaimed the young man. "If I weren't to find you, it would be easier to stay there to fatten the earth."

The professor brought his finger to his lips: "Quiet. Let old people say such things. At your age it's necessary to go ahead undismayed without delaying too much to collect those who fall from tiredness. For the rest, why do we agonize? I don't have the least doubt that we'll have years to stay together and live happily."

Giorgio smiled with a sign of agreement, he too pretending a security he didn't fully feel.

"I'll telegraph Berlin today" he added.

"Today? Why? Raucher recommends that you don't hurry your decision.... You might regret it."

"I don't want to regret it."

"No," insisted the professor, "don't telegraph today, I'm begging you...I, the one, who is pushing you to leave. Tomorrow."

"Is that so important to you?"

"Yes."

"Alright then, tomorrow."

"Thank you."

Breaking away from his son, Giacomo Moncalvo drew near the window from which you could see a large part of Rome. Giorgio followed him in silence.

They both leaned on the windowsill, touching elbows, ears inclined to the breath of the immense city that seemed to sleep in the sun. Waves of warmth and light came from the facades of the houses, the roofs, the street; there was a heavy sleepiness which passed from things to men and extinguished the sensations and broke the will, giving the spirit the impression of losing itself in the infinite as in a shipwreck without pain or terror.

"Ah, if it could always be like this, if you wouldn't wake" think the people who give in to the strange fascination.

"If there was no awakening," thought the two next to each other at that window and who in a few hours would be separated by so much sky and sea. "If there weren't an awakening, if the hour of separation might not sound," they thought, without having the power to take back the proffered words or revoke the decisions taken. They sensed that there was no remedy, that it was necessary to resign themselves to destiny.

And two weeks later, Giorgio Moncalvo set sail from Brindisi.

After the bell had rung the signal for departure, professor Giacomo, who had accompanied the travelers on board, came down the gangway. He sat down on a dockside bench and followed with eyes and spirit the ship that moved away, growing smaller until it seemed only a black point on the horizon.

When even the point had disappeared, when only a thin streak of smoke marked in the azure sky the route of the invisible ship, he shook himself and with lowered head took his way back to the hotel through the calls of the porters, the racket of the carts and the agitated movement of a cosmopolitan crowd. He had never before experienced so acute and fearful a sense of solitude, he who after the death of his wife and the absence of his son had lived alone for so many years in the modest house sacred to meditation and study.

He had lived alone but comforted by a sweet hope of having his son with him before long; burning with the same love of science, satisfied as he was by the joy that came from the search for the truth. Today that possibility no longer existed; today his son, brought back so recently to the paternal roof, was torn from his side, flung thousands and thousands of miles away to places where everything was hostile.

By telling him: "Go follow your master, face the danger of inclement weather, of contagious diseases, of hostile men," Giacomo believed Giorgio would be saved from an even greater peril. He'd thought to obey the imperious voice of his conscience and yet his conscience wasn't serene. Did he have the right to do what he had done? Was it really his place to send Giorgio into chaos? Would a mother have acted this way? And what if something happened to him? If Giorgio didn't return?

In the evening the professor left. Arriving in Naples the next morning after a sleepless night, he bought a couple of newspapers and his eye fell on a bit of news in the Vatican chronicle of the *Tribuna*:

> It's now confirmed that another honor from his Holiness will be accorded to the extremely wealthy Hebrew banker Gabrio Moncalvo, president of the International Bank, whose financial relations with the Vatican are well known. The Commendatore Moncalvo is the father of the present Princess Oroboni, who was converted on the occasion of her marriage. We've heard from the best sources that the Commendatore and his wife will soon enter the bosom of the Church; indeed according to some others the date of the baptism will be the same as the honor.

Several bittersweet remarks followed in the piece which noted that some years back Commendatore Moncalvo had been a candidate in the electoral district of Lazio with a program that was decidedly anticlerical.

All things considered, the news shouldn't have made a

strong impression on professor Moncalvo, who for a while now had appreciated the politico-religious gymnastics of his brother at precisely their correct value. In fact, since the death of Clara he had not gone to Palazzo Gandi at all. Still, in this moment the letter in the *Tribuna* increased his sorrow. Here was yet another voice repeating the unhappy truth: "you are alone."

Oh how they break up, how the families dissolve. Giacomo Moncalvo turned his thought to his far away childhood in the humble paternal house in which he and Gabriele had taken their first steps. They hadn't resembled each other and yet they loved each other, reconciling after their brief quarrels by a look or a word from their older sister. And in that evocation of time gone by, where the images of grandparents and parents faded into fog, the professor saw along with his older sister, the figurine svelte and sinuous of two much younger children: Lisa who one day would be his wife, Rachele who would become the wife of Gabrio. Now Lisa was dead and Clara—once so happy about the double marriage—was dead as well. And now Gabrio and Rachele wanted nothing more than to deny the past, while the children born from those marriages, Giorgio and Mariannina, met only to do each other harm. Now one had sold herself for a title and the other was a voluntary refugee, seeking peace and oblivion in risky adventures.

Such is the fate of the Moncalvos, he mused, a family perhaps envied by all the world. One had glory, one riches, one a coat of arms. No one had happiness.

But from these purely personal considerations, Giacomo Moncalvo rose to others more general and perhaps even less sanguine. No, this moral decay wasn't an isolated phenomena of which some of the Moncalvos had given such a miserable spectacle. Almost everywhere there was a lowering of character, a failure of convictions, a cynical scorn for the heroic virtues of renunciation and sacrifice, an unbridled rush towards ephemeral honors and improvised riches. What does it matter that science extends every day its dominion over nature? What does it matter that every day the confines of knowledge expand if man fails to grow equally in goodness and dignity? If he only becomes smaller in an ever larger world?

Notes

1. A prestigious Italian Academy, literally the Academy of Lynxes (as the lynx's eyes symbolized the sharpness necessary to scientific investigation), founded by Federico Censi in 1603 mainly for scientific inquiries, was revitalized in the late nineteenth century as the national Italian Academy for both science and literature.

2. A neighborhood in Rome near Villa Borghese which was developed in the 1880s on the grounds of the beautiful Villa Ludovisi, victim of the urban speculative development of post-unification Rome.

3. In English in the original.

4. In German: "Know you the land where lemon blossoms blow/And through dark leaves the golden oranges glow." From Johann Wolfgang von Goethe's novel *Wilhem Meister's Apprenticeship*, in *The Essential Goethe*, edited by Matthew Bell and translated by John R. Williams (Princeton: Princeton University Press, 2016), 454. These verses inspired the composition of several lieder by Ludwig van Beethoven, Franz Liszt, Franz Schubert and Robert Schumann, as well as an opera, *Mignon* (1866), by Ambroise Thomas.

5. Title bestowed in Italy by the King of Savoy during the Monarchy and today by the President of the Republic. In the order of chivalry, it is a rank higher than officer and knight.

6. Filippo Cifariello (1864-1936), Italian sculptor, famous in his day for his neoclassic style.

7. In French: "Nowadays we are people who keep to our place in society."

8. Giacomo Boni (1859-1925) was an archeologist famous for his work on the Trajan Column and his excavation of the Roman Forum. He became a senator in 1923.

9. On this date, the Italian army invaded Rome and annexed the city to the Kingdom of Italy. It marked the end of the Papal State. On February 3, 1871 Rome was proclaimed the new capital of Italy. Note: Vatican City was not established as a political city state until the Lateran Treaty of 1929.

10. Rome residence of the King and Queen of Italy, previously the residence of the Pope. Queen Elena of Montenegro and Princess Yolanda were the wife

and daughter of King Victor Emmanuel of Italy.

11. The breach of Porta Pia took place on September 20, 1870 and it refers to the battle that won Rome to the Kingdom of Italy.

12. On November 3, 1867, Giuseppe Garibaldi and his volunteer fighters were defeated in Mentana by the Papal troops, aided by French soldiers who were equipped with the new and more technologically advanced Chassepot rifles.

13. *Butteri:* Shepherds on horses who tended cattle and sheep typically from the Maremma southern area of Tuscany but also in some parts of Latium and, in the early twentieth century, also in the countryside around Rome.

14. Francesco Domenico Guerrazzi (1804-1873), patriot and writer from Tuscany, known for his political activism and popular historical novels, especially *La battaglia di Benevento* (1827) and *L'assedio di Firenze* (1836).

15. Reference to a famous scene of cannibalism in Dante's *Inferno* (Canto XXXIII), where Count Ugolino della Gherardesca is portrayed among the political traitors, as he gnaws on the head of the Archbishop Ruggiero degli Ubaldini.

16. In English in the original.

17. In French: "The gods are gone." An expression taken probably from the title of a collection of articles, *Les Dieux s'en vont, D'Annunzio rest,* written between 1903 and 1907 by Filippo Tommaso Marinetti, in which the Italian author with great irony described the funerals of general Giuseppe Garibaldi and poet Giosuè Carducci.

18. In French: "Death passes quickly."

19. "Now that the snows have come/Pressing like a funeral sheet on the earth and souls/And the light sound of life/Is lost in the winter air/You, pass, O sweet spirit...." From Giosuè Carducci's poem: "Ave (In morte di G.P.)" in *Nuove Odi Barbare* (Bologna: Zanichelli, 1886), 93.

About the Author

Born in Florence on February 8, 1839, Enrico Castelnuovo lived almost all his life in Venice, where he, still a small child, moved with his mother after his father abandoned the family and went to live in Egypt. Raised with modest means by his mother with the help of her relatives, he was not able to afford a classical education and, after attending a technical school (despite his strong interest for literature and the humanistic subjects), in 1854 at the age of 15, he began working for his uncle's olive oil import company. In the late 1860s he worked for a few years as a journalist, and during this period he traveled often to Milan where he met some of the most prominent cultural figures of the time, among whom, Giovanni Verga, Giuseppe Giacosa, Arrigo and Camillo Boito, Leone Fortis and Paolo Ferrari. In 1863 he married his cousin, Emma Levi; they had three children: one died soon after his birth; Guido (born in 1865), became a renowned mathematician and taught at the University of Rome; and Bice (born in 1867). Guido and Bice were raised by their father, after Emma Levi tragically died soon after having given birth to her daughter, Bice. At the end of 1872 Castelnuovo left his journalistic career to teach at the Superior School for Commerce in Venice (today known as the University of Ca' Foscari), which was founded by Luigi Luzzatti, his brother-in-law, and which he directed from 1905 until his retirement in 1914. He was a prolific writer, who published between 1872 and 1908 more than ten volumes of shorts stories and novels, while working full-time at the school. The first of Castelnuovo's fourteen novels, *Racconti e bozzetti*, appeeared in 1872, the last, *I Moncalvo* in 1908. Enrico Castelnuovo died in Venice on June 22, 1915.

About the Translators

Brenda Webster was born in New York City, educated at Swarthmore, Barnard, Columbia, and Berkeley, where she earned her Ph.D. A novelist, freelance writer, playwright, critic and translator who splits her time between Berkeley and Rome, Webster is also the president of PEN West. Webster has written two controversial and oft-anthologized critical studies, *Yeats: A Psychoanalytic Study* (Stanford) and *Blake's Prophetic Psychology* (Macmillan). She has translated poetry from the Italian for *The Other Voice* (Norton) and *The Penguin Book of Women Poets*. She is co-editor of the journals of the abstract expressionist painter (and Webster's mother) Ethel Schwabacher, *Hungry for Light: The Journal of Ethel Schwabacher* (Indiana 1993). She is the author of four previous novels, *Sins of the Mothers* (Baskerville 1993), *Paradise Farm* (SUNY, 1999), *The Beheading Game* (Wings Press, 2006), which was a finalist for the Northern California Book Award, *Vienna Triangle* (Wings Press, 2009) and *After Auschwitz: A Love Story* (Wings Press, 2014). Her memoir, *The Last Good Freudian* (Holmes and Meier, 2000) received considerable critical praise. The Modern Language Association published Webster's translation of Edith Bruck's Holocaust novel, *Lettera alla Madre,* in 2006. Webster's novel, *Vienna Triangle,* "navigates between the late Sixties and *fin de siecle* Vienna in a dramatic exploration of family romances inside and outside the circle that so famously gathered around the father of psychoanalysis, Sigmund Freud" (Sandra Gilbert). Of her novel, *After Auschwitz: A Love Story,* the journal *Hadassah* wrote: "The book's pain is offset by Webster's compassion for her characters, her evocation of both the joys of life and the darkening days of old age and, above all, the acknowledgment that 'after Auschwitz' there can be the golden glory of Rome."

Gabriella Romani is Associate Professor of Italian and Director of the Charles and Joan Alberto Italian Studies Institute at Seton Hall University. She holds a *Laurea* from the University of Rome La Sapienza and a Ph.D. from the University of Pennsylvania. She has taught at Barnard College and Princeton University before arriving at Seton Hall in 2005. With Brenda Webster she co-translated Edith Bruck, *Letter to My Mother* (2006). She is the co-editor of *Writing to Delight: Nineteenth-Century Italian Short Stories by Women Writers* (2007), *The Printed Media in fin-de-siècle Italy* (2011) and *The Formation of a National Audience: Readers and Spectators of Italy, 1750-1890* (2017). She is the author of *Postal Culture: Writing and Reading Letters in Post-Unification Italy* (2013). Her main research interests are in nineteenth-century Italian culture and literature.

Wings Press was founded in 1975 by Joanie Whitebird and Joseph F. Lomax, both deceased, as "an informal association of artists and cultural mythologists dedicated to the preservation of the literature of the nation of Texas." Publisher, editor and designer since 1995, Bryce Milligan is honored to carry on and expand that mission to include the finest in American writing—meaning all of the Americas, without commercial considerations clouding the choice to publish or not to publish.

Wings Press produces multicultural books, chapbooks, ebooks, CDs, and broadsides that, we hope, enlighten the human spirit and enliven the mind. Everyone ever associated with Wings has been or is a writer, and we believe that writing is a transformational art form capable of changing the world, primarily by allowing us to glimpse something of each other's souls. Good writing is innovative, insightful, open-minded, and interesting. But most of all it is honest.

Likewise, Wings Press is committed to treating the planet itself as a partner. Thus the press uses as much recycled material as possible, from the paper on which the books are printed to the boxes in which they are shipped.

As Robert Dana wrote in *Against the Grain,* "Small press publishing is personal publishing. In essence, it's a matter of personal vision, personal taste and courage, and personal friendships." Welcome to our world.

Colophon

This first edition of *The Moncalvos,* by Enrico
Castelnuovo, has been printed on 55pound EB
"natural" paper containing a percentage of recycled fiber. Titles have been set in Minion and
Adobe Caslon type, the text in Adobe Caslon
type. All Wings Press books are designed
and produced by Bryce Milligan, publisher
and editor.

On-line catalogue and ordering available at
www.wingspress.com

Wings Press titles are distributed
to the trade by the
Independent Publishers Group
www.ipgbook.com
and in Europe by
www.gazellebookservices.co.uk

Also available as an ebook.